MURDER AT ALMACK'S

Brookston was just about to inform Lady Jersey that he was in no need of her assistance when a sudden flurry of activity attracted their attention. Lord Palmering had once again risen abruptly from his chair and was clutching his throat, his face an unattractive beet red.

"This is the final straw!" exclaimed Lady Jersey.

Lord Palmering slowly raised his arm and pointed toward Lily, who had also risen and was watching him fearfully.

"Poison!" he croaked, his voice carrying through the sudden silence as others turned to stare at him. For a moment everyone seemed to freeze; then Palmering pitched forward across the table.

"It's worse than you thought, Sally," said Brookston in a low voice. "Palmering hasn't just died at Almack's. It appears that DeBracey has won his wager. I believe that Palmering has managed to get himself murdered . . ."

—*from* "Murder Most Indiscreet," by Mona Gedney

BOOK YOUR PLACE ON OUR WEBSITE AND MAKE THE READING CONNECTION!

We've created a customized website just for our very special readers, where you can get the inside scoop on everything that's going on with Zebra, Pinnacle and Kensington books.

When you come online, you'll have the exciting opportunity to:

- View covers of upcoming books
- Read sample chapters
- Learn about our future publishing schedule (listed by publication month *and author*)
- Find out when your favorite authors will be visiting a city near you
- Search for and order backlist books from our online catalog
- Check out author bios and background information
- Send e-mail to your favorite authors
- Meet the Kensington staff online
- Join us in weekly chats with authors, readers and other guests
- Get writing guidelines
- AND MUCH MORE!

**Visit our website at
http://www.kensingtonbooks.com**

MURDER AT ALMACK'S

Jo Ann Ferguson

Mona Gedney

Valerie King

ZEBRA BOOKS
Kensington Publishing Corp.
http://www.kensingtonbooks.com

CONTENTS

Invitation to Trouble

Jo Ann Ferguson

One

"How desperate do you believe me to be?" Amelia Wallace regarded her bosom bow, Lady Iris Dougherty, with a smile. Her dear friend was set all on end by the fact Amelia's escort for the upcoming gathering at Almack's had developed a frightful rash from something he had eaten. So frightful, poor Lewis had taken himself from London back to the country.

"As desperate as you truly are." Iris wagged a finger at Amelia, a trait Amelia found uncommonly vexing, for Iris was a year younger. Already married for several months, pretty Iris with her perfect blond curls and stillwater blue eyes and magnificent figure had taken it upon herself to make certain Amelia also found marital bliss.

Mayhap not bliss, for Iris had suggested a parade of possible suitors with an urgency that suggested she believed any husband was preferable to none.

Amelia did not agree. Even knowing that her red hair and hazel eyes and far less magnificent figure made her unlikely to turn a gentleman's head, she was not going to allow her well-meaning friend to persuade her to make a huge mistake she would regret for the rest of her life.

"Iris," she said, coming to her feet and getting the tray of chocolate cakes she knew her friend adored, "it is but a party. There will be others."

"Are you bereft of your good sense?" Iris rolled her eyes, always dramatic. "This is *the* gathering of the Season so far. An assembly at Almack's, sponsored by the patronesses, and some lucky young women, who charm them with their wit and loveliness, will be given vouchers to attend Almack's for the rest of the Season. What could be more important?"

"I cannot attend without an escort." She sat on the comfortable dark blue settee in the center of the small parlor where she had been reading when Iris called. This was her favorite room in the house, for she loved its blue-and-white-striped wallcovering and the frieze of vines and fruit creeping along the tops of the walls and across the ceiling to a plaster medallion. "You know that would be a *faux pas* beyond any imaginable."

"Exactly." Taking a cake, Iris smiled over it. "That is why I have arranged for Lord Foxington to escort you."

"Lord Foxington!" She was glad she had not selected a cake, for she was certain it would have crumbled when her fingers clenched against her palm. "Really, Iris, do you think someone like him would act as an escort for someone like me?"

"First of all, you should not heed all the *on dits* you hear." That finger pointed at Amelia again as if Iris were a governess and Amelia her naughty charge. "Lord Foxington is a well-respected man."

"True, but it is said he seldom utters a word of any interest." She put her hand over her heart. "Dear Iris, you know I am as taciturn as a mute when I am with those I do not know well. The reason I agreed to let Lewis Patten escort me was because he has never let a second go past without filling it with conversation."

"I have met Lord Foxington on several occasions, and I can tell you he is a gentleman of first consequence. I would not have arranged for him to escort you otherwise."

Amelia wanted to groan, but knew it would only make Iris more determined to list all the reasons why Amelia should allow the viscount to accompany her. Quietly, she said, "The invitations have not yet been delivered. I may not even be on the guest list, although you assure me I will be."

"You will be." She chuckled. "And you will be arriving on Lord Foxington's arm, which is a brilliant idea, if I may say so."

"I believe you just did."

Iris waved aside the comment. "Do not be petulant when I am doing the very best I can for you. After all, if Lord Foxington keeps his tongue between his teeth throughout the evening, you will not need to fret about him saying a mistaken thing that will reflect poorly on you. Oh, Amelia, it shall be utterly perfect, and, by the end of the evening, I daresay we shall be planning what you will wear to Almack's the following week when only the pink of the *ton* are welcome. *Then* we shall find you a suitable match."

This time, Amelia could not stifle her groan. Not that it mattered, because Iris was already outlining everything they needed to have ready before the gathering. Was this, she wondered, how it felt to be on a ship that had lost its rudder and its sails and was adrift with no hopes of rescue?

Her uneasiness was soothed when it was announced other callers had arrived. Her relief was short-lived as two young women walked into the parlor.

Susan Little and Paulina Middington looked enough alike to be sisters, for both had hair only a shade darker than Iris's. Susan was the younger, and she was a bit plump while Paulina had a lanky beauty that suggested she would be most happy riding across an empty meadow. Paulina was the daughter of a baron and Susan the granddaughter of a marquess, and Amelia was unsure which one was more anxious to garner the attention of the *ton* and make an enviable match.

When each one kissed her cheek, even as they were prattling about the upcoming gathering that had been announced last week at Almack's, Amelia would have guessed both of them had been present when the patronesses spoke of their intention to have a special gathering. She smiled when Paulina sat next to her and selected a cake from the plate.

"It will be an invitation almost as precious as a voucher to Almack's," Susan gushed. "I have heard the patronesses will be very selective about those who receive invitations."

Iris smiled. "You have heard correctly."

"What word do you have of this?" asked Paulina, leaning forward. "Oh, do tell, Iris, if you know anything about which names are on the list."

"I could not say." She smiled at Amelia. "If I spoke out of turn, then *I* could be banished from Almack's." She giggled. "You would not want that, would you?"

"If you want the truth," Susan began.

"Susan!" chided Paulina.

Amelia laughed. "Iris's place at Almack's is secure. She is only hoaxing you."

"This is no laughing matter," Paulina returned with sudden fervor. "Our futures are dependent upon this."

"It may leave us brokenhearted."

Susan shook her head in dismay. "Oh, Amelia, if you go with that outlook, you are certain to fail to attract the attention of the patronesses. I so want you and me to get those invitations."

"And me?" Paulina fired a frown at her friend.

Susan's smile was strained. "You and I have already expressed our hopes for each other. Must you ask for reassurance at every turn?"

"It is so important." Her frown deepened. "After all, aren't you the one who said you would want to die if you did not get an invitation?"

Amelia raised her hands. "Now you are being silly. Nothing is that important."

The shocked expressions she received from all three of her callers were an obvious disagreement. With a sigh, she decided silence would be the best course. Mayhap, if good fortune smiled on her, Iris was wrong, and she would not be invited to this gathering. Never had staying home with her parents while she spent the evening reading ever sounded so good.

* * *

"Why would I even consider attending such an assembly?" Stuart Foxington leaned back in his chair at the club where he usually found the company of his comrades pleasant. Not today, because he had no sooner entered than he was met by an overly enthusiastic Edward Dougherty, who seemed determined to persuade him to set aside other plans for this flummery.

"Because I am asking, old chap." Dougherty hefted his glass and downed his brandy in one gulp. Refilling it, he smiled. "It will keep harmony in my home, and you know you do owe me a favor or two."

"From our youths, mayhap." Stuart watched his friend drink the brandy with rare agitation.

Dougherty, a spare man with not an ounce of extra flesh on him, had been a friend from the days when Dougherty's hair was the pale gold of his new wife's. Now it had darkened to a muddy brown. Muddy. That was an apt description for his friend's expression as well.

"Then, the repayment is long overdue." Dougherty reached for the bottle again.

Stuart halted him, lifting the decanter away and pouring the last of the brandy into his own glass. He did not drink it, but he wanted to keep Dougherty sober enough to explain why his tie-mate had abruptly decided to take on the role of flesh-broker. True, Dougherty was very pleased with his decision to wed, but that did not mean he had to insist everyone else do the same. And, if Stuart wished a wife, he would go about finding one without the aid of a matchmaker or well-meaning friends.

"How desperate is this young woman if she needs *me* to escort her?" he asked.

Dougherty laughed, the sound warning he was only a bit foxed. "Do not denigrate yourself, old chap. You do have some redeeming qualities." He began to count on his fingers. "You have those dirty acres in Devon and enough blunt to keep you well-larded for the rest of your days."

"So she is a penniless miss?"

"Of course not. Her family is quite comfortable." Striking the tip of his next finger, he said, "And you have that fine title."

"So she is a fortune-hunter with an aim of bettering herself?"

"Of course not. Her father is not titled, because he is a younger son. However, there are both a marquess and a duke not far away in the family line." Squinting, Dougherty tapped another finger. "And you do have those deucedly dark eyes and hair that women seem to find irresistible. I have heard Lady Dougherty speak often of how her friends have taken note of your broad shoulders that seem perfect for the uniform you have set aside along with your commission." He laughed again. "Her words, I assure you, not mine."

"I would hope so." Stuart took a sip of the brandy, realizing he could use its calming effect when Dougherty was leading the conversation in such a peculiar direction. "May I assume you will not take no for an answer?"

"And hurt the young woman's feelings?"

"How would she—? Dash it, Dougherty! You have already asked her if she would allow me to escort her, haven't you?" He pushed himself out of his chair and went to the window overlooking St. James's Street that was awash with a storm.

"Me? No, but Lady Dougherty is calling there this afternoon to make the arrangements."

Foxington faced his friend, who stood several inches shorter than he. "And if I had said no?"

"You would not do that."

"No?"

Dougherty's expression of bonhomie tumbled into a frown. "You know I am thinking of your welfare. You have kept too much to yourself since your return from the Continent."

"I find I enjoy my own company as much as anyone else's since my return."

"Bah!" Dougherty sat on the arm of a chair. "You are morose and dull, and you have abandoned all your friends, save for me."

"Mayhap I should have kept one of the others," he grumbled.

"So will you give Miss Wallace a look-in?"

"It seems I would be considered uncivil to say no at this point."

"Good." Dougherty's breath sifted out of him in a relieved sigh.

Stuart frowned when he saw his friend's shoulders sag as if allowing a heavy load to slip from them. "What is it? This seems to matter more to you than pleasing your wife by finding an escort for Miss—"

"Wallace." He reached for his glass, then saw it was empty. He plucked Stuart's from the table and finished the brandy. "I am glad you will be there. It may come in handy to have a man with military experience if trouble comes."

"Trouble? What sort of trouble?"

Dougherty shrugged. "All I have heard are rumors. However, what I have heard was enough to convince me that you would be the best escort for Miss Wallace. She is my wife's dearest friend, and I doubt Lady Dougherty would forgive me if something happened to Miss Wallace."

"And you want me to be certain of that."

Dougherty sounded completely sober when he said, "Yes."

Two

"Miss Amelia, your hair is impossible!"

In the glass's reflection, Amelia could see her abigail's frown. Nancy never watched her tongue when they were alone. And, if the truth needed to be told, Amelia's hair *was* impossible. Not just its unfashionable red, but its mass of curls that seemed resolved never to remain properly in place.

Amelia stood and took the comb from her abigail. While Nancy watched, tapping her toe, Amelia forced her hair into a bun.

"You simply need to be patient," she said, putting the comb on her dressing table.

"I doubt I ever shall be able to control it."

"It is a chore." She offered Nancy a smile in hopes it would soothe the older woman's obviously ruffled sensibilities. Nancy had been her mother's abigail until this trip to London, and she wished to prove to Mrs. Wallace that she could handle working for both women. If Amelia had been born with her mother's smooth dark hair instead of her father's wiry curls, Nancy would have been far more successful.

Amelia reached for another pin to stick into her hair. The motion sent her hair bouncing onto her shoulders again, scattering the pins already in it. Picking up a ribbon, she tied her hair at her nape.

"You cannot be thinking of receiving Lord Foxington like that!" gasped Nancy.

As if on cue, the sound of a door opening and a deep voice stating that he was calling for Miss Wallace resonated up the stairs and into the bedchamber. Nancy rushed to the bedroom door to peek out.

"'Tis Lord Foxington!" she gasped as she closed the door.

"He is early. Mama is still attending Lady Simonson's at home."

Receiving the viscount alone would make her a pariah among the Polite World. For a moment, the naughty side of her mind suggested she should do just that to insure an invitation to this assembly was not delivered to her. Then good sense eclipsed that thought. She would not shame her family by acting out of hand.

Nancy came back to the dressing table. "Then, he should cool his heels while we tend to matters here."

"Nancy, you would not suggest that I keep Lord Foxington waiting in the parlor while we continue the struggle with my hair." She did not add that she was tempted to remain here until the viscount grew tired of waiting and took his leave. Reminding herself that the poor man was as much a victim of Iris's matchmaking as she was, she wanted to do nothing to add insult.

"But to receive him in such *déshabillé* . . ." Nancy put her hand to her forehead, smoothing back her gray hair. "Your mother will be aghast."

"My mother will understand. She taught me the importance of making all callers welcome."

Not giving Nancy another chance to argue, Amelia went out of her room and down the wide stairs. Her hair might be held back by a green bow, as if she were still in the schoolroom, but it matched the ribbons woven through the sleeves and hem of her gown. She would not disgrace her family.

Nancy trailed after her, and Amelia took a deep breath as she paused before reaching the doorway of the room where she and her mother enjoyed working on needlework in the afternoon sunshine. She hoped this call would not be as bad as she suspected, then realized nothing could be that horrible. Or so she wanted to believe.

She forced a smile as she walked into the parlor. Sunlight glistened off the striped wallcovering and seemed to bring the friezes to life. A man set himself on his feet from where he had been in the chair Iris had used yesterday.

"Go in," ordered Nancy in a whisper. "Now that you have come down, you must go in and greet Lord Foxington."

This man was Lord Foxington? She had envisioned him as sort of a beetle of a man, hiding within his hard shell and not letting anyone close without flitting away. Instead, he was a well-favored man with hair that caught blue fire in the afternoon sunshine.

"Good afternoon," he said in a mellow baritone that seemed to match the breadth of his shoulders and the dark depths of his eyes. "Miss Wallace?"

His question warned she had been gawking too long. She hastily murmured what she hoped he would believe was a warm greeting. As she went to sit on the dark blue settee where she had spoken with her friends yesterday, she was glad her mother was not here to chide her for her ineptitude in receiving the viscount at her father's house. She bumped a book, and it clattered to the floor. Hoping her face was not flushed, she picked it up and set it on the table beside her. She adjusted the bookmark, glad it had not fallen out.

She watched Lord Foxington sit again. He had a smoothness in his motions that suggested he would be comfortable in the saddle or during a dance.

Tea was brought, and Amelia tried to think of the easy patter her mother devised whenever she had guests. She could not convince her lips to form a single word. She poured tea for the viscount. When it splashed, she could not keep from chirping, "Ouch!"

Lord Foxington affixed her with a steady stare, and Amelia wished she could pull back that single word.

Bother! She was allowing her own disquiet to panic her. Iris had arranged this meeting, and she had to trust her friend. With Nancy sitting in the corner, there would be no question of impropriety.

She almost laughed. *That* was not what she had dreaded. It was not having anything to say to Lord Foxington.

"It is very kind of you to call, my lord," she said, finally falling back on the trite.

"Yes."

"Thank you for taking time from your day to call."

"You are welcome."

The silence stretched until she wanted to shriek out for him to speak to her . . . about anything. She could hear carriage wheels on the street, and from the lower floor, the servants' voices drifted into the parlor. When laughter, quickly muffled, sounded, she yearned to excuse herself and go to where people were comfortable with each other.

Usually she enjoyed silence, taking advantage of it to read or to consider her own thoughts or to admire the flowers she was arranging in a vase. She could sit with her parents in this very parlor all evening, and no one needed to say a word. Yet, while she sat here with Lord Foxington, each second seemed to last a separate eternity.

"More tea?" she asked, hopeful he would say no and take his leave. She ignored the pulse of guilt at the thought.

"Thank you."

As she reached for the teapot, her gaze was caught by Nancy's. She did not need her abigail's glower to know she must make another effort to put the viscount at ease and draw him into conversation.

"Spring appears to be coming early this year," she said. Mother often spoke of the weather when receiving guests.

"It often appears to, I have seen."

"And then cold weather returns."

"Yes."

She waited for him to say more, then wondered why he would. This conversation was guaranteed to create *ennui* as taxing as any she had ever experienced. Bother! Pulling every word from his lips would make for an interminable call, and the idea of a full evening in his company set her to pondering how she could, if she received an invitation, send her regrets to the Almack's patronesses without doing herself damage in their eyes.

He shifted in his chair, and she looked up. Her anticipation of his departure must have been visible, because his eyes slitted before he said, "This is a futile exercise."

"Yes . . . I mean . . ."

"You may as well speak your mind, Miss Wallace. It seems this call cannot take much more of a turn for the worse."

For the first time, she did not lower her gaze away when he spoke to her. He was correct. Anything she said, anything she did, could not make this conversation more uncomfortable.

"I have to concur."

From her left, Nancy cleared her throat quietly.

Amelia paid her no mind, for, at last, this conversation was moving forward.

"It seems we both are afflicted with that most accursed thing—friends who care about us," Lord Foxington said with a hint of a smile.

"True." Knowing she could not allow this to falter, she hurried to add, "It is difficult to be ungrateful for their good intentions."

"I find it quite easy."

She smiled and held out the plate of cakes. "You are clearly wiser than I."

"I doubt that." Instead of taking a cake, he stretched to pick up the book from the table. "You handled this with a care that suggests you have been reading it."

"Yes." She set the plate back on the tray beside her. Again she should say something more, but she always had found her reading a most intimate subject which she did not discuss even with Iris.

"A biography of Queen Elizabeth, I see." He turned the book to open its cover. "Do you admire her?"

"Deeply."

He smiled. "And I have to, as you said moments ago, concur. She was a woman worthy of admiration, although I doubt she was easy to be around."

Amelia laughed, startling herself. "An understatement, my lord. Anyone that focused on a single goal would be difficult."

"If not deadly."

"For those who crossed her or she believed stood in her way. She was a woman who was willing to do what she must to safeguard the throne of England."

He set the book back on the table. "Admirable, but dangerous. Do you consider you have much in common with her beyond the shade of your hair?"

"Me? Admirable, but dangerous?" With another laugh, she shook her head. "I daresay not."

"Lord Dougherty seems to believe you have many commendable qualities which should be displayed at the patronesses' masquerade."

"Masquerade?"

He smiled, and she wished he would continue to do so, because it added a warmth to his face that had been missing when he spoke so politely with her. "You didn't know it shall be a masquerade?"

"To be honest, my lord—"

"Which I trust you will continue to be."

"I had no idea what sort of assembly it would be, other than Iris—Lady Dougherty's assertion that I must attend, or I was doomed for all time in the eyes of the *ton*."

"That was quite honest."

She put her fingers to her lips, wondering why she was being so outspoken when moments before she had been unable to find a single word to speak. A glance at Nancy, who was now frowning as if she had pricked her finger, urged her to say, "Pardon me, my lord."

"To the contrary. Please speak your mind. It is refreshing." He tapped the cover of the book. "Good Queen Bess would not have hesitated. You have friends who care deeply about you, Miss Wallace."

"I am lucky."

His laugh startled her, but not as much as his words when he replied, "I am uncertain if I would call blatant matchmaking good fortune."

"Matchmaking? I believe it was only for this single evening that you agreed to be my escort."

"Come now, Miss Wallace. You must be aware that all people who have ventured into marriage are quite insistent that none of their friends elude the parson's mousetrap."

She raised her chin. "You can be reassured, my lord, that I have no interest in speaking vows with you in front of the vicar. I intend that the man I marry will not have to have his arm twisted to be my husband."

Stuart laughed. By Jove, the woman did have more wit about her than he had suspected when this call was arranged. Dougherty was a good friend, and his wife was a diamond of the first water; but conversations with them seemed to focus completely on the latest gossip from the *ton* . . . and when Stuart would find a wife and obtain an heir to his title.

"Well put, Miss Wallace." He started to raise his cup to his lips to finish the tea within it, but paused when she stiffened. Did she think he intended to use the tea as an excuse to put an end to the conversation?

Then he heard the hurried footfalls she must have noted. He came to his feet as a woman, who must be Mrs. Wallace, appeared in the doorway. She was shorter than her daughter, and her hair was a sedate brown instead of a fiery Queen Elizabeth red. However, her still slender form and finely drawn features identified her as Miss Wallace's mother.

"Lord Foxington!" she gasped, untying the ribbons on her bonnet. "I had no idea the hour was so late. Forgive me for not being here when you arrived." Her glance in her daughter's direction suggested she was relieved to find Miss Wallace unravished.

"Miss Wallace has been kind enough to speak with me while we awaited your return." He set his cup back on the tray. "I trust you will forgive what may seem incivility, Mrs. Wallace. I was about to take my leave."

"Of course." She could not hide her eagerness to discuss his call with her daughter.

Dougherty owed him a duty for allowing another matchmaking mama to get ideas in her head. Thank goodness, Miss Wallace was of a far more commonsensical stock.

Smiling at Miss Wallace, he said, "I trust you are agreeable, then, to the arrangement for me to escort you to the masquerade."

"Yes."

"Mayhap we might speak more of Queen Elizabeth at that time."

Her lovely green eyes glittered with delight. "I would greatly enjoy that, my lord."

"As I would." Taking her hand, he started to bow over it.

"Of course, we may be fortunate and neither be invited to this soirée," she said softly.

He laughed, earning a frown from her abigail and a gasp of astonishment from her mother. Miss Wallace wore a chagrined smile, and he knew she believed she had spoken out of turn again. Mayhap escorting her to this silly gathering and watching over her if trouble began would not be such a chore after all.

Three

Miss Wallace's hopes were for naught, Stuart realized when he returned home several days later to find an embossed invitation waiting on his desk. The paper was an exquisite cream, and the seal identified it as coming from Lady Dougherty, who clearly was acting for this event as a secretary for the Almack's patronesses.

"You look less than pleased, my lord." Tinkcom, his butler, came in with a tray topped with a light meal. Setting it on the desk, for Stuart had developed the habit of eating there, the round man added, "It arrived not more than an hour past."

Stuart picked up a muffin. He had not had breakfast this morning. Taking a bite, he regarded the invitation. Matters were becoming quite clear. Dougherty and his wife had arranged for Miss Wallace to be on the guest list for this gathering, and then they had asked him to play her escort with some wild tale of trouble. Blast and blast again his sense of honor! How many more predicaments would it get him into?

"Is there an answer, my lord?" asked Tinkcom with a hint of impatience. Hint? His butler seldom was circumspect about his opinions.

"You can tell Lady Dougherty—"

"The answer is not to be returned to her, but to Lady Cowper. The messenger was not the usual lad from the Doughertys' household, for he wore a different livery." The butler allowed himself a smile. "I was given the impression that the staffs of several households have been pressed into service to deliver these invitations."

Stuart did not silence his groan. This gathering of young misses was becoming the social event of the Season and, as such, would most likely prove to be even more vexing than he had first imagined.

"Is there an answer, my lord?" Tinkcom was once again his sedate self.

"You may send word to Lady Cowper that, with the greatest pleasure, I accept her invitation."

He thought he heard his butler snort with something that sounded suspiciously like amusement. Why shouldn't Tinkcom enjoy this jest perpetrated on him? If he had followed his first inclination and told Dougherty he could not escort Miss Wallace to the gathering, he would not be caught up in this skimble-skamble.

Finishing the muffin, he opened the invitation. Dougherty had not said what time the gathering was, and Stuart doubted if Miss Wallace would appreciate arriving so late that the patronesses were displeased. He laughed under his breath. What a silly state of affairs! He had thought he was done with such posturing when he sold his commission at the end of the war and sought a quieter life.

He opened the invitation. A slip of paper spiraled to the carpet. He picked it up, realizing it had been folded within the sealed invitation. With a frown, he read the words.

"Is this someone's idea of a jest?" he asked aloud.

If so, it was not a very good one. Ringing for his carriage to be brought, he knew he would not make a good second impression on Miss Wallace by calling without an invitation like this. However, certain matters—like threats for her safety—took precedence even over the canons of society.

"Lord Foxington is here?" Amelia's voice came out in a graceless squeak, but the footman who was announcing the viscount did not smile. She appreciated, as never before, how well her mother had trained the household staff.

"He—and these are his words, Miss Wallace—begs your indulgence and asks you to see him posthaste even if you are not at home this afternoon."

"Tell him to come in, Gordon." As the footman walked toward the parlor door, she called, "Tell him slowly . . . and after you send for Papa."

"Mr. Wallace does not like to be disturbed."

Did Gordon think she was not aware of her father's habit of enjoying a pipe and a book each afternoon as soon as the midday meal was over? Instead of retorting with that, she said, "Tell Papa that Lord Foxington is calling. He is sure to want to join us."

Amelia ignored how the footman's lips quirked in a smile he was trying to hide. She suspected before the hour was over, there would be gossip in the kitchen she had wanted her father with her during this call in hopes that Lord Foxington would offer for her. What flummery!

Putting her book on the table next to where she was sitting, she smoothed the front of her light yellow dress that while one of her favorites, was hardly suited for receiving callers because she often used it while tending flowers in the small garden behind the house. Patting back her hair, she knew it would have to do as well. The dampness from the rain pelting the windows made it curl even more tightly than usual.

"A caller?" asked her father as he came into the parlor. His thinning red hair sifted the smoke curling up from his pipe. Dressed even more casually than she, he carried the book he must have been reading. His spectacles had slid to the very tip of his nose.

Before she could answer, the footman announced Lord Foxington.

The viscount's face was as cold as a statue in the center of an elegant square. His eyes could have been two pieces of unfired coal, for not a single spark brightened them.

"Miss Wallace . . ." He looked at her father as Papa cleared his throat. "Sir." He bowed his head. "I am glad to see you here."

"Lord Foxington, you appear all on end." Papa gestured toward the settee where she sat, listening. "Why don't you sit and explain why you are giving my daughter this unplanned look-in?"

"Gladly."

Amelia hoped no one else heard her breath draw in quickly when the viscount sat beside her. The settee was not large, and she doubted she could move without brushing against him. Why would Papa suggest he sit *here?* He must be as distressed as Lord Foxington.

Without a further greeting, Lord Foxington asked, "Miss Wallace, did you receive an invitation to the masquerade at Almack's?"

"I don't know."

"Please check."

She could not mistake the tension in his voice. Rising, she tried to swallow her gasp when her leg brushed his. A sensation, startlingly like an ember bursting on a fire, raced through her. She looked back and saw her astonishment mirrored in Lord Foxington's eyes. When her gaze was caught by his, a smile eased—for only an instant—his rigid face. Then it was gone, so speedily she could have believed she had only imagined that smile. Her rapid heartbeat refused to let her dismiss that fleeting connection as a fantasy.

Papa's voice, asking Lord Foxington about some tidbit of news, spurred her feet to take her to the bell. She sent the maid who answered to see if anything had been delivered to the house. Because she could not loiter by the door like a naughty child, she walked back to where Papa and Lord Foxington were discussing the book her father had been reading.

The viscount gave her another lightning swift smile that sent luscious warmth thundering through her. With care, she sat next to him. If she chanced to touch him now . . .

She was not sure what might happen, but it would be more unsettling.

"Both Mrs. Wallace and I have enjoyed reading Mrs. Stanhope's most recent novel," Papa was saying. "Mayhap you have read it."

"Which one?" Stuart had little interest in this topic, but he would speak of anything to keep his mind off the reason why he was calling.

Wallace replied, *"Treachery or the Grave of Antoinette.* A most intriguing story."

"No, I haven't had the pleasure of reading that."

His tone must have revealed too much because Wallace replied, "Mayhap you are like Amelia. She prefers much heavier fare, I must own."

"Biographies of Queen Elizabeth as I recall."

His hope that Miss Wallace would smile withered when she glanced at him and quickly away. He might be able to bamboozle her father into believing there was nothing amiss, but she had seen right through any pretense.

The maid who had answered the bell hurried back into the room. She eyed him openly, then looked away when she realized he was aware of her scrutiny. No doubt this call was setting off all sorts of rumors among the household. That gossip would be silenced in the wake of what he suspected would be revealed to Miss Wallace and her father.

"It arrived only a short time ago," the maid said as she handed a familiar-appearing folded sheet to Miss Wallace. Again the maid looked at him before scurrying out of the room.

"Is that what you have been waiting for?" Wallace asked, popping his pipe between his teeth and setting a cloud swirling around his head.

"It is, I believe, an invitation to the masquerade at Almack's." She struggled to smile. "I cannot say it is something I have been waiting for." Her eyes remained troubled as she looked at him. "Did you receive one as well, my lord? Is that the reason for your call?"

"I did receive one." He motioned toward the folded sheet. "Please open it."

"Now?"

"If you would be so kind."

He watched as she carefully broke the green wax sealing the folded sheet. Pieces of it dropped onto her lap, teasing him to let his gaze slide along her. He must not let that pleasurable sight blind him to the reason why he had called.

"Is there another piece of paper inside the invitation?" he asked.

She nodded. "Yes, it is folded within it."

"May I?"

Silently, she handed it to him.

He opened it and fought not to snarl the curse burning in his throat. The words were identical to what he had already read.

"May I?" she asked.

He held out the slip of paper. "Are you sure you want to see it?"

"The message was clearly meant for me to read."

"True." He gave her a taut smile. "Prepare yourself, Miss Wallace."

She took the piece of paper, and her face bleached, adding fullness to her lush lips. His gaze jerked away from them when she whispered, "'Stay away from the masquerade, or you will be sorry.'"

Her father reached out and snatched the paper from her fingers. "What is this? A hoax?"

"I don't believe it's a hoax," Stuart replied.

Miss Wallace regarded him steadily. Her voice was far more even than his or her father's as she asked, "Do you wish me to believe that you believe it is some sort of threat?"

"It would appear so." He came to his feet, unable to sit. "Mr. Wallace, Lord Dougherty requested that I escort your daughter to this gathering because he had previously heard rumbles of trouble."

"Do you think I will allow Amelia to walk into what might be a dangerous situation?" Wallace stood, his fingers clamped so tightly around his pipe that Stuart was not surprised when it snapped. "Deuce take it!"

Miss Wallace said, still as serene as if they were discussing the rain pelting the windows, "I assume you have received a comparable note, my lord."

"An exact duplicate."

She put her hand on her father's sleeve, and Stuart was astonished to have disappointment flush through him that those slender fingers were not on his arm. Was *this* the danger suggested in the note? Letting his mind be betwattled by this young woman who had not made any secret that she was accepting his company only as a favor to her bosom bow?

"Then, Papa," she said, "it seems logical to believe this so-called threat and the rumbles of trouble are simply part of an attempt to make the masquerade as entertaining as possible."

Her father did not answer for a long minute. He looked from his daughter to Stuart when he said, "That is possible. I do not know you well, my lord, but I do know my daughter is not one to panic. She seems to believe the note does not portend some disaster. If I have your word that you will safeguard her . . ."

"You do, sir." He cursed himself. If he had said that he did not want the responsibility, this ado would be over. "But it might be wiser—"

"Ah, my lord," Miss Wallace said as a footman entered the room, "here is your cloak. I thank you for coming here to express your concerns about my safety."

While her father spoke to the footman about bringing him another pipe, Stuart asked in a near whisper, "Why are you pretending this is nothing? Up until now, I would have labeled you a uniquely rational woman. Are you so desperate to achieve recognition from the patronesses that you will risk yourself?"

"Of course not!" Her lowered voice took on an edge he had expected to hear when she discovered the note within her invitation. "However, I have several friends who would not be kept from Almack's door that evening even if the devil himself greeted them."

"So you are thinking of attending the gathering in a misguided effort to protect them?"

"Yes, although I hope my efforts will not be misguided."

"How do you intend to protect them?"

A shiver raced along her so fiercely he could see it. "I don't know, my lord, but I do know that I would never forgive myself if I did not try."

Four

How hard could one's heart thump and still remain within one's chest?

Amelia clasped and unclasped her hands with anxiety. This coming evening was enough to make her swoon. Not only must she remember every lesson she had been taught about such gatherings, but she had to keep that dreadful note in mind. She had been glad to see Lord Foxington shared her disquiet over what she had convinced both Papa and Mama was simply a joke. If he had not added his words to hers, she doubted her parents would have relented. For that, she was grateful to the viscount, glad he understood her determination to make certain nothing happened to her friends.

"You don't even know if they received such a note, too," she whispered to herself, not wanting to attract her abigail's attention.

A wasted effort, because Nancy asked, "Did you say something, Miss Wallace?"

"Just repeating my lessons to myself." Her smile must appear strained, because her lips were reluctant to move. "I don't want to do anything to distress my family tonight."

"How could you?" Nancy smiled, obviously in a generous mood. "Your costume is perfect."

"Thanks to you." She touched the flounces sewn onto the full skirt that suggested she was about to enter the fabled French court at Versailles.

Nancy rushed to the window when the sound of carriage

wheels rattled to a stop in front of the house. Peeking out, she crowed, "Lord Foxington is here."

"Hush! What if he were to hear you? And come away from the window."

"So he doesn't suspect you might be looking to see his arrival?" Her abigail laughed. "If you want my opinion, Miss Wallace, 'tis high time such a fine-looking gent came calling. You have kept your nose too deeply in your books to notice other men, but you have noticed this one."

"Nancy!" She was astonished, for her abigail had never been so blunt.

"Don't give me a scold, for you know I am speaking the truth. Lord Foxington is far better looking and far better spoken than his reputation suggests." She smiled. "And he likes looking at *you*."

"Don't have me betrothed and married off before I go down the stairs. Remember he is escorting me only as a favor to his friend."

"Mayhap it started that way." Nancy added nothing else, and there was no need. Her satisfied smile said it all.

Knowing she would not alter Nancy's opinion a jot, Amelia picked up her mask that was waiting on the bed. She slipped her hand through the strings of the small bag that held her invitation.

Did sheep feel this same sense of inevitable doom when herded to the slaughter?

Stuart heard light footsteps on the upper floor as he was greeted at the door by the Wallaces' butler. He smiled, for that sound meant he had not been mistaken when he saw curtains pull back from two different windows as he stepped from his carriage. Neither of them would have been drawn aside by Amelia, he was most certain, but well-trained servants would have alerted her of his arrival.

He looked up when those footsteps reached the staircase. The only word that came into his mind as he saw her walk toward him was *breathtaking*. He had paid little mind to fashion's caprices even before he had left for the Continent. Undoubtedly, he would have given it a great deal more of his attention if he had seen any woman dressed like this.

The dress with its silvery trim accented every curve, drawing his eyes to her firm bosom and slender waist. Drapes of fabric sewn to the skirt matched what flowed along her as she seemed to glide across the foyer. Pearls and more of the silver-edged lace were woven through her auburn hair which was already cascading from its disciplined curls into a rambunctious tangle on her shoulders as if determined to choose a style for itself.

In one hand, she carried a befeathered mask of the same silk as her gown. On her other arm, a small bag was nearly lost in the folds of her gown. Her fingers were tight around her mask, he noticed, when she paused in front of him.

"Good evening, mademoiselle," he murmured.

"And to you, *mon seigneur.*"

He lifted her hand and bowed over it. As he was about to release it, he brought her fingers to his lips. Her lacy mitts offered a tantalizing sample of her soft skin, and he slowly lowered her hand, not wanting to release it.

The thought astonished him. He was not a rake who found the very scent of perfumed skin an intoxicant. Instead, he kept his attention on far more profound pursuits. In his head, Dougherty's laugh sounded along with a scold that even the most serious man should not banish amusement from his life.

And Amelia Wallace was unquestionably amusing. Not just her sharp mind and clear opinions, but her loveliness that he was proud to have by his side tonight.

"You look beautiful," he said and was rewarded by her eyes that sparkled as brightly as her gown's silver trim.

"And you most odd, if I may say so."

He looked down at his own costume which consisted of a buckskin coat over a long waistcoat of a generation past. Leather boots reached to his knees. "I would not look odd if I were among other backwoodsmen in the wilds of America."

"Do you think *that* is a good idea?"

Putting his hand on the dagger he had hooked to his waist, he smiled coldly. "I think it is an excellent idea under the circumstances."

Whatever she might have said next went unspoken, because her parents came down the stairs to greet him. He could not mistake their uneasiness, and he marveled that they were trusting him with their daughter when they clearly were not persuaded the notes were a hoax. Swallowing a promise to watch over her, for that might induce Mr. Wallace to insist she remain at home, he bid them a good evening as the front door opened. He would have been glad to speak his mind if he had been sure Amelia would not go to Almack's on her own to ascertain her friends' safety.

And he had promised Dougherty to watch over her tonight. Too many promises tangled them up more tightly than fish in a net.

Amelia tried to smile when Lord Foxington handed her into his carriage which was too grand for a backwoodsman. Sitting on the tufted leather seats, she tried not to bump Nancy's knees. The tiger must have helped her abigail in while she was saying good evening to her parents. When Lord Foxington sat beside her, she saw his grim expression in the moment before the door was closed and the carriage draped in shadow.

Silence, that dreadful silence, filled the carriage while she waited for him to say something. If he did not want to upset their chaperon, he could speak of other matters. He was well-acquainted, she guessed, with many of the guests this evening. Then she realized he never had spoken of *on dits* as her friends did.

"I should say how much I appreciate your accompanying me tonight, my lord." Her voice quavered on each word as if they were riding over a featherbed lane instead of the city street.

"You are welcome."

She dampened her lips, wishing she had chosen words that would have required more of an answer. Nancy's knee bumped hers a bit harder, and she guessed her abigail was urging her to say something more.

"Did you speak with Lord Dougherty about the invitations?" she asked.

That got his attention. Moving so she could see his face that was nearly lost in the darkness, for the long nights of summer were still months away, he said, "I did, and he was as astonished as you and I at what was included with them. Lady Dougherty claims to know nothing of the matter."

"Iris would not just *claim*. She would be honest."

"You are very loyal to your friends, Miss Wallace." His laugh was short and harsh. "I trust that will not prove to become a problem for you this evening."

"Are you saying one of my friends . . . ?" She clamped her mouth closed. To say too much when Nancy must be avidly listening would be foolish. Her abigail would fly up to the boughs before ordering the carriage back to the house.

"Someone must have," came his grim answer.

"I realize that, but I would prefer to believe it was a stranger."

His hand settled on hers. If he had intended to ease their trembling, his touch achieved exactly the opposite result. Her fingers quivered beneath his as the amazing awareness that suffused her whenever he was near flared into a sweetness scrambling every thought in her head. When his thumb slipped beneath them, caressing her palm, she looked up at where he was slanting so slightly toward her. His gaze cut through the dark to capture hers, and she discovered there was a danger to her that had nothing to do with what might be nothing but a malicious prank. Her heart began that frantic pounding against her breast as his thumb's gentle, questing motion suggested he would be more bold if they were alone within the cloak of these shadows.

"Miss Wallace," her abigail said, excitement filling her voice, "we are here."

Amelia was not sure if she withdrew her hand or if Lord Foxington lifted his hastily away. Either way, she regretted the loss of that warmth as she looked out at the busy street and the dozens of carriages disgorging their passengers at the door to Almack's.

When the door of their carriage was opened, Lord Foxington stepped out. He turned and held up his hand to her. Now, in the light from the lantern on the carriage and what streamed out of the assembly rooms, she could not mistake his expression. His fingers closed around hers again, and she knew he wanted to hold her far more intimately. It was an exhilarating undercurrent to the activity around them, because her own thoughts were taking the same brazen turn.

As she started to step from the carriage, he grasped her by the waist and swung her, with a rustle of petticoats and silk, down to the street. She gasped in surprise and heard Nancy mutter something that did not sound complimentary to the viscount.

"Forgive me," he said as he gestured toward the street. "I did not want you to ruin your slippers in yon mud puddle. I know Sir Walter Raleigh put down his cloak for the queen, but I find I am without a suitable garment to do the same this evening. Mayhap I should have come as a courtier instead of a woodsman."

She laughed, and heads turned to them before bending toward each other with whispers that soon would be repeated throughout the *ton*. Boring Lord Foxington was escorting shy Miss Wallace . . . and making her laugh.

He must have taken note of the prattling, which did not surprise her, for he added, "Nothing like titillating our fellow guests before we even bid good evening to the patronesses, is there?"

"Gallantry should always be celebrated," she returned.

"Egad, I suspect I will rue my chivalry this evening."

She let him draw her hand within his arm. "Shall we, *mon seigneur?*"

His hand clasped hers against his sleeve. "Take care when you ask that, mademoiselle, for you may get a most unexpected answer."

She smiled as he swept her toward the door. The answer could not be unexpected when she anticipated so many responses to that question . . . and all of them with his lips against hers.

Five

"Isn't this the very best of the best?" Susan grabbed Amelia's hands and squeezed them.

Amelia smiled at her friend, for she had never seen Susan so happy. The young woman, who was dressed like a milkmaid, had just returned from her conversation with Lady Cowper, and she could not stop babbling about how kind the Almack's patroness had been. Her eyes glistened as brightly as the double rows of candles on the chandeliers hanging from the assembly room's lofty ceiling. No music from the gallery set high in the wall could be as sweet as Susan's voice this evening.

"She knows my mother and my aunt and my cousin," continued Susan, babbling as her face reddened with the excitement.

"Of course, she does. The patronesses know everyone in the Polite World." Before Susan's smile could slip, Amelia added, "And now she has had the chance to get to know you."

"And you!"

"Thank heavens that interview is over." She lowered her voice as she jabbed some recalcitrant hair back over her ears. "And thank heavens it was Lady Cowper who is interrogating us instead of Lady Jersey. I doubt I would have endured the sharp edge of her tongue long without speaking my mind."

"Amelia!"

She laughed along with her friend, letting Susan believe

she had been jesting. However, she had been honest. Lady
Cowper had been the pattern-card of kindness to her; but
Amelia doubted if the patroness shared any of her interests, and, ungrateful wretch that she was, she had wanted
to get back to enjoy Lord Foxington's company.

From where she was standing, she could see him talking with Lord Dougherty and a gentleman she did not
know. Lord Dougherty was dressed as a cavalier, and the
other man in some sort of costume she guessed was supposed to be medieval. It was a dark brown, and he wore
both a sword and a knife.

Susan giggled. "Doesn't Sir Bernard look like a muff in
that outfit? I daresay Paulina was not pleased to see him
arrive to escort her while wearing that."

"Where is Paulina?" she asked, still admiring how Lord
Foxington's simple clothes accented his strong build. Although he had spoken to her of books he had read, she
doubted he led a sedentary life.

"Over there speaking with Lady Cowper."

Amelia pulled her gaze from the viscount to see her
friend was now the one being interviewed by the patroness. Paulina's shoulders were stiff, and Amelia wanted
to rush to her side and offer her sympathy.

"Who would have guessed he would look so dashing?"
continued Susan.

"He? Who?"

Her friend's eyes twinkled. "Why, sadly flat Lord Foxington, of course."

"Susan, you should not speak so about him."

"I am only repeating what others have said. I do not
know how you endure that boring man."

Trying to make her shrug nonchalant, Amelia replied,
"We have mutual friends whom we wish to please by appearing here tonight."

"Is that the whole of it?" Susan bent toward her and said
in barely more than a whisper, "I heard about how he res-
cued you from a puddle out front."

"He was being kind. Nothing more."

"If it was nothing more, why are you glowing at the very mention of his name?"

"Mayhap," came a petulant voice, "she is not glowing because of *him* but because of *her.*"

Amelia sighed when she heard Paulina's tone. It warned her that her friend's conversation with Lady Cowper had not unfolded as she had hoped. Her struggle to smile for her friend was futile because Paulina's mouth was in a straight line and her eyes filled with tears. Spots on the veil of her costume that was the complement to her escort's medieval attire warned some of those tears had already fallen.

Taking Paulina by the arm, Amelia led her to a dusky corner as far as possible from where Lady Cowper stood. Susan followed. Amelia wished Susan would have the good sense to know that her excited anticipation of the announcement of who would receive the vouchers would only exacerbate Paulina's dismay.

Paulina dropped without any grace onto a chair and put her fingers over her face. Kneeling in front of her, Amelia drew down her hands and folded them between her own.

"Don't try to comfort me with platitudes," Paulina said with a sob.

"I would not do that. I know you are distressed." Amelia patted her hands.

"Who knows?" tossed in Susan. "You may have made yourself memorable to Lady Cowper, so she wishes to see you again."

"You are such a block!" Paulina started to jump to her feet, but Amelia motioned for her to remain sitting.

Coming to her feet, Amelia faced Susan. "I have never known you to be cruel before this. Such words will not curry favors for you with the patronesses."

"Why are you blaming *me* when I did not make a complete jumble of this?" Susan flung her hand toward Paulina, who was looking daggers at her. "I told you, Paulina, to prepare yourself for this interview."

"I did!"

"Obviously not well enough. Now you have lost your last chance to join the Polite World at Almack's."

"You don't know that for certain."

"Don't I? Look at you! All upset, and you are in a coil so tight you could break at any moment. I warned you that if you did not prepare well, you would appear to be an encroaching mushroom."

"Susan!" chided Amelia, shocked her friend would use such a derogatory term. Paulina was of a fine family, and she was not trying to take advantage of her betters. "Susan, I think you have forgotten yourself in the exhilaration of the evening. Mayhap it would be for the better for you to excuse yourself."

"Me?" She fired back a furious scowl at Paulina. "Why are you scolding me when *she* is the one who has ruined the evening by piping her eyes?"

Amelia did not answer. Words clearly would be ineffectual with Susan tonight. She stared at her friend, keeping all expression from her face. Slowly Susan's bravado crumpled, and, with a mutter, she turned on her heel and walked back to where she could bask in the expectation of winning one of the coveted vouchers.

"Thank you," Paulina whispered.

"I have no idea what got into her to make her act in such an uncivil manner."

Paulina's mouth worked before she spat, "You do not know her well. She can be arrogant and silly as you just saw. If she ever had a rational thought in her head, it would die of loneliness."

"I thought I did know her well, but 'tis clear I was mistaken." Not wanting to scold Paulina for being as unprettily spoken as Susan, she sat next to her friend and again pushed her hair back from her cheeks. She should have known that her hair would be as bothersome as everything else this evening. "You must put a good face on this tonight."

"How?"

"I wish I had an answer for you."

Amelia was still searching her mind for some consolation to offer her friend when the man Susan had pointed out as Sir Bernard came over to ask Paulina to stand up with him for the next dance. When Paulina started to demur, Amelia gave her back a gentle shove. Paulina rose and put her hand on Sir Bernard's with a pretty grace Amelia doubted she would ever be able to copy.

Watching the two walk to where others were gathering for the dance, Amelia sighed. She had been afraid of this from the moment Iris first spoke of this gathering. Some young women would be ecstatic to be granted entrance into the *ton's* inner sanctums, but the rest would be heartbroken like Paulina.

She looked around the assembly room, but she did not see Lord Foxington. Just now, she would have appreciated his irreverence about this evening. Mayhap he had gone to join some of the other men in the pursuit of chance's favor in one of the card rooms, although she had thought he would do her the courtesy of telling her that he was taking his leave.

Bother! She was in a grim mood now. Sitting here and suffering from the dismals would gain her nothing. A smile teased her lips. Nothing was exactly what she had hoped to achieve tonight, although her parents would be so proud if she was granted a voucher.

"No thank you," she said to herself as she stood. This was too much of a bumble-bath already.

As she crossed the room, looking for Iris, who had requested that Amelia seek her out after her conversation with Lady Cowper, she realized she had misjudged the tension throughout the room. Susan was not the only one who was all a-titter with contemplation of being awarded such a prize. Clumps of people were gathered in earnest conversation that faded into silence whenever anyone approached. Suspicious glances followed her across the large space. Not just her, but anyone who was not part of one of the clusters of guests.

Where was Lord Foxington? She could not fault him for escaping this strain, but she wished he had taken her with him.

She sighed. No guest must leave until the official pronouncement was made. By that time, the nervousness in the room would smother her.

"There you are!"

Amelia turned and was nearly knocked from her feet when Iris threw her arms around her. Regaining her balance, she smiled until she felt more strands of hair falling around her face.

"I was looking for you, Iris." Her smile broadened when she saw the Grecian gown her friend wore. Its white silk was draped across her with bands of gold. "What a beautiful costume! You look lovely tonight."

"As you do."

She put her hand up to the wisps still clinging to her face. "I should have come as a vagabond. I fear that is the only way this silly hair would be appropriate."

"Nonsense. You look perfect." Iris's voice became an eager whisper. "As perfect as a young miss should when she is about to receive a voucher to attend Almack's for the rest of the Season."

"Me?" She wanted to groan out a denial. Coming to the occasional assembly would be fun, but to be sucked completely into the whirl of the Season would demand so much of her time.

"I knew you would, Amelia, because I knew you would charm Lady Cowper." Iris's smile became triumphant.

"Or is it rather that you persuaded her?"

"What does it matter?" She laughed. Lowering her voice again, she added, "Tell no one what I have told you. Let Susan Little and Evelyn Barry be surprised."

"Not Paulina?"

Iris's smile dropped away. "Dear me, she will be disappointed, won't she?"

"Terribly." She did not want to envision her friend's tears falling anew when this announcement was made. "If you urged Lady Cowper to extend the invitation to me, couldn't you suggest she invite Paulina, too?"

"That would not do."

"Then give Paulina my voucher. It matters so deeply to her."

Hearing a squeal of excitement, Amelia looked across the room to see Susan and Evelyn Barry, a petite brunette, hugging each other. Clearly the tidings would not remain a secret. She scanned the room, seeking Paulina. There must be something she could say to comfort her friend, although she was not sure what. She saw Paulina standing beside Sir Bernard before she walked out one of the doors beyond the gallery.

Amelia attempted to follow, but she was halted by the press of the guests who were eager to congratulate her. Some of the felicitations were sincere, but others, coming from those who had hoped to be anointed with a voucher, were feigned. This had been, Amelia decided, the very worst idea anyone had ever had. Two young women were thrilled, and so many were disappointed. The author of that silly note which had been put into the invitation was right. She was sorry she had come here tonight.

Six

"Are you enjoying yourself?" Amelia smiled as she walked to where Lord Foxington was resting one shoulder against the ornate draperies by one of the windows near the musician's gallery.

"I would say I am most definitely enjoying myself." He chuckled. "As for the rest of this clutter, I cannot say the same. I have never been fond of crowded confusion. And you? Are you enjoying yourself?"

"No."

"A straightforward answer that will not serve you well when you are the talk of the *ton* at the next gathering at Almack's."

She rolled her eyes, then looked about, hoping nobody had taken note of her action. "I know I should be grateful."

"So I would be wise to withhold my congratulations?"

"I wish you could offer them to someone else."

"Your friend Miss Middington, I assume."

She nodded. "Paulina was very distressed before the announcement was made. Now . . ." With a sigh, she glanced around the room. "Mayhap she has already taken her leave."

"I saw Miller a few minutes ago."

"Who?"

"Sir Bernard Miller. His face was as long as a winter night. 'Twill do his intentions toward Miss Middington no good when the very sight of him is certain to be a reminder of her disappointment."

"He has a *tendre* for her?"

"I suspect so, for he was prattling nonstop about her when he joined Dougherty and me earlier."

"If he were to say something to her—"

"Would that ease her despondency?"

Amelia closed her eyes and sighed. "I doubt anything will."

"I know one thing that will ease yours."

She opened her eyes as his finger beneath her chin tilted her face up toward his. Knowing the peril she was provoking by not looking away, she gazed up at him. How could anyone believe this man to be boring? His touch enthralled her, and his smile suggested adventures that would be far from dull. He might be sparing of words with others; but he never used them to spare her feelings, and she appreciated that honesty.

Her eyes focused on his mouth as she imagined it against hers. When his finger coursed along her jaw, a chaste caress that seemed as intimate as a kiss, she looked away.

"Would you care to dance?" he asked.

Was his voice breathless, or was her heartbeat thundering in her ears distorting the sound? She wanted to shout that of course she wanted to dance with him, but, even in the midst of this enchantment, she could not forget herself . . . or the other guests who would take note of every social solecism she might make. She must be even more cautious now that she had been anointed with that irksome invitation to Almack's.

"I would enjoy dancing very much," she said, trying not to sound as agog as his voice had in her mind.

"It will grant you a reprieve from your adoring fellow guests."

Amelia laughed as his teasing words freed her from the bonds of despair that had clamped around her as soon as she heard of this gathering. She wanted to thank him for his kindness, but such careless words might be overheard and misinterpreted . . . or interpreted all too correctly.

Lord Foxington chuckled, too, as he held out his crooked arm. When she put her hand on it, he said, "That is better. You have had such a doleful expression one would believe you were not highly honored with the accolades heaped on you tonight."

She laughed again and put her fingers to her lips. "Please, my lord, you are going to draw everyone's attention to me if you keep me giggling."

"I believe I am too late for that."

"Yes." She sighed, her brief good humor vanishing. "I have garnered, most unfortunately, much interest with this evening's events."

"I was not speaking of this evening's events."

At his abruptly somber tone, she looked at him again. "No?"

"No. I was speaking of how charming you look in your delightful costume which has drawn the eyes of many in the room tonight." He lightly touched the lace on her shoulder. "Including mine, again and again."

When his fingertip brushed her skin, she knew he had taken note of her quivering reaction because his smile returned. But it was not the same smile, for this one had nothing to do with amusing words. Instead, it suggested other ways than trading words that he would like to amuse her.

"Shall we?" he asked.

"Yes," she whispered.

He had led her a trio of steps toward where the others were preparing for the next set before she realized that her answer had not been to his invitation to dance, but to another invitation she had created within her fantasies. Again she lowered her eyes before anyone could sense her thoughts. She could not forget that Lord Foxington had escorted her to this assembly simply as a favor to his good friend. If she let her hoydenish yearning for his kiss betray her, she was certain to end up as dismayed as Paulina.

Amelia used the time spent dancing to try to regain her composure. What had happened? Just days ago, she had been asserting that she did not want to have Lord Foxington for her escort tonight. Now the idea of his kisses filled her every thought.

As they went through the pattern of the dance, she could not help noticing how his smile broadened when she returned to take his hands. Mayhap these silly desires were nothing more than the excitement of the evening. Mayhap he was simply trying to make this important evening memorable for her.

She did not realize she had laughed aloud until he asked, "What is so amusing?"

Before she could compose an answer that would not disclose the truth, she was swept away into another repetition of the dance's steps. She could not hope he would forget the question and her lack of response, so she had one ready when she came back to him again.

"You and I," she said.

"Us? So amusing?" He spun her about so swiftly her dress flared out around her ankles. "What is amusing about us?"

"Neither of us wished to attend this evening, but here we are having a pleasant time."

"Very pleasant." His voice took on the warmth again that sent something tingly whirling through her.

This time she did have an answer, but had no chance to speak it as the dance came to an end. Instantly, they were surrounded, and she found herself once more the focus of the conversation. She tried to hide her dismay. She thought she was successful until Lord Foxington's hand on her arm guided her away from the crowd as he asked them to excuse her for she was overmastered by her good fortune.

Amelia released her breath with a long, slow sigh as the guests went in search of the other two women who had found favor with Lady Cowper this evening. "Oh, my, if I had had any idea it would be like this, I believe I would have said something quite saucy during my conversation with the patroness."

"I fear 'tis too late by half for that." He smiled.

"Do not think I am being ungrateful," she hurried to say, realizing how insulting her remarks could be construed to be. "I should have gone with my initial instincts and accepted I am far more comfortable sitting at home with a book I can enjoy."

"With all the invitations I heard being offered to you, I doubt you will ever finish reading another book."

"I could not possibly call on everyone who has spoken to me tonight."

"It will be expected you do."

"Bother," she muttered as she jabbed at her hair that was tickling her back.

"That sounds as if something is more direly wrong than unwanted calls."

She smiled at him as she put up her hands to catch another section of her hair that had escaped from its pins. "My accursed hair is falling down, and I cannot wander about while looking like a hoyden."

His fingers sifted into the loosened strands, and that delicious joy flowed through her as it did each time he touched her. She should tell him to unhand her this very moment, to recall they stood within the so-very-proper walls of Almack's, but she said nothing as she let herself be lost within the tempting fire of his eyes.

"Your hair is trying to tell you something," he said so quietly his words would reach no farther than her ears.

"What is that?" Her voice quivered on each word.

"That something this beautiful should not be restrained."

"Mayhap someday it will be permissible for a woman to be seen with her hair loose."

"It is permissible now." His eyes twinkled as one closed in a wink. "Just not in public!"

She was glad that despite being ginger-hackled, she did not blush, for her cheeks were as hot as a cobble on a sunny day. "My lord, you should not say such things."

"I know, and I usually don't. You seem to be bringing out the worst in me." He twisted a strand around his finger. "Or mayhap the best."

"I will leave that decision to you."

He chuckled. "I should know better by now than to try to offer you such flummery."

"Flummery?"

"Mayhap that was not the right word, for there is nothing foolish about speaking the truth." Again he smoothed the strands curling along his finger. "And it is the truth that this is lovely."

"I should go and put my hair back in place." She did not move away.

"Yes, you should." He did not release her hair.

"If I am seen in such a disheveled state, it would reflect badly on my family."

"Yes, it would."

"Are you going to agree with everything I say?"

He unwound her hair from around his finger. "I think, knowing me, that is highly unlikely."

"Good." She started to turn, then asked, "Could you point the way to a private place where I can tend to this?"

"I would be glad to show you." His smile became roguish. "After all, I am your escort tonight, so it behooves me to escort you to such a private place." He settled her hand on his arm and led her toward a nearby doorway.

Amelia knew she was chancing trouble by not disagreeing with him. To leave the assembly room with him would start tongues wagging, a situation that he would appreciate no more than she would. Yet she said nothing, not wanting to ruin the fantasy that they would be alone and he would draw her into his arms and—

"Ah, there is your abigail," Lord Foxington said, shattering that dangerous dream as he motioned to Nancy to join them. "This way," he added when Nancy reached them.

Her abigail glanced at Amelia with a question she did not speak. Again Amelia knew she must say something. She heard herself babbling about her hair refusing to stay put and the need to redo it. Even in her ears, her voice sounded odd—strained and taut.

When Lord Foxington pointed along a hallway where she should be able to find a room to tend to her hair, Amelia was glad he did not follow. She needed time to tend to her equilibrium as well. It might not be as easily repaired as her hair, but she must be more serene before she returned to the assembly room . . . and to his side.

"Lord Foxington has been very attentive to you since the announcement was made of your acceptance here," Nancy said as they found the first two doors closed. "He must be very proud to be your escort tonight."

"I am not sure how much it matters to him that the offer of a voucher was made to me." She wished Nancy had not spoken of this, for she was unsettled by the idea that the viscount was being kind to her only because of that bothersome invitation. She wanted to defend him to her abigail, but, as she thought of it, she had to own that he had been absent until it was known she had been one of the three chosen.

"Your mother and father will be pleased," Nancy added. "I fear they despaired of you ever catching a gentleman's eye when you preferred to remain at home with your nose in a book."

She did not reply as she put her hand out to touch a half-open door. Pulling it aside slowly, for she did not want to disturb anyone inside, she took a single step into the room.

Then she froze. She could not move. She could not scream. She could only stare at Susan, who was lying on the floor, gazing at the ceiling with eyes whose last sight must have been the person who had driven the knife into the center of her chest.

Seven

At a scream, Stuart ran along the corridor Miss Wallace and her maid had entered only seconds before. He recognized that sort of shriek, for he had heard it when men first saw the carnage of battle. But what was that sound doing within the walls of Almack's?

A door opened nearly in his face. He shoved it closed, ignoring the curse shouted at him, as he rushed in the direction of that scream. When another sounded, he heard footsteps behind him. Lots of them. The shriek must have reached into the assembly room.

When a woman ran toward him, he reached out to halt her. Miss Wallace's *duenna,* he realized with horror.

"Where is she?" he asked. "Is she hurt?"

"She is dead."

"Dead?" He could not believe what he was hearing.

"Dead."

He leaned the sobbing woman against a closed door and ran to an open door. He threw it aside so hard it crashed against the wall.

Slender arms were flung around his neck as a soft body pressed against him. Red curls brushed his cheek, and he breathed in their sweet fragrance as he buried his face in her hair. At the same time, he wrapped his arms around Miss Wallace's waist. She shivered as if it were the coldest wintry night, but the very motion sent waves of heat through him.

If this was her abigail's idea of a jest. . . .

"She is dead," Miss Wallace whispered.

"Dead?" he repeated as he had before.

When she drew out of his arms, he reluctantly released her. Only then did he see the horrible sight on the floor in front of a draped table. He knelt beside Miss Little and put his fingers to her neck.

"I checked," Miss Wallace said. "There is no pulse, and she is not breathing."

A scream came from the doorway, and he heard shouts and the unmistakable thump of a body hitting the floor. Not just one, but several along with more calls for help and for smelling salts.

He ignored them with the skill to focus on a single matter that he had honed on the battlefield. The knife in the young woman's chest had unique carving in the haft. He seemed to recall seeing it before, but could not recall just where. He did not remove it, for the authorities would want to see it, he suspected.

Looking up at Miss Wallace, whose face was almost the shade of the corpse in front of him, he asked, "Did you discover her this way?"

"Yes." Her eyes widened. "Are you suggesting—?" She choked back the rest of what she had been about to say.

He came to his feet and put his arm around her shoulders, drawing her close again. "I am not suggesting anything. I am simply asking what others will." He glanced toward the door and motioned to Dougherty.

His friend elbowed his way through those clogging the doorway and into the room. "What has happened?" He gulped loudly. "By all that's blue, Foxington! What is this?"

"You know quite well. Send for the watch and a coroner. You had better send someone to the closest church, too. They will know what to do."

He nodded, backing toward the door with an expression that suggested Miss Little's ghost was already visible in the simple chamber.

Stuart sat Miss Wallace on a padded bench by one wall

and went to the door. He called to several other men he knew would be steady even in this situation. He gave them quick orders, and they hurried away.

Stuart looked along the corridor and was glad that Miss Wallace had not panicked and shrieked in hysterics, although he suspected she might be the only woman in the assembly rooms who had not. Several women had apparently swooned even before they had reached the room, for they cluttered the hallway with their unconscious bodies. Their escorts and their watchdogs were hunched over them with *sal volatile,* and the unmistakable reek of burning feathers was already taking over Almack's.

Hearing a rustle behind him, he turned to see Miss Wallace pulling a cloth off the table and draping it over her friend.

"She should not be stared at so," Miss Wallace whispered as she knelt to draw the tablecloth over the corpse's face.

"I could close the door."

"No!" She shuddered. "I do not want to be shut in here with *that.*" Her voice softened even more. "But I do not want to leave Susan alone."

He put his hand on her shoulder, and the gratitude in her eyes threatened to undo him. He could not forget that the woman lying on the floor had been her friend.

Walking around her and the body, he pulled another cloth from the table. He glanced toward the door and saw that the curious crowd had grown in number as they jostled each other to see the macabre sight within the room.

"It is a true pity," murmured one young woman who was eyeing him with obvious interest even as he covered up the corpse. "After all, *she* was one of the lucky three who was offered a voucher to another evening here at Almack's."

He was unsure whether to roll his eyes or curse when her companion agreed readily, so he did both. A woman was dead, and the only thought in their heads was of the accursed vouchers. When had entrance to these assembly rooms become more important than a woman's life?

"Don't heed them," Miss Wallace said as she sat back on her heels.

Surprised that she was attempting to comfort him, he nodded. "I will try not to."

People were shoved aside as two men he did not know came into the room. Their rough clothes identified them immediately as the watch. A third man motioned for the gawkers to disperse. For a long moment, no one moved; then the crowd began to thin around the doorway.

"Who be you two?" asked the shorter of the trio. The distinctive odor of cheap gin flowed out of his mouth on each word.

"Lord Foxington," he answered, helping Miss Wallace to her feet as he stood. "And this is Miss Wallace."

"Did you find the murdered woman, my lord?"

Again Miss Wallace quivered, and he could not fault her. The word *murder* was an ugly one, so ugly he had not allowed himself to think of it.

"I found her," Miss Wallace said. "My abigail and I were looking for a place to redo my hair, and we came in here and saw her."

The short man nodded and rubbed his chin that was dark with whiskers. "That be good."

"Good?" she echoed.

"That there be two of you. She can say you didn't kill the victim, and you can say the same." He gestured for them to move aside. "I need to see the victim."

Stuart said quietly, "You may want to avert your eyes, Miss Wallace."

"There is no need. This sight is burned into my memory."

In spite of her brave words, he edged forward slightly so he stood between her and the corpse as the cloths were lifted away. He heard a gagging sound. Not from her, but from by the door.

Sir Bernard Miller was standing in the doorway and staring at the corpse. "What is *that* doing here?"

"Take care how you speak, Miller," Stuart retorted. "The young woman—"

"What is my dagger doing here?" He pressed one hand over his stomach as his face turned a sickly shade of green. His other hand groped at his belt, clearly hoping to find his knife was still there.

"This is your knife?" asked the tallest of the trio from the watch.

Stuart released Miss Wallace and went to put his hand on Miller's arm. "Take care what you say," he reiterated, this time his concern aimed at the baronet. "The wrong word will find you on your way to the hangman."

Miller stumbled toward the bench where Miss Wallace had sat so briefly. Dropping to it, he cradled his head in his hands. "I had nothing to do with this. Tell them that, Foxington. I had nothing to do with this."

"Do you know when your knife was taken?"

"No." One hand again fumbled along his waist to the empty sheath in a desperate, futile attempt to prove that the knife he had already identified was truly not his. He moaned and hunched even more deeply into himself.

"Do you have an idea who might have taken it from you without your knowledge?"

Miller looked up. His lips trembled before he said, "It could have been anyone in that crush. I was bumped into several times, and it could have been plucked from me any of those times." He choked as he looked at the corpse. "Or when I was dancing. I danced with Miss Little. Do you think she took the knife?"

"It does not appear to be self-inflicted, for the angle would be difficult."

With a moan, Miller hid his face again.

Someone pushed past Stuart. Miss Middington, he discovered, when she sank to her knees beside Miller. She hid her face against his legs as her shoulders quaked with emotion.

As Miss Wallace went to offer solace to her friend, he

spoke with the man who was examining the corpse. He learned nothing he had not already guessed. The knife had been driven into Miss Little's chest from close range, and the horrible deed must have been by someone she knew. There was no sign of a struggle as there likely would have been if a stranger had skulked up to attack Miss Little.

The man made a pointed request for everyone to clear the room, and Stuart had to concur. Remaining here would gain no more answers. If the murderer lingered nearby, the danger might not be past.

He assisted Miller and Miss Middington to their carriage. After telling Miller he would share anything else he heard, Stuart smiled grimly when he saw Miss Wallace helping her abigail toward his own carriage. Their steps were labored, and he could see how the older woman was leaning more heavily on Miss Wallace with each passing second. He hurried to them and lifted her abigail onto the seat before Miss Wallace collapsed under her weight.

"Thank you," Miss Wallace said. "What will happen now?"

"I suspect there will be an inquest headed by the coroner."

"To uncover the murderer?"

He sighed. "They are not always successful, especially when there are no witnesses to the murder."

"Please don't use that word."

He enfolded her to him again, not caring who might chance to see. Amid these extraordinary circumstances, the canons of society must be shunted aside. He rested his cheek on her springy curls and wished he could lose himself in their luscious scent, allowing it to wash away the horror of what remained inside Almack's.

"Let me take you home now," he murmured.

She nodded and started to step away.

He kept one arm around her as his other hand rose to cup her cheek. When she closed her eyes and rested her head against his palm with a trust he found amazing when the murderer might be close by even now, he pushed all thoughts of the tragedy from his head and savored her soft skin against his hand. He let his fingers sift up through her hair. Her eyes opened, and he saw that fiery spark return. Her lips parted in what appeared to be an invitation for him to taste them. Would those light pink lips be as delicious as the aroma from her hair?

As he bent toward her, he halted himself. There was enough madness about them already. To compound it by giving in to the temptation to kiss her would be foolish. He had promised to escort her here tonight and return her home. That should be the end of it. After all, she had been forthright with him during his call and let him know she neither expected nor wanted more.

Tonight. . . . He could not allow himself to be caught up in the insanity of the evening and mistake her preference for his company as anything but her appreciation of a kindred soul.

When he stepped back and held out his fingers to hand her into the carriage, he saw the confusion on her face. Had he been in error? Was she hoping he would kiss her? He swore silently. This was all becoming too convoluted. The best thing would be to return her to her home and bid her farewell.

If that was so, why did the very idea curdle his stomach as much as the sight of the corpse had?

Eight

Amelia doubted she had ever been so happy to see her own front door. When Lord Foxington helped her out of the carriage, he did not release her hand as they walked up to the door that was being held open. A footman rushed to the carriage on Lord Foxington's orders to bring Nancy into the house.

Her mother rushed down the stairs and hugged her. "We heard—We heard horrible things."

"*On dits* are moving faster than the swiftest horses tonight," Lord Foxington said quietly. "Dougherty, I assume?"

"Yes." Mama stroked Amelia's hair. "Iris insisted on word being sent here straightaway, along with a message to reassure us that you were unharmed. How are you, my dear child?"

"I am all right, Mama." She did not like lying to her mother, but she hated even more the idea of having to explain to her mother exactly what she had seen.

Papa stepped forward and shook Stuart's hand. "This family owes you a great debt of thanks for watching out for Meelie at Almack's."

"Meelie?" He chuckled as he stepped aside to allow the footman to help Nancy, who was bemoaning her bad luck at being at Almack's tonight, up the stairs.

"A childhood nickname I should not have spoken." Papa winked, and she knew this was his way of trying to lighten her spirits. His graying hair drooping over his spectacles was a comforting sight. "Lord Foxington, if you would like something to drink . . ."

"No, thank you. I think it would be wiser for me to bid a good evening to your daughter and be on my way."

"Very well. Good evening." Papa put his hand on Mama's elbow and steered her up the stairs.

Amelia knew they would not go far, because not even tonight's appalling events could excuse untoward behavior. When the foyer was empty, save for her and Lord Foxington, she was uneasy with him as she had not been since the beginning of his first call.

"I suppose I should say thank you, too," she said.

"I would reply it was my pleasure, but there was little pleasurable about the end of this evening." He stepped closer as he folded her hands between his. "Although there was much pleasurable about dancing and talking with you." An abrupt grin warned her of his intention as he added, "Meelie."

"That is a silly schoolroom name."

"I am simply curious how you got it."

"It is like Amelia."

"True, but Meelie doesn't suit you. There is nothing mealy or mealy-mouthed about you." He ran his finger along her cheek. "Your skin is as smooth as the finest satin, and I vow I have never met another woman who is more ready and willing to speak her mind with absolute honesty."

"Such a *bon mots* from you?"

"From sadly flat Stuart?" He chuckled. "Why do you look so dumbfounded? Surely you have heard that name associated with me."

"Yes, but I didn't realize you had."

"I find the label rather fitting." He laughed. "I fear I would have been sadly lacking as a courtier in Queen Elizabeth's court, and such a fault often ended with one being shorter by a head. That would leave one with quite a flat appearance."

Amelia smiled, and tears filled her eyes. She had not guessed it would feel so wondrous to wear an expression that had been commonplace.

"Are you sure you are all right?" he asked, again serious.

"No." She could not be false with him when he had endured what she had. "I don't think I will be all right for a very long time. And you?"

Instead of answering, he raised her hand to his lips. He kissed it quickly, but the warmth lingered even after he released it.

When he bid her a good evening, she could only nod in response. She held that hand in her other. She did not move as he walked out of the house, closing the door behind him. Even when the tears she had not let fall before streamed down her cheeks, she remained where she was. Only now, when he had left, did she discover how much she had depended on his strength.

And now it was gone.

Amelia dabbed away another tear as she emerged from the churchyard where Susan's funeral had come to an end. She did not look back at the disturbed earth or the other mourners who were gathered around the grave on the incongruously sunny day. If she did, she might see Lord Foxington again. She had hoped he would approach her during the walk from the interior of the church to the newly dug grave, but he had acted as if he did not see her.

Letting that add to her distress was silly, but she could not help wondering why he was ignoring her. Mayhap it was as simple as the very sight of her reminded him of what they had seen at Almack's when she went to redo her hair. How innocent the hours before that seemed now.

"Amelia?"

She did not try to smile as she waited for Iris to catch up with her on the uneven walkway. Her friend's face was stained with tears, and more clung to her golden eyelashes.

Iris took her arm, drawing her beneath one of the trees near the wall surrounding the churchyard.

"Amelia, did you notice who did not attend this service?" Iris asked, her voice low and conspiratorial.

"I paid no attention." The only one she had taken note of was Lord Foxington.

"Evelyn Barry!"

"She and Susan were not more than acquaintances."

Iris's eyes twinkled with excitement. "I hear it is more than that. I hear she is frightened to leave her house, for she fears she will be attacked as well. She believes Susan was killed because of the voucher to Almack's."

"That is silly."

"Is it?"

"Yes, for I am here, aren't I?" She folded her arms in front of her. "Iris, it isn't like you to spread *on dits* at a funeral."

"Mayhap you should not have attended."

"Nonsense! Susan was my friend, and I will not allow some absurd rumors to keep me from paying my respects. If Evelyn Barry wishes to be an utter cabbage-head, that is her choice."

Iris glanced around before saying, "Mayhap you should be more cautious until the truth is uncovered in this. If there is even the slightest chance that Susan's death was connected to her being given that voucher, then you could be in danger, too."

Amelia sighed, wishing her friend had not chosen now to believe the gossip that always surrounded any event— good or misfortunate—among the *ton*. "Iris, you are overreacting. After all, Evelyn Barry is not the only one among those attending the gathering at Almack's who is not here today."

"That is true." Iris's excitement deflated. "Paulina Middington is not here."

"I had not realized that. She and Susan were together so often."

"But hardly friends, you must own. One always tried to outdo the other."

She smiled sadly. "That is true, but there must have been a friendship amid the brangles. Otherwise, they would have sought others' company."

"True." The word was reluctant. "I have heard—"

"Not another rumor, I hope."

"Only that Paulina Middington has gone to the country to mourn in private."

"That should show you what good friends they truly were." Amelia patted her friend's arm. "And now as you are *my* good friend, Iris, I must ask if you will excuse me. I should not delay my parents—"

"They have already left. I told them that we would bring you home."

"We?" Her heart leaped with an anticipation she could not govern.

"Lord Dougherty and I."

"Oh . . . Thank you."

Iris shook her head. "I was afraid of this."

She did not need to ask what *this* was, but she wanted to avoid taking the conversation in the direction of Lord Foxington. "I hope I did not sound ungrateful for your offer."

"He has been moping for the past two days from what Lord Dougherty tells me. Now you are doing the same."

Again Amelia had no reason to have her friend explain whom she meant by *he*. "It is a terribly tragic time."

"Yes, but it is more than that, isn't it?" The glitter returned to her eyes. "Do you have a *tendre* for him?"

"That is a farradiddle."

"What is silly about such a question?"

Amelia kept her voice low, hoping no one would chance to overhear the conversation now that it had taken this turn. "I have spoken to him on only three occasions."

"That is more than he has spoken to many people."

"Don't disparage him, Iris, simply because he does not feel a need to fill people's ears with his opinions."

Iris pressed her hand to her dark bodice. "Dear me! You do have a *tendre* for him."

"You are being silly."

"Am I? You are determined to defend him. That is a sure sign of a heart that has been touched by another."

Amelia decided it was not worth arguing about . . . most especially when Iris might be right. In the two days since the assembly at Almack's, her stomach had tightened each time the front door opened. Her hope that Lord Foxington was calling was dashed again and again, but she could not keep herself from eagerly listening for his voice.

"Do not look so down-pinned," Iris said with a smile. "I daresay he is suffering from much the same *tendre.*"

Although she wanted to ask why Iris believed that, she replied only, "I doubt he is that unwise."

"Don't you know, Amelia? The ways of the heart are seldom wise."

She was spared from having to answer when Lord Dougherty walked over to collect them so they could go to the waiting carriage on the street. Iris exchanged a glance with her husband, but Amelia could not guess what it was meant to convey. Not asking would be advisable at the moment, she was certain.

Yet, no matter how hard she tried to halt them, her eyes scanned the churchyard and the street. She knew she had been a fool when they were caught by Lord Foxington's. Although he stood almost twenty yards away, near his own carriage, it was as if everyone between them had vanished.

There must be some way to express those thoughts she dared to let him view, but she could not imagine what it might be. And if he became privy to the ones she could not trust even with herself, she was unsure what he would do.

So she simply stared. She had no idea how long she had or how long she might have, because Iris's hand on her arm turned her toward the Doughertys' carriage. The connection was shattered, and she was as bereft as she had been the night she had stood alone in the foyer after he had left.

Even Iris was quiet as they were driven toward Amelia's house. Lord Dougherty glanced at Amelia several times and seemed about to speak, but he remained silent as well.

Amelia murmured her thanks as the tiger helped her out of the carriage. She hurried up the steps, hoping for a haven in the cocoon of her home. Pausing only long enough to let her parents know she had returned, she continued to her bedchamber.

She closed the door and then went to latch the door to the dressing room. She never had shut her abigail out of her room, but she needed privacy to gather her scattered thoughts. Her laugh was terse. Her thoughts were not the least bit scattered. Each one was focused on Lord Foxington.

"How did this happen?" she asked as she sat beside the window offering her a view of the houses on the other side of the road. She wished one of the passersby would pause and answer her question. A silly wish, she knew. "I told him I wanted nothing more from him than his company at the gathering. That was all he wanted, too."

She sighed. Talking to herself would resolve nothing other than persuading the household that she was addled. Her parents would grant her privacy to deal with this, knowing she would seek them out for advice when she was ready. She wondered if she ever would be.

Shadows were creeping along the floor when a knock sounded at her door. "Yes?" she called.

The door swung open, and a footman bowed his head. "This was just delivered for you, Miss Wallace."

"Thank you," she said, taking the folded page he held out. Her fingers trembled as she wondered if Lord Foxington had written to her. Mayhap he was even asking permission to give her a look-in. Her heart pounded with an excitement she could not restrain at the very idea of him calling on her. "Is someone waiting for a reply?"

"No."

"Thank you," she said again, wanting to be alone while she read the note.

He bowed his head and left, closing the door after him.

The page was not sealed with wax, and her heart emptied of hope. Surely Lord Foxington would have ensured that any note from him would not be read by anyone else.

Unfolding it, she gasped when she read:

You have been warned once. This is your final warning. Stay away from Almack's, or you will be sorry.

Nine

Stuart heard the door to the street open as he was on his way up the stairs. Dash it! He had not expected any caller. Gathering up the ends of his loosened cravat, he began to tie it. He looked down to see Tinkcom greeting someone. A flash of red was his only warning before the form pushed past his butler and ran up the stairs to him.

Amelia Wallace! What was she doing here? Even if her life was as dull as his without the conversations—and the chaste touches—they had shared, he had not guessed she would call like this.

"Stuart! Thank heavens you are here." She threw her arms around his shoulders and pressed her face to his half-tied cravat.

He was doubly shocked. Not only had she flung herself into his arms, but she had spoken his given name with an ease that suggested she used it often in her thoughts. He did not allow himself time to enjoy that idea. Instead, he led her up the stairs. She held on to him on each step as if she feared he would tumble onto his face. When they stood at the top, he cupped her elbows and drew her back far enough so he could see her ashen face.

"What is wrong . . . Amelia?" Dash it! He should not encourage the continuing of this conversation by offering even this small intimacy. When had he become such a hypocrite? He had been fantasizing about far more intimate exchanges than using their first names.

"I think Iris is right."

"Iris? Lady Dougherty? Right about what?" It was not like Amelia to be barely coherent.

"About someone trying to kill me, too."

"What makes you think that?" He drew her into his book room and shut the door, not caring how much it shocked his butler. After sitting her on the dark leather settee, he went and drew the drapes on the front window. If she was seen within here, her reputation could be destroyed. He grimaced. It would not do his any good either, for Dougherty would be ready to have banns read straightaway.

Picking up a bottle of wine and two glasses from a sideboard set beneath the window, he walked back to where she still had not answered. He filled both glasses and gave her one. When she gulped it as if she had not had anything to drink in weeks, he handed her the other glass. He poured more into the empty goblet as she sipped with a bit more self-control. The wine in the glass rocked like a stormy sea, and he put his hand over hers which was trembling wildly.

"Tell me," he commanded softly.

"I don't know where to start."

"At the beginning is usually the best place."

"At the beginning is when Susan was killed." She shuddered so hard, he plucked the glass out of her hand before she could spill it on herself. After drinking half the wine, he handed it back to her. She nodded her thanks and whispered, "Please don't think I am want-witted and hysterical."

"Even if you were hysterical, you have every right to enjoy a good *crise de nerfs* in the wake of what has happened." His fingers were beneath her chin, tipping it up, before he realized he was allowing his sympathy for her to grant him free rein to muddle this situation even further.

She raised her other hand to settle on his wrist, and

he struggled to keep his mind from whirling out of control with the sensations exploding within it. Other touches, far less chaste than this, had not had such an effect on him.

"This is no *crise de nerfs*," she said, her gaze slipping along his face. He wondered what she was seeking, but had no chance to ask, for she added, "I received another note."

"May I see it?"

"Yes, I brought it to show you because you were the one to recognize the other note might be a real threat." She put her wine on a bookshelf behind the settee, then reached into the bag he had not noticed she was carrying.

As she faced him, something sparked in her eyes. Something that set an answering ember within him afire. His fingers coursed along her soft cheek, and she closed her eyes as the barest ghost of a smile played across her lips.

"Look at me," he commanded softly.

She did, and he knew he had been a widgeon to ask this. Emotions swirled within her light green eyes, daring him to discover which each one was. That was a task that could take a man a lifetime.

He withdrew his hand and then held it out for the piece of paper she held. He tried to ignore how the light extinguished in her eyes as she placed the slip on his palm. Like him, she must be aware of the perils of pursuing these hints of pleasure. Or was she too frightened to govern her feelings?

With an inward curse, he silenced that thought. He should not be contemplating what sort of affection she might have for him . . . as he had so often in the past two days.

"Aren't you going to read it?" Amelia asked when Stuart did not move. *Stuart!* Had she really called him that aloud? She should apologize for being so unmannered, but that would have to wait. Now she wanted to know his reaction to this note.

"Yes, of course."

She flinched at his gruff reply. Reaching for the wineglass again, she faltered when he swore. Out loud and quite vividly.

Without apologizing for his words, he asked, "Have you shown this to anyone else?"

"No. I did not want to upset my parents, who are quite distraught already, and the watch and the coroner have been ineffectual in discovering who killed Susan. Not going to Almack's tomorrow evening is the simplest solution."

"But you will have to send Lady Cowper your regrets along with a reason why you have not been seen among the *élite* of the *élite*. She will view your refusal to attend the weekly soirées at Almack's as an insult to her and the other patronesses."

"I have thought of that, but what excuse can I give her other than the truth? To speak of that would be to risk causing more panic among the *ton*."

"Your mourning for your friend?"

"I had thought of that, but Susan's mother urged me not to let her daughter's death be the cause of me losing out on this opportunity." She shivered. "I was shocked when she said that, because going to Almack's was of the least concern to me at my friend's funeral."

"But of the greatest concern for everyone else."

"So I need another excuse not to go to Almack's tomorrow evening."

"You could ruin your name."

"That is not a feasible solution." She glanced at the door. "Think of what that would do to my parents."

"I did not mean it to be taken as a valid suggestion."

Amelia stood and kneaded her fingers. "I am sorry, my lord."

He scowled as he set himself on his feet. "Why are you returning to such formalities now?"

"I was not thinking clearly when I greeted you, I am afraid."

He took her hands before she could rub all the skin from them. "Nor am I when I stand here with you."

"You should not say such things."

"I did not intend to add to your distress." He released her hands.

Her fingers were reaching for his before she could halt them. She needed the warmth of his touch to combat the icy fear within her.

"Mayhap your idea is not without merit," she said.

"To ruin your name?" His frown deepened, gouging lines in his face. "You need to think clearly now, not jump on the first solution that presents itself. There must be another way."

"Short of insulting Lady Cowper to her face, can you think of another?"

"I shall."

"But when?" She laced her fingers through his. "I have no idea if I have time to consider other options. There must be a method to ruin my reputation only slightly. Don't you know of a way?"

"You are asking *me* how one should ruin a woman's reputation only slightly?" He smiled. "Ask me about some aspect of history or about a topic to be brought before the Lords, and I will give you a valid, well-thought-out answer. To this, I fear I have no knowledge."

"None?"

His laugh was hushed and husky as his fingers closed around hers. "Ah, you have caught me in a falsehood, for I have heard many tales at the club. Some of the stories of escapades with a lovely, willing lass might have actually been true."

"Then, help me."

"Ruin your reputation only slightly?"

She nodded. Going to the window, she threw open the drapes. She looked back at him and arched a brow.

He smiled. "Are you so sure someone will be peering in the window to see your misadventures?"

"If not . . ."

"Then they will have to be repeated where they are certain to be seen?" He walked toward her. "Do you consider this attempt to tarnish you only a practice?"

"Don't tease me."

"But you tease me with too many thoughts of holding you like this."

She was amazed she could even breathe when his arm slipped around her waist and pulled her to him. The loose ends of his cravat brushed her skin above the curve of her dress's neckline. Could he feel her heart that seemed determined to batter its way out of her chest?

"And you should put your arms around me, Meelie," he whispered, drawing her gaze up to meet his.

"Around your shoulders?"

He nodded. "But slowly."

"Slowly?"

His hand took hers and pressed it to the front of his waistcoat. "Slowly." He lifted his fingers away.

Hers slid up his chest, savoring the firm muscles beneath his shirt's fine lawn. When they reached his coat, they glided beneath it to curve along his shoulder.

"And the other?" she whispered, struggling to speak as her breath came swift and shallow.

"Very slowly." His voice was as unsteady as hers. "Very, very slowly."

She stroked his chest as she let her fingers find their way up it and behind his nape. "And now?"

"I will take it from here, Meelie."

His lips caressed hers with a gentleness that sent an ache deep within her, an ache for more than just this sample of rapture. When he raised his mouth from hers, she whispered his name. He kissed her again with an unbridled passion she offered back to him. His arm tightened around her, drawing her even nearer until she was no longer sure which frantic heartbeat was his and which was hers. She did not care. She only wanted this luscious kiss to continue and continue and continue . . . until the fear beyond it vanished.

And then she wanted him to kiss her more.

Ten

Amelia looked up in hope when she heard a guest being greeted at the door. Was that Stuart . . . at last? It had been only yesterday that she had gone to him with the appalling note, but it seemed so long since he had held her in his strong arms and eased her fears with his fiery kisses. When he had asked her to remain at home or go out only with friends she trusted while he showed the note to people who might be able to help her, she had promised.

Who had been so bamboozled by him that they had been the first to label him boring? He was a spellbinding man who had let her see through the magic he had cast to keep others from intruding into his life to discover how compelling he truly was.

She touched her lips which still tingled with the memory of his against them. She wished he would escort her to Almack's tonight, but he had arranged for Iris to accompany her in case his efforts to uncover the truth about the note's origins took longer than he hoped. However, she would see him there tonight.

"Such a faraway expression. Am I disturbing you?" came a voice from the doorway.

"Paulina!" She jumped to her feet and went to hug her friend. "I had heard you were going to leave Town and mourn in the country."

"There are all sorts of silly rumors circulating through the *ton*." She handed her shawl to the footman who had followed her up the stairs and then linked her arm through Amelia's. "Do you think I would abandon you?"

Sitting next to her friend, Amelia said, "But I did not see you at the funeral."

"I went to the service, but I could not go to stand beside the grave. I don't know how you could. After all, you were the one who found her."

"I had to go. She was my friend." She tried to submerge the memory of Susan's body on the floor of the room at Almack's. "She would have done the same for me."

"You should not be so certain of that. She was likely to forget it because she was so caught up in doing something else that would put her in good pax with the Polite World. Even you, who never speak a cold word about anyone, must own that Susan was a bit of a block."

"How horrible to speak so of the dead."

Paulina's smile grew stiff and cold. "You know I said much the same when she was alive. She thought only of garnering a titled husband and a fortune to offset her family's recent misfortunes."

"She did not think only of that."

Paulina gave her an expression of disbelief.

"All right," Amelia conceded, "but she was a good friend."

"I am not denying that, but she was so determined to obtain *entrée* into the highest realms of the Polite World. Who knows what she might have done in her efforts to obtain that position?" Paulina's eyes widened. "Do you think she had a hank on someone?"

"Blackmail? Susan?" Amelia shook her head. "You are letting your distress overmaster your good sense. Can we speak of something else?"

"Shall we speak of your visit to Almack's tonight?"

She rose and shook her head. "I most definitely do not want to speak of that." Going to the window that overlooked the garden in the back, she stared out as she said, "I would prefer to speak of something else."

"Mayhap you do, but no one else in the *ton* does. Everyone has been curious who would receive the voucher that should have been Susan's."

"Not everyone." She turned. "Paulina?"

Her friend's face grew rigid. "No, I was not the recipient. Some chit whose mother was once the mistress of a friend of Lady Cowper's has received it."

"I am so sorry."

"Do not feel sorry for me. There will be other opportunities, I am sure." Paulina came to her feet. "Lady Dougherty will be stopping by later this afternoon to bring you to tea at my house."

"Today?"

"You will be done long before you need to worry about getting ready for this evening."

Amelia did not want to own that her dismay had not been because of preparations for Almack's, but because she did not want to miss the chance to see Stuart if he called. Stuart! She must send a note to his house to let him know that she was calling at Paulina's with Iris, for she did not want him worrying needlessly. "Thank you, Paulina, for the invitation. I will be there and look forward to a conversation with you and Iris."

"I have invited Evelyn Barry, as well. I thought it would be wise for all of us to get better acquainted."

She nodded, fighting the sickness souring in her stomach. Despite Paulina's remarks about Susan, she was eager to attach herself to Evelyn Barry in, if Amelia was not judging her friend's expression inaccurately, hopes of still obtaining one of the coveted vouchers for herself.

"Will you bring your voucher so we all might see it?"

"If you wish."

Paulina smiled broadly, but before she could reply, Amelia heard a much deeper voice ask, "Am I intruding?"

Seeing Stuart in the doorway, Amelia had to fight her feet that wanted to send her running to him. She locked her hands together behind her back to keep them from reaching out to him as she said, "Of course not. Do come in."

"Ah, Lord Foxington." Paulina glanced at Amelia and smiled. "I suspect I should not be surprised you are calling."

"I wanted to ascertain for myself," he said, bowing his head toward Paulina before entering the room, "that you are well, Amelia."

She refrained from looking at her friend because she did not want to see Paulina's superior smile at the way Stuart addressed her. She refused to be dishonest now and pretend she and Stuart were no more than acquaintances. His friendship was precious to her. And the dream it could become far more than *amitié* was a bulwark against the terror stalking her.

"I am fine." She gave him a smile, not wanting to see such worry carving furrows in his brow. Had he discovered something to share with her? "Will you join us?"

He nodded. "That would be my pleasure."

"You must excuse me," Paulina said. "I will see you later this afternoon, Amelia. Lord Foxington."

He bowed over the hand Paulina held out to him and said nothing as she went from the room and down the stairs. Only when the street door shut behind her did he turn to Amelia. He closed the distance between them in a single step. Clasping her face, he kissed her deeply.

She smiled up at him when he released her and whispered, "That is a lovely way to say good morning."

"I can think of even lovelier ways while I hold you in even lovelier ways." He chuckled. "You're blushing!"

"I do not blush!"

"Then, you must be furious with me because your cheeks are an alluring shade of pink." He ran his finger across her lips. "Or could it be that you are imagining what I am?"

"I think it would be better if I did not answer that."

He laughed and, taking her hand, placed it on his arm as he led her out of the room and down the stairs. When

Nancy fell in line after them, he nodded to her, and Amelia guessed he had sent for her abigail when he arrived.

The sunshine was dimming as they went out into the garden. He walked with her to a bench beneath an arbor where the leaves were only beginning to turn green. Sitting, he glanced at where her abigail sat far enough away to allow them privacy to talk but close enough to give countenance to the call.

"What have you learned?" Amelia asked, unable to wait any longer for the news he brought.

"Nothing."

"Nothing at all?"

He shook his head. "Either no one knows or no one will own to knowing."

"Be honest with me," she said.

"Of course."

"Do you think it's possible? Do you think this has anything to do with the decisions Lady Cowper made that evening?"

"It is too early to tell."

"I know."

He stood. "I called because I wanted to inform you that I would continue asking questions. I should be seeing Dougherty at our club, and he always seems to know things others do not."

"Because Iris heeds every word of gossip among the *ton*."

"Mayhap that is a habit all of us should acquire."

"I will talk with her as well when I go with her to call on Paulina this afternoon for a tea to allow us to become better acquainted with Evelyn Barry."

His eyes widened. "I must own I had not thought Miss Middington would accept defeat with such aplomb. I must have misjudged her." Taking her hands, he asked, "Shall I call for you this evening to escort you again to Almack's?"

"I would greatly appreciate that."

"Just appreciate?"

She looked past him to her abigail and then smiled. "That is all I should say for now."

"Then, I will look forward to you saying more—and saying much less—when I accompany you this evening." Lifting her hand, he pressed his mouth to it.

She longed for his lips on hers, but that must wait for tonight. She had never guessed she would look forward to her next visit to Almack's so much.

Stuart heard his name shouted and echoing off the high ceilings of the usually tranquil club. He rushed out of the room where he had been waiting for Dougherty to arrive and ran into the man himself.

"Why are you bellowing like a bull in rut?" Stuart asked.

Dougherty grabbed him by the sleeve and tugged him back into the room. "You need to hear this! Evelyn Barry's carriage was upset near St. James's Park."

"Was she badly injured?"

"A broken leg as well as a broken arm." He clenched his hands behind his back. "She was fortunate it was not a broken neck."

"What happened?"

His friend shrugged. "Does it matter? First the Little girl and now Miss Barry. Is there a curse on that accursed idea of Lady Cowper's to give out vouchers to Almack's?"

Stuart reached for his hat and cloak before running back out into the hall, calling for his carriage to be brought posthaste. When Dougherty followed along with a demand for what he was doing, Stuart replied, "I don't have time to explain. I need to make sure Amelia is all right."

"Amelia?" Dougherty's face became as white as his cravat. "By this hour, she should be in the carriage going to Miss Middington's with Iris."

He smiled grimly as Dougherty used his wife's first name instead of her title. His friend now shared his anxiety. He hurried down the stairs to the ground floor, hoping he and his friend would not share grief at another tragedy.

"I wonder what is keeping Evelyn," Paulina said as she handed Amelia a cup of steaming tea. "It is not like her to be late."

"We had to take a different route here," Iris replied. "I heard there was an upset carriage blocking traffic. Paulina, this tea smells heavenly."

"My own personal blend. Do try it."

Amelia lifted her cup to take a sip, but froze when she heard a slamming door and angry voices followed by furious footsteps on the stairs. She stared in disbelief when Stuart burst into the room with Lord Dougherty, Paulina's butler, and a fourth man whom she did not recognize on his heels.

"Put it down, Amelia," Stuart ordered.

She began, "Stuart—"

"Put it down."

"Put what down?"

"That cup of tea! Heaven knows what she put in it."

When his gaze shifted toward Paulina, Amelia stared at her friend. Paulina's face reddened, then grew icy white. Beside her, she heard Iris set her cup with a crash onto the tray.

"You put something in our tea?" Amelia asked, not wanting to believe her own words.

Paulina jumped to her feet. "You are talking nonsense!"

"Am I?" asked Stuart, entering the room, his eyes riveting on Paulina. He picked up Amelia's cup and held it out. "Prove me wrong. Drink this."

"I will not be treated like this in my own home."

"You can answer my questions now or answer the coroner's later." He sniffed the cup. "He might be able to tell what is in this far better than I can, but I suspect whatever is in this would make both Amelia and Lady Dougherty quite ill."

Paulina folded up and dropped heavily back into her chair. Pressing her hands over her face, she said, "I did not want to hurt anyone badly. It was an accident."

With a gasp, Amelia realized her friend was not talking about adulterated tea. She edged toward where Stuart stood. Slipping her hand in his, she whispered, "Are you speaking of Susan's death?"

"Yes," Paulina replied. "I just wanted to scare her when she was acting so high-and-mighty. Then she paraded her voucher before me, and—and—I don't know what happened next. It is just a blank."

"And Evelyn Barry?" Stuart asked more quietly. "Did you intend to just scare her, too?"

Paulina's head jerked up. "She isn't dead, too, is she?"

He shook his head. "No, your plans to have a wagon cut her off did not go awry. She will not be able to go to Almack's tonight, but she is in no danger of dying. You should have selected your allies with more care. The teamster you hired has already begun confessing." He looked over his shoulder, and the fourth man stepped forward. "The constable will want to speak with both you and Sir Bernard, Miss Middington."

As Lord Dougherty led his weeping wife from the room, Amelia picked up her reticule. She opened it and pulled out the voucher she had been given. Tossing it onto the table next to the tea tray, she said, "Here it is. It is yours, if you want it."

Paulina inched forward, then snatched the voucher from the table. She pressed it to her chest as the constable began to question her.

Glad for Stuart's arm around her, Amelia went with him down the stairs and out onto the street. She saw the Doughertys' carriage being whipped up as if they could flee from the memory of these events.

She sat in Stuart's carriage and shook. When he sat beside her, she pressed her face to his chest. "Thank you," she whispered. "How did you know?"

His thumbs tilted her face back. "I didn't. When I heard of Miss Barry's accident, Dougherty and I hurried here. We reached the house just as the constable did. When he explained why he was there, I figured I would take a chance and see if she would confess to everything." His lips tilted in a smile. "It was no less than any courtier should do for a redheaded queen."

"If I were as wise as Queen Elizabeth, I might have seen this myself."

"But she was blinded, too, by friendships." His finger stroked her cheek. "You know she will never be able to use that voucher, Meelie."

She smiled at the pet name she had hated until she heard him speak it. "I know, but I thought it might make her feel better during what is ahead of her."

"It is just as well you gave it to her, because you will not be needing it."

"I should think not. I would rather—"

"You will not need it when you arrive at Almack's as my wife, Meelie."

"Your wife?" She stared at his slowly broadening smile.

"Say you will marry me. I could not bear being apart from you so much during these past few days." His kiss was swift but melted the icy fear lingering within her. "Say you want more than this and you will marry me."

"Yes," she whispered. "I will gladly marry you, even if I do have to go to Almack's with you."

His roar of laughter bounced off the sides of the carriage before he pulled her into his arms. This kiss was most definitely not a quick one.

Murder Most
Indiscreet

Mona Gedney

Rose Battinger frowned as she finished reading her sister's letter a second time. Lily's penmanship had never been anything more than passable, and she had clearly written this note when she was laboring under great emotion, sprinkling the paper liberally with tears and ink blots. Nonetheless, Rose finally managed to decipher it, and the news was as bad as she had feared it would be.

"What does Lily have to say, my dear?" inquired Rose's aunt, who had been watching her anxiously. Elvira Battinger, an elderly spinster, had made her home with her brother and his family since her girlhood, remaining with Rose after he had died and Lily had married. "Is the poor child still unhappy?"

Rose nodded, her face stiff as she tried to control her distress. "Yes, Aunt, it is more of the same, I'm afraid, only worse. Lord Palmering has taken away her pin money again, but this time he has also forbidden her to leave the house unless he is escorting her—and of course he will take her nowhere."

Lily's marriage to a peer of the realm had turned out to be anything but the fairy-tale romance she had dreamed of—unless one thought of Rapunzel, locked in her tower. Lily was no longer waiting for her prince to come and rescue her, however. Her prince had already come, and he had proven to be a toad in disguise. Rose was certain, too, that her sister had not told her the worst. On Lily's last visit home fourteen months ago, Rose had seen bruises on her sister's arms that she had not been able to explain—and just six months ago, the graceful Lily had written that she had inexplicably fallen down the stairs and broken her arm.

For a moment Rose thought fondly of some of the strange tales she had heard of the power of a gypsy's curse, and she wished earnestly that she were acquainted with gypsies. She had never cared for her sister's husband, but her feeling toward him had long since changed from mild distaste to adamant dislike.

"Do you mean that she cannot even drive out to the park or go shopping?" demanded Aunt Elvira, shocked by such a notion. "Why, certainly he can't hold her prisoner in her own home!"

"He can do anything he pleases, Aunt! And it's his home, even though it was our father's money that kept him from losing it to his creditors, and even though it is Lily's settlement that supplies him with every pound he spends," said Rose impatiently, pacing the length of the drawing room and crumpling the letter in her hands. "You know very well that he has complete power over her. The law gives him all the rights and her none at all. Her money is his to use as he wishes."

She had not shared her suspicions about Palmering's abuse of Lily with her aunt, for there was nothing she could do about it, save worrying herself into a frenzy.

Elvira lapsed into troubled silence, twisting her handkerchief in her hands. "But she is such a dear girl," she faltered, "and so lovely, too. It isn't as though he married some unattractive, graceless woman that he would be ashamed of. Why would Lord Palmering treat her in such an abominable manner?"

"Because her birth makes her beneath him—at least in his eyes—and because she is an inconvenience," replied Rose, her voice grim.

"But your mother was his equal in birth," said Elvira. "After all, she was the daughter of an earl."

"Yes, and you know very well that he cast her off when

she married Papa. He did not come to see her—nor even send a message—when we wrote to tell him that she was dying and wished to see him once more." Rose's voice was now as stiff as her face, for she could not speak of that most unhappy time without breaking down, and she was determined not to do so.

Her aunt shook her head. "Poor Sarah. Even though she was so happy with your father, she was brokenhearted to be separated from her father."

"And that was entirely her father's fault," returned Rose. She shook her head as she thought about it. "I know that Papa thought he was in some way making up for that by marrying Lily to Lord Palmering, but Palmering is like all men of his class—he cares for nothing but position and appearance. Lily was all very well when he needed her money. Now he has complete control of all that she has, and she has become just a brewer's daughter, too far beneath him to be noticed."

"He did not behave so when dear Edward was alive," murmured Elvira, dabbing at her eyes with the handkerchief.

"Of course he did not!" returned Rose, pausing for a moment in her pacing to stand at the window and look down at the south lawn where three spaniel puppies were rolling in play. The dogs had always been Lily's delight, but her husband would allow her none, saying that they were a nuisance and too expensive to keep. Nor would he allow her to come home to visit. Not since their father's funeral had she been permitted to spend time with her family.

"While Papa was alive, he could still have changed his will. I told him that he should place Lily's money in trust, but he felt that he would be insulting Lord Palmering. I still cannot believe that Papa could not see Palmering for what he is. He was so delighted to have Lily marrying 'well' that he would not listen to reason, and now the blasted man can ride roughshod over her without anyone to stop him."

"But he seemed so truly the gentleman when he came to visit," sighed Elvira, still unable to reconcile appearance and reality. She lived with a perennially sunny vision of the motives and actions of others. "He spoke so pleasantly, and he complimented my roses and my watercolors. Why, he even took me up beside him in his curricle and drove me round the Park!"

"But that was well over a year ago, Aunt, before Papa died. And once he was gone, Lord Palmering made certain that Lily observed her year of mourning very strictly. I daresay she went out to no more than half a dozen engagements during the entire time, always swathed in black. It's only in the past four months that she has been allowed out at all, and he has already cut off her pin money twice."

She glanced down at the crumpled letter she had been clutching. "And we know that he has been seeing other women since Papa's death, for he makes no bones about telling Lily of the others. Why, she writes here that he has even had one of them to dinner in their own home and forced Lily to sit down to table with her—just the three of them."

"No!" gasped Elvira. Such an enormity was beyond her comprehension. Her own brother, although he had made his money in brewing, had been every inch the gentleman in his treatment of others, particularly the ladies of his family. "I know that a gentleman might very well have other love interests, but no well-bred man would treat his own wife in such a manner!"

"And there we have it in a nutshell, Aunt!" agreed Rose. "Any hunter in our stables is better bred than Palmering. Papa would have done better to marry Lily to an honest tradesman who would treat her kindly. I told them both that marrying a man with a title was marrying nothing but trouble! We had already seen proof of that with my grandfather's behavior. Men like that care for nothing but themselves and their own importance!"

"Your dear father was simply doing what he thought was best for Lily," said Elvira gently.

"I know that he was, Aunt," Rose replied. She could not remain angry with the memory of her indulgent father. He had always concentrated on doing what was best for his family; however, since he had never overcome his feeling of guilt for removing his beloved Sarah from her "better" world, he had unfortunately believed that marrying his daughters to gentlemen would secure their happiness. Rose had flatly refused, and he had allowed her to make that decision; but Lily had done as her father wished, and Lord Palmering had been her reward for obedience.

She sank down beside her aunt with a sigh. "It is fortunate that she at least no longer gives a fig about winning his affections. I tried to tell her from the first that he simply was not worth her while, but she is too much like you, Aunt." Here Rose paused to pat Elvira's plump shoulder. "She persists in seeing the best in everyone, even when there is no best to be seen."

"Perhaps we are being too harsh, my dear!" protested Elvira feebly, unwilling to think so poorly of a fellow human being, despite the evidence. "Lord Palmering must have some redeeming characteristics."

Rose smiled thinly, her green eyes narrowing. "Just one that I can think of, Aunt," she conceded. "He is, after all, mortal, so he must at some point die—preferably sooner than later."

"Rose!" exclaimed Elvira, her pink cheeks flushing even pinker. "I know that you cannot mean such a heartless comment. You are overwrought."

Rose shrugged, her smile fading as quickly as it had come. "If it pleases you to think so, I shall not correct you. But at least if he were to die, Lily could come home freely and live with us once again. Her stepson would not wish her with him in London. After all, he would have the title and Lily's money—she would merely be in the way."

"It would be wonderful to have her home again," agreed

Elvira. "You would think that Lord Palmering would be glad to have her come to us, particularly since he is not allowing her to go out. I cannot understand why he has refused her permission to come each time she has asked or you have written to ask him on her behalf."

Rose sprang to her feet, the anger that she had been trying to control overwhelming her again. "He simply likes to show his power over her!" she exclaimed, pounding the fist of one small hand into the palm of the other. "I believe that he wishes her to be miserable! He is a despicable man, and I cannot allow him to do this to Lily!"

"But what can you possibly do about it, Rose?" Elvira straightened the ribbons on her lace cap and regarded her niece seriously. Long experience had taught her that Rose was a formidable force when she was in this state of mind, and she tried to brace herself for what was to come.

"We have no brother to speak for Lily," Rose replied, "so I shall do it myself. Thank heaven that Papa at least left me in charge of my own inheritance! I will go to London and offer Palmering ten thousand pounds if he will allow Lily to live with us!"

Elvira shook her head. "Just think how it would make him look, having his young bride leave him to go back to her family. He will never do it, my dear, even for so handsome a sum."

"We will see about that!" responded Rose, her small chin jutting out. "He will at least allow her to come home for a holiday. I shall write him a letter immediately, laying out my proposal, but I shall press my suit in person as soon as possible."

She pulled her aunt to her feet and gave Elvira her orders. "Pack your trunk, Aunt! We are going to London to rescue Lily!"

Unaware of Rose's plans, Lord Palmering was happily pursuing his own pleasures in London. Lily had been informed, to her great surprise, that she was to accompany him to Almack's. She had been there only twice, although she had received her voucher two years ago from the good-natured Sally Jersey.

When Lord Brookston, a friend of Lady Jersey's and a stickler for form, had expressed his surprise at Lady Jersey's decision to admit the daughter of a brewer to the hallowed precincts of Almack's, she had reminded him that Lily Battinger was also the granddaughter of the Earl of Sharrington. Aside from that, she had observed tartly that the poor child might as well have something good happen to her since she was to undergo the pain of marrying Palmering. As she had pointed out to the other patronesses, who had also questioned her decision, Lily was a very pretty girl with a genteel manner. And, she had added, laughing, it would anger the odious Palmering to have her admitted, for she was certain that he would like to keep his fiancée as far as possible from the critical eyes of the *ton*. Since they all disliked Lord Palmering, they had reluctantly agreed with Lady Jersey's decision, Lady Sefton adding as a reluctant stamp of approval that the child at least dressed well, not as though she had purchased her gowns in Cranbourne Alley as many of the provincials did.

So it was that Lily's only visits to Almack's had been before her marriage. After she became Lady Palmering and was subject to her husband's orders, she was no longer allowed to attend the weekly balls held there during the Season. The news that she was to go to the Rooms with her husband that evening made hope flutter in her heart once more. Perhaps, she told herself, she had judged her husband too harshly, and this evening was an indication that things were about to change between them. However, once they arrived at Almack's that evening, Lily found herself abandoned almost immediately, as her husband threaded his way through the crush.

"Isn't that your pretty little protégé?" inquired Lord Brookston of his companion, nodding toward Lily, who was glancing uncertainly about the room. "I don't recall seeing her for a good many months."

"Oh, that poor child!" exclaimed Lady Jersey. "At least she is finally out of mourning and Palmering has allowed her to leave the house! You wouldn't believe what that abominable man has done to her, Brookston!"

"Then, you would be mistaken, ma'am," he assured her, his expression grim. "I would believe anything abominable that you were to say about him."

Brookston paused and glanced about the crowd. "There is your favorite now," he observed. "Palmering appears to be endearing himself to some of your guests in his own inimitable manner."

In the distance they could see Lord Palmering, a tall, rather heavy man, bending far too close to a slender, doe-eyed young woman. As they watched, another gentleman approached the pair and clapped his hand upon Palmering's shoulder. Palmering knocked away the newcomer's hand and turned to face him.

"It would be just like that reprehensible man to make a scene. Come along and help me put a stop to this, Brookston!" exclaimed Lady Jersey, pulling him along in her wake. Scandal might be gossiped about within the sacred walls of Almack's, but no scandal was enacted there. Those in attendance might themselves be the subjects of the latest crim. con., but at Almack's they appeared to be paragons of virtue.

"Perhaps you would allow my wife a little more breathing space, Palmering," said the young man. Here the gentleman deftly inserted himself between Palmering and his victim, tucking the young lady's hand possessively within the crook of his arm. "I am certain that you can find someone else who would be more receptive to your attentions."

"Oh, I believe that she would be receptive enough were you not present," returned Palmering, his pale eyes glittering dangerously. "Or at least I have found her to be so."

The young man stiffened, and his wife clutched his arm nervously. "Don't listen to him, Albert. I've done nothing wrong, but he won't leave me alone."

"Come now, Chesterton, why should you be distressed to discover that your lovely young wife and I have spent a little time together? We are both men of the world, are we not?" asked Lord Palmering, more than a hint of mockery in his voice.

"Not in the way that you mean it," replied Mr. Chesterton grimly.

He did not blame his wife, for Alison Chesterton was very young and they had been married scarcely three months. She could not be expected to recognize the danger presented by a man like Palmering. He had no scruples where young women—married or unmarried—were concerned. He had figured in countless scandals over the years, and some of them had ruined the young women involved with him, though Palmering himself had gone unscathed.

Alison glanced up at her husband timidly, a little frightened by his stern expression.

Seeing her distress, Palmering laughed, but the laughter did not reach his pale blue eyes. "Be careful, dear lady," he warned in a theatrical whisper. He ignored Chesterton and lightly brushed his lips across Alison's free hand before she could snatch it away. "A jealous husband can interfere with your small pleasures and quite cut up your peace."

Still laughing, he bowed to the Chestertons and strolled away. When he caught a glimpse of Lily through the crowd, he impatiently motioned to her to join him, and she hurried to his side.

"We might as well have some of the impossible supper they offer here," he said abruptly. "They are all anxious for me to be gone, so I shall not give them the pleasure of seeing me leave too quickly." He had seen Lady Jersey and Brookston making their way toward him, and he guided his wife's steps toward the room where the supper was laid out.

"But why should they wish you gone?" asked Lily, bewildered. "And who is it that you mean?"

"Never mind! Sit down here and I shall bring you some of that vile orgeat," he ordered brusquely.

Lily sat down as she was bidden, saying, "But I would prefer lemonade—" Her husband, however, ignored her words and strode in the direction of the supper table.

Brookston and Lady Jersey, who had followed them and witnessed this byplay, glanced at each other and then back at Palmering, watching him as he collected refreshments and returned with them to his wife. He did not sit down beside her, however, turning his attention to another young woman instead.

Lady Cowper, who had just joined them, followed their gaze. "What has that dreadful man been doing now?" she demanded.

Sally Jersey shrugged in disgust. "Brewing scandal-broth again, I daresay," she responded.

"Why he was ever allowed admittance to Almack's is something I shall never understand," complained Lady Cowper. "He has been nothing but an embarrassment for years."

"It has worked out very well for him, however," commented Brookston, staring at Palmering with distaste. "I believe he is invited to very few private parties these days. Where except Almack's could he prowl freely among so many innocent young women?"

"Oh, pray don't say such things!" exclaimed Lady Cowper in horror. "You make him sound like a wolf among lambs!"

"And so he is," returned Brookston, "except that he preys upon young women—whether they are married or not. As long as they are vulnerable, he will strike."

Married women were often granted some freedom of behavior, particularly after they had provided their husbands with an heir, but the unmarried were held to stricter standards of behavior. After all, no gentleman wished to purchase damaged goods at the marriage mart. After marriage, of course, it was up to the husband to protect his property.

Lady Cowper regarded him with dismay. "Whatever shall we do?" she asked, turning to Lady Jersey. "Perhaps we should blackball him so that he can no longer attend the balls here."

Lady Jersey, relaxed now that the immediate crisis had been averted, turned away and tapped Brookston on the arm as she passed him. "You should know by now, Emily," she said to Lady Cowper, "that you must not let Brookston perturb you. There is no need to enact a Cheltenham tragedy, for he quite enjoys seeing you fret. He would doubtless love to see us order Lord Palmering from these sacred precincts, forbidding him entrance here ever again."

"Nothing would delight me more," Brookston assured her. "I only beg that you will tell me when you are about to do so. I would like to be there to applaud you."

"Who is he accosting now?" demanded Lady Cowper, seeing Palmering bow to another young lady.

"Miss Pinkering," replied Lady Jersey, "but she is perfectly safe. Her father is with her, so Palmering will not linger." She nodded with satisfaction as she saw her prediction fulfilled, but then she frowned and shook her head.

"It appears that he has suddenly remembered that he is married," she said. "I daresay his wife wishes that he had not recollected it."

The three of them watched as he bore down once more upon the hapless Lady Palmering.

"Unfortunate child," sighed Lady Cowper, shaking her head. "How unkind fate has been to her."

Lady Jersey nodded. "Her fortune and her father's desire to marry her well made her the natural prey of a man like Palmering. She is pretty enough and not ill-bred, despite her father's background. Blood will tell, after all, and she *is* the granddaughter of an earl. She lacks town-bronze, of course, but she will never acquire any since her husband keeps her under lock and key."

"Such Turkish treatment!" exclaimed Lady Cowper, who was normally a quite gentle soul. "He should be ashamed of himself, of course, but unfortunately he seems to think the whole business quite laughable. DeBracey told me that he knows of at least a dozen men—fathers, husbands, brothers—who have tried to call him out, but of course Palmering is too cowhearted to accept a challenge."

"Did he also tell you that at White's they are making wagers about how long it will be before someone puts a period to his existence?" inquired Lady Jersey. "I understand that DeBracey believes it will occur before May Day."

The three of them turned to look at the man in question. He had seated himself beside his wife and was obviously berating her. He was still speaking to her, but Lily had turned her face away from him.

A waiter moved deftly among the guests, removing plates and cups from tables, pausing briefly at Palmering's table. Unfortunately, Palmering rose abruptly from his chair at that precise moment, sending the waiter's tray spinning, and it required considerable dexterity on the part of the servant to keep it from crashing to the floor.

"A very nimble move," observed Brookston as the waiter brought the tray under control. Then he frowned, for Palmering had grabbed the man's arm. "But it appears that he has irritated Lord Palmering."

"Brookston, go and put a stop to that before the ridiculous man finally manages to create a disturbance," commanded Lady Jersey.

"Must you always try to prove your manhood by picking on those who cannot strike back at you?" inquired Brookston in a low voice as he disengaged Palmering's hand from the waiter's arm. Grateful, the waiter hurried on his way before anything else could transpire.

Palmering, his face scarlet, sank into his chair, still glaring at Brookston. Unperturbed, that gentleman bent closer and said, "I would strongly suggest that you enjoy your supper quietly and that you not continue to take out your anger upon Lady Palmering."

Lily, who had been listening, flushed, but she smiled gratefully at Brookston.

"That's right! Make sheep's eyes at any man who pays attention to you! That is why I can't allow you out of the house!" growled Palmering, reaching for his cup and drinking deeply.

Brookston smiled back at Lily and bowed. "My apologies, Lady Palmering. I fear that I have increased your husband's ire. I am sorry that you are being subjected to it."

He glanced coldly at Palmering, his voice growing as frigid as his expression. "Do not forget that here you are under the eye of the *ton,* Palmering. You would be wise to hold your temper and pretend to be well-bred, at least for the moment."

Then, bowing briefly again to Lily, Brookston turned and walked away. It was a thousand pities, he reflected, that a pleasant young woman had to be subjected to such indignities. No matter what her background, she deserved better treatment. However, he could do nothing about it, so he resolved to go home and put the whole unpleasant matter out of his mind.

When he reached Ladies Cowper and Jersey, he bowed again. "Ladies, if you will excuse me, I believe that I have had quite enough of Palmering this evening, and no quantities of weak tea can atone for it. If you wish to keep the young bucks coming to Almack's, I fear you will have to do something more than allowing the waltz in order to enliven the balls. Perhaps you should offer stronger liquid refreshment. If even the older ones like myself are going home early, you clearly have a problem that should be addressed."

"Nonsense, Brookston!" retorted Lady Jersey. "You simply have not looked about the Rooms and found a lovely young woman to dance with. That would keep you from being bored and fretting over refreshments. It is high time you married anyway—stay for just a moment, and I shall find you a likely partner."

Brookston was just about to inform her that he was in no need of her assistance when a sudden flurry of activity attracted their attention. Lord Palmering had once again risen abruptly from his chair and was clutching his throat, his face an unattractive beet red.

"This is the final straw! The man is going to die of apoplexy right here and now!" exclaimed Lady Jersey. "He has never had the least consideration for anyone else!"

Lord Palmering slowly raised his arm and pointed toward Lily, who had also risen and was watching him fearfully.

"Poison!" he croaked, his voice carrying through the sudden silence as others turned to stare at him. For a moment everyone seemed to freeze in a tableau; then Palmering pitched forward across the table. In the stillness, all that could be heard was the sound of breaking glass and the heavy thud as the weight of his body pulled him from the table to the floor.

Alistair Fitzgerald bent over Palmering for a moment, then stood up and shook his head. Lily collapsed into her chair, and the crowd about her began to murmur.

"It's worse than you thought, Sally," said Brookston in a low voice. "Palmering hasn't just died at Almack's. It appears that DeBracey has won his wager. I believe that Palmering has managed to get himself murdered."

Lady Cowper moaned and put her hand to her forehead, but Lady Jersey glared in the direction of the corpse. "Palmering has always been completely tasteless. I might have guessed that he would be so even in his death."

"Really, Sally, you must be more discreet," said Lady Cowper. "The man is dead, after all."

"Well, that is my point precisely," retorted her friend indignantly. "He was under no obligation to die here! I shall call the servants to remove his body. We cannot leave him lying there on the floor."

Here she turned to Brookston. "And you must take his poor wife home immediately, Basil. She is clearly in no condition to go home without a proper escort. I do wish that she had someone there to look after her; but there's only Palmering's son, of course, so she will have to rely upon her abigail."

Brookston looked at Lady Palmering with some misgiving, but he saw to his relief that she had not dissolved in tears. Instead, her fair skin was even paler than usual, and her eyes did not appear to be focused on the scene before her. A stout matron was leaning over her, waving smelling salts briskly under her nose, but there was no response.

"Come along, Lady Palmering, let me see you home," he said in what he hoped was a reassuring voice. Lily turned to look at him, still with that strangely unfocused gaze that made him feel that she was not really seeing him.

"Is he dead?" she asked, glancing toward her husband's body.

Brookston nodded gently. "I am afraid so." He took her elbow and helped her to her feet. She did not argue, but came along with him meekly, not looking again at the body of her husband. The crowd parted as they made their way toward the door, every eye staring at her curiously. To his relief, she seemed oblivious to them all.

As he helped her into his carriage, her arm was icy to the touch. Once in the carriage, he tucked a lap robe around her and wished that he had a flask of brandy with him so that he could have her swallow some. Her silence was beginning to trouble him, and he was afraid that she was suffering from shock.

When they reached her home, he escorted her to the door and asked the butler to send down Lady Palmering's maid. The butler's blank stare told him that there was no such person.

"Very well," Brookston said briskly. "Show us to the

drawing room, then bring in a glass of brandy for your mistress and send down the most capable maid you have. Lady Palmering has suffered a severe shock and will need to be attended."

The butler recognized the tone of a man accustomed to having his orders obeyed, and he hurried to do as he had been told. Brookston guided Lily to a chair and once more wrapped the robe around her shoulders. As soon as the butler returned with the brandy, Brookston poured some and lifted the glass to her lips.

"Just take a sip, Lady Palmering," he said gently. "It's strong, but it will make you feel a little better."

Lily sipped obediently and choked, but he saw with relief that a little color had crept back into her cheeks. "Very good," he said encouragingly. "Try just a little more—think of it as medicine."

Accustomed to doing as she was told, Lily sipped again and choked again, but this time she looked directly at him.

"Thank you, Lord Brookston," she said in a low voice. "It was very kind of you to see me home."

"I'm sorry about what happened, Lady Palmering," he replied gravely. "Is there anyone that I can summon to be with you? Do you have any relatives in town?"

Lily shook her head and, to his alarm, closed her eyes.

"What of friends here in London? I could go and fetch someone to stay here with you."

Again she shook her head, and a tear slipped silently down her cheek. "My sister and my aunt live at Darrowby. That is one hundred miles from here."

"If you will write a letter, I will see to it that they receive it, Lady Palmering. You should not be here alone."

"But she is not here alone, Brookston." An elegant, whipcord-thin young man in tightly fitted evening dress lounged in the doorway. "She is a married woman, so naturally her husband lives here." He paused a moment for dramatic effect, his lip curling slightly. "And—it may have escaped your notice, of course—I am also here."

Brookston, who disliked Palmering's son, Lord Tiller, almost as much as he had disliked his father, kept himself from responding in kind. After all, Lady Palmering was present, and Lord Tiller, although he clearly did not yet know it, had lost his father.

"Yes, so I see, Tiller, but Lady Palmering needs to have a woman with her tonight."

Tiller's thin eyebrows arched. "Indeed?" he commented. "And may I ask why?"

Brookston steeled himself. "I regret to be the one to tell you this, but your father collapsed and died tonight." He hesitated a moment, and added, "I'm sorry."

Lord Tiller stood perfectly still. "Dead?" he asked blankly. "But I saw him at dinner."

"He and Lady Palmering went to Almack's afterwards," said Brookston.

Tiller nodded. "I know. That seemed a strange thing for him to do. He doesn't go there often, and he certainly never takes—" Here he paused and glanced at Lily. "And he certainly never takes her with him. It was all very odd."

He sat down abruptly. "And now you say he is dead."

Brookston nodded, deciding that he would not mention what Palmering had said before dying.

Just then he was saved by the arrival of a small, rather frightened maid. "Take your mistress upstairs and stay with her tonight," he commanded. "And be certain that she drinks a cup of hot tea, well-sweetened, before she goes to bed."

"A pretty thing, giving orders to my servants, Brookston," complained Tiller petulantly as the maid led Lady Palmering from the room. "You take too much upon yourself."

"I will be taking a little more," responded Brookston shortly. "Lady Palmering did not have an opportunity to write a note to her sister and aunt, but if you will give me their direction in Darrowby, I will send for them."

"To come here?" demanded Tiller.

Brookston stared at him. "Yes, naturally to come here,"

he returned. "Lady Palmering has been widowed, and her family should be with her."

"Perhaps they should," Tiller responded, "but they may stay at a hotel. There is no need to have the commoners outnumbering the peers in the household."

Apparently feeling that he had made his point, the young man bowed briefly and turned to leave the room.

"Insolent pup!" exclaimed Brookston, but his quarry apparently had become conveniently deaf and continued out the door.

Seething, Brookston returned home determined to show young Tiller, now Lord Palmering, that he needed to mind his manners. He greatly disliked the disrespectful manner in which he was treating Lady Palmering, and he disliked even more the contemptuous way in which he himself had been dismissed. Brookston did not consider himself a particularly proud man, but he was accustomed to thinking well of himself and to being treated as a man of consequence. Tiller's manners were in definite need of mending. He decided that he himself would set off for Darrowby at dawn the next morning and escort Lady Palmering's sister and aunt back to London.

Still motivated by a strong sense of sympathy for Lady Palmering and by an even stronger feeling of indignation toward the new Lord Palmering, Brookston set forth for Darrowby at daybreak. His enthusiasm was somewhat dampened by the cold drizzle that began to fall, but he rode on until late afternoon, when the storm broke in earnest. To his relief, he finally saw a small inn and hurried toward its welcoming lights.

"Landlord! I need a room immediately, and some hot water so that I can clean up." Brookston took off his hat and shook the water from it. Seeing the fire in the bar, he moved briskly toward it and took a comfortable position with his back to it.

The landlord, a small, round man with gray hair, looked at him uneasily. He recognized a member of the quality, and he did not wish to offend his unexpected guest.

"I'm afraid that there's not a room to be had, sir," replied the landlord unhappily. "We have only two guest chambers, and they are both taken by the ladies."

"I see," said Brookston, glancing about the tiny bar. It was a snug, cheerful place, ringed with casks and dotted with nets filled with lemons, firelight flickering on the polished wooden floor. Clearly this room was too small to accommodate him. The two small tables all but filled the available space.

"Isn't there any other place that I could sleep?" he asked, feeling aggrieved. "You can't expect me to go back out into the rain."

"No sir, of course not," the landlord assured him, sounding still more unhappy. "There's always the stable," he added, snatching at straws.

"The stable?" asked Brookston in disbelief. "You think that I should sleep in the stable with the livestock?"

"Naturally not, sir," replied the landlord hastily. A prolonged pause fell as he regarded his boots thoughtfully.

"Well?" demanded Brookston. "If I don't sleep in the stable—which I will not do—where will I sleep?"

"You could sleep on the settle in the common room, sir," said the landlord, brightening as he thought of this solution. "I could keep the fire burning instead of banking the coals, and we have an extra blanket."

"Sleep on a wooden settle?" asked Brookston. "Are you suggesting that I sleep on an uncushioned settle?"

The silence that ensued informed him that that was precisely what the landlord had suggested.

"How many ladies are there?" inquired Brookston abruptly.

"Two," answered the landlord.

"And you have two chambers?" continued Brookston. The landlord nodded.

"Are the ladies strangers to one another or are they traveling together?"

"They are traveling together."

"And so they are friends?"

Again the landlord nodded. "I believe that they are related, sir."

"Better still," said Brookston jubilantly. "Our problem is then solved."

The landlord looked at him blankly.

"Just have them share a chamber," explained Brookston patiently, "and I will take the other one."

"But the ladies are already in their chambers, resting before dinner," said the landlord.

"And I am certain that once you explain the situation to them, they will be happy to allow me one of those chambers," repeated Brookston. "Leave me with a tankard of ale to warm myself by the fire while you go upstairs to make the arrangements—and do be quick. I need to change from these wet things as soon as possible."

"Do you, indeed? Well, perhaps you should ask for a screen so that you may change beside that fire. I'm certain that the landlord would be happy to accommodate you."

Both men looked up. In the doorway stood a dark-haired young woman, her gaze fixed upon Brookston.

"I'm afraid that such an arrangement would not be at all satisfactory, ma'am," he returned smoothly. His voice was well-modulated and polite. The young woman was well-dressed and well-spoken, but his manner would have been the same if she had not been. "I am in need of a private chamber."

"Indeed?" asked the young woman coolly, sizing him up from heels to crown in a manner he found extremely irritating. He was a man accustomed to deferential treatment, and this minx appeared to be taking his measure in a manner he found intrusive and presumptuous. Almost immediately he found himself growing stiffer, drawing himself up to his somewhat impressive height so that he could look down at her.

"Yes," he responded briefly. "I understand that you and your companion are occupying the only two chambers available. It would seem to me that the two of you could stay together for this one night so that I might also have the comfort of a bed."

The young woman appeared not at all impressed by his manner or his height. She regarded him seriously for a moment before replying. "Yes, I can see that you would think that an excellent idea. I, on the other hand, do not find it so. The beds are small, and I have no wish to be uncomfortable myself or to inconvenience my aunt—who is, I might add, already asleep in her chamber."

Here she turned to the landlord, who had been following this interchange with increasing discomfort. "Do you have any other places available for this gentleman?" she inquired.

He nodded, not raising his eyes to hers or to Brookston's. "I suggested to his lordship that the common room has a settle in front of the fire."

"His lordship?" inquired the young lady, her brows rising. She surveyed Brookston once more. "I can understand your distress more readily, sir. I had no notion that you were a member of the peerage."

"I have not told you who I am," protested Brookston, glancing at the landlord.

"I should imagine that your manner has told him," commented the young lady dryly. "And I suppose you feel that this should make a difference in my attitude toward your request."

Brookston said nothing, but he naturally felt that it should indeed have some slight effect on her thinking.

She waited for his reply, then shook her head. "I am afraid—my lord—that I still feel that my aunt deserves her rest, as do I. And I am relieved to hear that you have the common room at your disposal. I would not sleep well if I thought you did not have a place to rest."

Turning, she walked from the room without a backward glance. The landlord, feeling Brookston's eyes upon him, bowed swiftly and followed in her wake.

Irritated, Brookston turned back to the fire, attempting to finish thawing from the cold spring rain. It appeared that he would have to make do without a chamber, but he was determined that he would not be relegated to the cold common room and the hard settle. The tiny bar at least had the advantage of warmth. There was no proper place to sleep, of course, but he would think about his options as he had his dinner here before the fire. With that in mind, he set off to find the landlord and discover what was to be had for dinner.

The landlord and his wife, accustomed only to the local clientele, were bustling about the tiny kitchen. His wife had three plump fowls turning on the spit, which she planned to dress with liver and sausages, and she was laboring over oyster fritters. Brookston assured her that this would be very satisfactory and, highly gratified by his approval, she returned to her cooking.

A brief glance into the common room revealed that, weather notwithstanding, it was filling with locals who were bending over their cider and pint-pots of ale. Brookston's nose wrinkled at the blend of pipe smoke, wet hair, and damp wool, mixed now with the smell of the smoke from the fire and the wet fur of a large, woolly dog resting in front of it. He had never considered himself a fastidious man, but he determined immediately that he would neither eat nor sleep in this room tonight.

Accordingly, he turned back to the kitchen.

"I will have my supper in the bar tonight, landlord," he announced. "And if you will bring me a blanket afterward, I will sleep in that room as well."

The landlord looked at him and hesitated before speaking.

"Well, what is it, man?" demanded Brookston, impatient that his gracious acceptance of uncomfortable circumstances was being received with no recognition of the sacrifice he was making.

"The young lady plans to have her dinner in the bar tonight, my lord," he explained reluctantly. "It would not be seemly for a lady to eat in the common room, and we have no private dining room."

"Why can she and her aunt not dine in their chambers?" demanded Brookston.

"The young lady said they are too small to dine in," replied the landlord, regarding the toes of his boots studiously.

Brookston swallowed the words that rose in his throat. Clearly, the landlord felt that he could contend with the company in the common room. He could not, in good conscience, argue that the ladies should be placed there, either, but he was determined that he would also enjoy the comparative privacy and comfort of the bar.

"I believe that I will join the ladies for dinner," he announced. "Please lay a place for me as well."

The landlord, not eager to argue with his betters, bowed, and Brookston returned to the snug little bar and his place before the fire, carefully arranging one of the tables close by it.

When the young lady reappeared an hour or so later, she was alone. Seeing Brookston seated at the table, she frowned.

"I did not realize that anyone else would be here, sir," she said, pausing.

Brookston, who had already begun his dinner, glanced up at her. "I trust that you are not thinking that I should leave, ma'am," he commented. Then, noticing that she was alone, he added, "Is your aunt not hungry?"

She shook her head. "She is still asleep. The journey and the emotional distress have taken their toll on her."

"Have you had a long journey today?" he inquired idly, standing to pull out her chair for her at the other tiny table.

"Long enough," she responded, seating herself reluctantly.

"Please understand that I am not trying to pry," he said, glancing at her. The young lady, he noticed, was handsomer than he had at first thought. Her features were daintily chiseled but distinctive, her arresting eyes an unusual shade of green shot through with gold, her skin pale against her dark hair. "I was simply making conversation."

"Of course," she replied, smiling briefly. "I believe that people of your station feel obliged to fill silence with idle chatter."

"And I suppose people of your station—whatever that might be—converse in intelligent silence?" he inquired, irritated.

Suddenly she laughed, a ripple of genuine amusement rather than an affected giggle. "Touché!" she returned cheerfully. "I yield. I did sound impossibly priggish."

Thrown off guard by her response, he glanced up at her sharply. When her eyes met his, he suffered a brief stab of delight. Her glance was intelligent and alert. To his surprise, he felt that he would, indeed, like to talk with this young woman, whether she wished to do so or not. And it occurred to him suddenly that this could be a most enjoyable interlude.

Instead of casting down her eyes, she continued to regard him steadily, but her eyes were somewhat kinder now, merriment having dispelled their coldness.

"Are you on your way to London?" he inquired.

She nodded, leaning over to pat a small, rough-coated terrier who had made his way into the room and demanded her attention.

"Is that your dog?" he asked curiously.

She laughed. "No. I don't usually travel with my dogs."

"But I take it by your reply that you do keep some," he returned.

She nodded, still patting the terrier, who was regarding her closely with bright, inquisitive eyes. "I should say that this one has hopes of sharing my dinner when the landlord brings it," she observed. "I daresay he wouldn't mind a bite of yours, either. I see that you still have a portion of it left."

When the landlord entered a moment later, carrying her meal on a tray, he attempted to send the dog from the bar, but the young woman stopped him. "He has been waiting patiently for a little of my supper," she said, "and I plan to give him some."

"Very good, miss," he replied, regarding the terrier disapprovingly, "but I must say that Rags is getting above himself."

"Rags? Is that his name?" she inquired, amused.

The landlord nodded. "He sleeps on a bundle of rags in the corner of the scullery, and my wife said that the patches of color on his coat look like rags—so Rags he has become."

"They have been very hard on you," said the young lady to the terrier after the landlord had left. "It seems to me that you are a good bit better than your name."

As she set about preparing a plate for Rags, Brookston cleared his throat. "It occurs to me that we know the dog's name; but I do not know yours, and I have failed to introduce myself. I apologize for being so—forgive me—so rag-mannered."

"Not at all," she returned cheerfully, cutting the sausage into bite-sized pieces as the dog watched eagerly. "I think, given our circumstances, that we will do quite well with no names at all. After all, we will soon go our separate ways, and it does not seem to me vital to know who you are."

He stared at her, taken aback by her response.

She saw his expression and laughed. "Besides, I know that you are to be called 'my lord,' and I have no desire to call you that. I shall like you far better if I think of you as a plain country gentleman, caught in this little inn by the storm."

"And so I am," he asserted, attempting to look as plain and countrified as possible.

She looked at him and shook her head, smiling. "I'm not certain that we can bend the truth that far, sir." She paused a moment, then added, "If we must have names, then you shall be Mr. Jamison, and I shall be Miss Dayton. For the evening, those will be our roles."

"And I take it, then, that you are not truly Miss Dayton," he observed.

"No more than you are Mr. Jamison," she returned. "The only one going by his true name is Rags."

Recognizing his name, the terrier glanced up from his plate of sausages and wagged his tail sociably.

"So, tell me, Miss Dayton, is it business or pleasure that takes you to London? It must be pleasure, surely."

Her face darkened at his words, and he hastened to add, "Forgive me. Your reason for going is none of my affair, of course. I asked because of my undeniable propensity to make idle chatter, as you were pointing out earlier."

She shook her head. "Your comment was innocent enough, and my rudeness earlier was really quite inexcusable. I am going on business, I fear."

He searched his mind quickly, trying to conjure up an innocent topic of conversation that would lighten the atmosphere.

"Perhaps you will have time to go the theater while you are there," he said. "Assuming, of course, that you enjoy the theater. Do you?"

She shook her head. "Not particularly, I am afraid. I am more inclined to enjoy country pleasures, which are rather scarce in London."

"Well, you can ride there, of course," he said.

"In a park with countless others," she returned. "The country is much better. I do not ride to observe people or fashions."

"Of course not," he replied, chastened. "I don't suppose I dare mention balls or shopping as pleasurable possibilities?"

"Well, perhaps an occasional ball," she conceded. "I imagine much of your time is occupied with such affairs."

Brookston was somewhat nettled by her comment, particularly because it was true and because she seemed to think so little of spending time in such a manner.

"I do have to be forced to go, of course," he said, "and, once there, I refuse to enjoy myself. After all, balls are a waste of time, and there is little of interest to be found in shops, particularly those that display art and books. I would much prefer sitting at home and staring into the leaves of the plane tree just outside my study window."

"I believe, Mr. Jamison, that you are making light of me," the young lady observed unsmilingly, although he noticed that the dimples around her mouth were deepening.

"I would never do so, Miss Dayton," he assured her gravely. "After all, being a country gentleman, I know the value of the pleasures you enjoy. I too, long to walk through quiet gardens in the peaceful twilight."

She nodded encouragingly, her expression equally grave.

"And to—to take out my gun and trek into the woods to hunt my dinner—"

Here she shook her head warningly.

"No, no, of course not—what could I have been thinking?" he corrected himself quickly. "I long to walk through the spring woods, admiring the snowdrops and the newborn rabbits."

Again she nodded, waiting for him to continue.

Brookston delved desperately into his scanty knowledge of sylvan delights. His own country activities had been limited to hunting, fishing, and attending the races—along with attending the occasional boxing match that was scheduled in some rural retreat.

"And, of course, when I am away from the country, I always long to return so that I may—so that I may—"

"So that you may," she repeated, gesturing with her hand for him to continue. "So that you may what, Mr. Jamison?"

"So that I may—walk in the kitchen garden with the cook and choose my own vegetables for dinner!" he finished desperately. "How the devil would I know, Miss Dayton? I am afraid that I needed more time to prepare for my role."

Her laughter echoed through the tiny bar, punctuated by a brief, sharp bark from Rags, who was eyeing Brookston's plate expectantly.

Brookston regarded him with disfavor. "Yes, I know now what I should have said. I should have said so I may walk with my dogs, should I not?"

She nodded. "Indeed, you should have, Mr. Jamison. I am shocked that it did not occur to you immediately since you are, after all, a country squire."

"Yes, well, perhaps if Rags had spoken up a little sooner, it would have occurred to me, but it appears as though he has just finished one meal and is longing for another."

"He does look a little thin, Mr. Jamison," she pointed out. "You, on the other hand, do not appear at all thin. I daresay that you could spare him a little of what you have left on your plate."

"I beg your pardon, Miss Dayton." Brookston was affronted by her remark. He prided himself upon his fine physical condition. He rode regularly, he was a very pretty whip, and he made it a habit to drop into Gentleman Jackson's boxing saloon on Bond Street several times a week. And now he was being unfavorably compared to a bony little terrier.

"I fear I have offended you, Mr. Jamison," said the young lady, her smile indicating that the fear was not distressing her at all.

"Not at all, Miss Dayton," he responded, with what he considered admirable coolness. Carefully he took his plate and leaned over to scrape the leftovers onto the terrier's saucer.

Miss Dayton, however, restrained him. At his questioning look, she pointed to the meat.

"The meat should be cut in small, bite-sized pieces, and you must never give a dog the bones of a fowl. They could choke him."

Brookston stared at Rags for a moment, thinking briefly—and fondly—of the part about choking. Rags, however, appeared to be able to read his mind and emitted a low, throaty growl as he eyed Brookston intently.

"Oh, very well," responded Brookston petulantly, and in no time at all Rags was consuming the last traces of his meal, his stubby tail wagging joyously. When he had finished, he turned in a circle and settled next to Miss Dayton with a satisfied sigh.

"I believe I know now why I have avoided the country all these years," he remarked, watching the slumbering Rags.

"Nonsense!" returned Miss Dayton, sipping her glass of claret. "You are simply accustomed to thinking only of yourself, so naturally it is a strain to turn your attention to someone else—even if the someone else is only a poor, scrawny dog."

Startled, Brookston stared at her. What she said was blatantly untrue, of course, and a reflection of her obvious distaste for the peerage. Naturally he thought about others. Why, only last night he had taken Lady Palmering home. Lady Jersey had commanded him to do so, of course, but he would have done it willingly enough anyway—if he had thought of it. And before that—well, before that there had been many other times when he considered other people, he told himself defiantly.

His companion had been watching his face with interest. "You hadn't considered that, had you, Mr. Jamison? Were you able to think of a time when you thought of someone other than yourself?"

"Naturally I was able to do so," he replied, and even to himself his tone sounded defensive.

"Were you able to think of more than one occasion?" she asked curiously, still studying his face.

Brookston was an inherently honest man, so his response was not immediate this time, and she said quickly, "Well, never mind. It was none of my affair to ask such a thing, after all."

It was not, of course, but it still annoyed him that he could not think of another time when his concern had been completely for another individual rather than himself. There were many, he had no doubt, for he did not consider himself a selfish man, but he was having some trouble recollecting them.

"Good evening, Mr. Jamison," said the young lady, rising from her place. "I have enjoyed your company. And yours, of course, Rags."

Rags and Brookston rose to their feet at the same time. "As have I," he responded, bowing. "Must you go up so soon?"

She nodded. "We will get an early start so that we reach London by tomorrow evening. Perhaps we shall see you on the road."

He shook his head. "I am going the opposite direction, I fear."

She looked shocked and dimpled deeply. "I am amazed to discover that you are riding away from London rather than toward it, sir," she said.

"Only for a brief time," he assured her, "and then I shall be back in London. Perhaps we shall see one another there."

"That hardly seems likely, Mr. Jamison," she replied. "I do not believe that we will be traveling in the same circles—but if I go the theater, I shall look for you there."

Here she curtseyed and he bowed briefly, and she left the bar, followed closely by Rags. Depressed, he sank into his chair next to the fire. He had enjoyed her company—genuinely enjoyed her company—and such an experience was a novelty to him. It was a thousand pities that it was over, he told himself. The next morning, he would rise early and discover her name and where she would be staying in London. At least he might have the pleasure of seeing her once more while she was in town.

Stretching his boots toward the fire, he dozed, lightly at first and then more deeply. He did not awaken until morning, to find that the fire had died to a few gray coals, that he was stiff and cold, and that the young lady and her aunt, whose names the landlord had never learned, had left for London an hour earlier.

Cursing, Brookston had his mount saddled, ate his breakfast, and rode on toward Darrowby. After some inquiry, he arrived at Ivy Manor, the home of Lady Palmering's family, and was disgusted to discover that they had already left for London. His uncomfortable journey appeared to have been for nothing.

"Why were they going to London?" he demanded of the butler. It was not possible that they could have had news of Palmering's death at the time they left.

The butler, convinced he was dealing with a madman, told Brookston gently that he did not know why the ladies had left. They were not in the habit of confiding their thinking to him.

Forced to be satisfied with that, Brookston began his weary journey homeward, deprived even of the knowledge that he had done a good deed. He had tried to help Lady Palmering, but her family appeared to be one jump ahead of him. Without giving much thought to the matter, he knew that he heartily disliked them, if only because they had caused him to undertake a luckless, tiring trip.

Nonetheless, the morning after his return to London, he called to pay his respects to Lady Palmering. The funeral, he knew, had been the day of his return. The same sedate butler showed him to the drawing room and left him to summon Lady Palmering. To his astonishment, when the door reopened, a small terrier bolted through the opening and came to rest with his front paws on Brookston's knee.

"Rags?" he asked in disbelief, and the terrier wagged his tail briskly in response, keeping his eyes fixed firmly on those of Brookston.

"Oh, I do beg your pardon, Lord Brookston," exclaimed Lily, hurrying over and removing the dog from his knee. "Rags has not yet acquired any company manners, I fear."

"Where did you acquire—Rags?" he inquired, certain that he knew and certain now of Miss Dayton's identity.

"My sister brought him to me," she responded, confirming his suspicion. "She and my aunt stayed at an inn on their way from Darrowby, and Rose purchased Rags from the landlord there. She thought that he would cheer me up—and he has, immeasurably."

Her tone and the fresh color in her cheeks supported her statement. Even in black, she looked radiant. If Brookston had been a less charitable man, or had he liked Lady Palmering less, he might have considered the possibility that the absence of the dark presence of her husband could have also been responsible for her much happier appearance.

Instead, succumbing to her innocence and her beauty, Brookston smiled at her. "I am pleased to see you looking so well, ma'am."

Lily colored slightly at this. "I know that I should not appear happy at such a time, Lord Brookston; but I have not seen my sister and my aunt for over a year, and having Rags is a great help to me, too."

"And you have every right to enjoy them," he said firmly. If anyone had a right to a little happiness, it was Lady Palmering, who had had so little to brighten her life since her marriage.

"You are very kind," she said gratefully. "And I am glad that you have come, for I wished to thank you for your help on the night of—" Here words failed her, and she looked down at her hands, which were folded in her lap.

"I wish that I could have done more," he replied gallantly. Then, hoping both to relieve her discomfort and his own curiosity, he added, "I am delighted to hear your family has arrived. Perhaps I might be able to meet your sister and your aunt, Lady Palmering."

"They are not here just now," Lily explained. "They had planned to stay at Grillon's Hotel; but Lord Tiller—I mean, Lord Palmering—insisted that they stay here with us, and they are back at the hotel, packing their things now. It was so very kind of him."

Brookston stared at her, remembering what the gentleman had said to him on the night of Lord Palmering's death. What, he wondered, had brought about such a change of heart on the part of a notoriously selfish young man?

"I should think your family would have expected to stay with you, Lady Palmering," he observed.

She flushed slightly. "Well, Lord Palmering—my late husband, that is—did not wish for me to have close contact with my family, and he would never allow me to invite them here. That is why it is particularly kind of his son to do so. He surprised me greatly with his invitation."

Brookston, too, was surprised—and more than a little suspicious. Miss Dayton might have accused him of not thinking of others, but, in comparison to the new Lord Palmering, he considered himself a paragon of kindness and selflessness. Again he wondered about this unusual behavior and determined to think about the matter later.

Assuring Lady Palmering that he would call again in the afternoon to meet her sister and aunt, he bowed and said his good-byes to her and to Rags, then strolled thoughtfully back to his club. He was cheered by the thought that he would soon meet Miss Dayton again, and the visit with Lady Palmering had left him with much to think about.

As he walked down Bond Street, someone clutched his arm, and he emerged from his reverie to see Lady Jersey staring at him.

"I said, Brookston, have you heard that they are saying that Palmering was murdered?" she demanded, apparently repeating a question she had already asked.

He stared back at her for a moment.

"Well, yes, of course I have, Sally. I was there—don't you remember?"

"Of course I remember, Brookston!" she responded impatiently. "That's why I am talking to you about it now. We must do something about it!"

He decided that reason was not going to work, so he waited to hear what her point was.

"They are saying that Palmering was murdered *at* Almack's!" she exclaimed, keeping her voice low. "If people believe it, this will be a terrible scandal!"

"Well, Sally, that *is* what Palmering said himself—and it certainly appeared to be the truth. After all, he did collapse and die immediately after saying he had been poisoned. You and I heard him."

"But I had every intention of ignoring it, Brookston—as would anyone of good sense. I certainly was not the one to begin the gossip about this!" Lady Jersey, an inveterate gossip, appeared perfectly serious. "This could ruin Almack's!"

Seeing that she was genuinely upset, Brookston tried to be reassuring. "Well, I shouldn't worry, Sally. It will be a nine-day wonder, and then the talk will die away."

She shook her head. "I understand that there are inquiries already being made. That poor child is going to be dragged into it and accused!"

"What poor child?" he demanded, startled by the news. "Do you mean Lady Palmering?"

She nodded. "After all, he pointed at her when he said 'Poison!' and everyone is talking about it."

"Hell and damnation!" breathed Brookston under his breath.

"Just what I said when I heard the news," said Lady Jersey approvingly. This was much closer to the comforting reaction she had expected. "Just as you said the other evening, we are having enough trouble just keeping the young men coming. Now people will be worrying about whether or not they will be poisoned as well. This could be the death blow for Almack's!"

"I wasn't thinking of Almack's, Sally," he retorted. "This will scarcely help Lady Palmering either."

"Well, naturally not," she returned, but then she brightened. "But at least, Brookston, if some one person is identified as the murderer, perhaps people will not hold Almack's responsible for his death."

Brookston turned and looked at her as though he had never seen her before. "Listen to yourself, Sally! Surely you don't mean that you would like to see Lady Palmering convicted for this!"

"Well, it would naturally be better if the murderer were someone that I don't like—" she began, but he interrupted her.

"I really don't wish to hear anything else you have to say just now, Sally," he said briefly, striding off toward St. James Street and his club, leaving her staring after him.

This certainly could not be true, he told himself. Too few people would be interested in the death of Lord Palmering. Even as he told himself that, however, he knew he was wrong. There were few things that the *ton* loved more than a scandal, and this had all the earmarks of a good one—an unexplained murder, a lovely young woman, a fortune that she had brought to the marriage. They would be delighted to follow the scandal, to discuss it with vigor, to argue their own points of view about the murder with fervor.

The gossip at his club confirmed his misgivings. Although no one blamed Palmering's lovely young wife for administering a dose of something lethal to him, most of them appeared to believe that she had been guilty of doing precisely that. As to what should be done about it, opinion was divided. Some, particularly those that were husbands, felt that the matter should be investigated closely so that she did not set a dangerous precedent. Most, however, felt that the event should be covered over as quickly and neatly as possible. She was, after all, the widow and grand-daughter of peers of the realm, and she had done nothing so desperate as shooting her husband before witnesses.

Alistair Fitzgerald, who had been the first to check Palmering's pulse, declared himself ready to go before any magistrate and proclaim that Lady Palmering would not have been close enough to her husband to administer any poison to him.

"Come now, Fitzgerald," Brookston heard himself replying. "We do not know if the poison was fast-acting or slow, so it could have been administered before he came to Almack's and only taken effect then. And as to being too far away from him, you know very well that she was sitting directly next to him, and part of the time he was away from the table, leaving his drink unwatched."

Fitzgerald stared at him, astounded. "You know what Palmering was, Brookston. Are you seriously suggesting that Lady Palmering should be accused of his murder?"

"No, of course not," he heard himself saying, and, indeed, he knew that he did not wish to accuse the young lady, whom he considered an unfortunate victim. "I am merely suggesting that there are any number of possibilities. For instance, I am almost certain that Palmering poured himself a drink from a silver flask that he was carrying. Who is to say that there was not poison in the drink he poured for himself?"

And, so saying, he removed himself from the club and went out for a breath of fresh air. It seemed to him that he was becoming embroiled in a matter he had no desire to be any part of. After strolling down Regent Street for a while and regaining his perspective, he decided that he would, as he had promised Lady Palmering, call to meet her sister and her aunt. Doing so would help to take his mind off the ticklish problem at hand. He did not add to himself that he looked forward to a meeting that he knew would surprise Miss Dayton.

When the butler opened the door for him this time, it was Rags that ushered him into the drawing room before the butler could announce him, nipping at Brookston's heels as though he were herding him.

Lady Palmering stared at her new pet in astonishment. "Rags!" she scolded him. "Whatever has come over you? Stop that immediately!"

Her voice was gentle, but it had an immediate effect. Rags, clearly already the abject subject of his new mistress, tucked his nub of a tail between his legs and slunk to her side, casting an apologetic glance toward his victim.

"Why, Mr. Jamison!"

Brookston had not seen Lady Palmering's sister, who was seated in a snug corner, next to a window overlooking the street. He was annoyed that she had been able to see him before he entered and to prepare herself for his arrival, while he himself had been caught off guard by the aggravating Rags.

Lily looked at her sister in surprise. "Why, no, Rose," she said. "This is Lord Brookston, the gentleman that I told you about who has been so kind to me."

It was Rose's turn to look surprised. "Indeed?" she said, rising and curtseying to that gentleman, who bowed in return. "Then, I am indebted to you, sir. My sister has told me of how you helped her."

Brookston thought of his conversation with Alistair Fitzgerald and had the grace to color slightly. "It has been my pleasure to be of service to Lady Palmering in whatever small way I could."

"Small way!" exclaimed Lily, extending her hand to him and looking up at him gratefully. "It may have seemed small to you, but escorting me home at the end of that dreadful evening and seeing to it that I was taken care of was not a small thing to me, sir. I daresay that you do so much for others that you did not consider what you did for me as anything worth commenting about."

To his profound irritation, Brookston felt his cheeks grow hotter still, and he assumed from Miss Dayton's knowing glance that she was reading the situation correctly.

"You give me too much credit, ma'am," he murmured, sinking gratefully into a chair and bending over to pat Rags. For once he was glad to have the little beast present. At least he could hide his flaming cheeks until they had time to cool.

Lily was looking at her sister with a puzzled expression. "But, Rose, why did you call Lord Brookston by another name? I believe you called him Mr. Jamison."

Rose glanced at Brookston, mischief in her eyes. "I believe I must have met Lord Brookston when he was ruralizing," she responded.

"Really?" asked Lily, looking at her sister with wide eyes. "You had not mentioned this to me, Rose. When did you meet?"

"Just a few nights ago," responded her sister. "When Aunt and I were on our way here, we stopped at a small inn. It was there I met Lord Brookston—only I did not know his name nor did he know mine."

"How very strange!" said Lily, her eyes wide. She thought about the matter for a moment; then her eyes widened still more, and she turned to Brookston. "Were you going to Darrowby, Lord Brookston?" she asked. "I remember that you asked me for the direction of my sister and my aunt when you escorted me home from Almack's, but I went to bed and did not remember until the next morning that I had not told you. Did you, indeed go there, sir?"

Seeing her looking at him worshipfully, for she was anticipating his reply, was grueling for Brookston. He knew that he had gone not just because of Lady Palmering, but because of his own irritation with Tiller. He nodded briefly and tried to look unconcerned.

"You see, Rose, I do have at least one friend here in London," she said, smiling at her sister.

"I had hoped, dear lady, that you would also count me among your friends here," said Lord Tiller, appearing in the doorway in time to hear her comment.

"Of course I do," responded Lily warmly, rising to curtsey and extend her hand to him. "You have been all kindness, sir."

Rose, who looked less impressed, also rose and curtseyed, murmuring her own thanks.

"I hope that you and your aunt have been properly looked after since your arrival from the hotel," he said, bowing and taking her hand as he did so. Brookston noticed with irritation that he did not let it go immediately.

"Indeed, we have, Lord Palmering," Rose responded. "Our reception has been most gracious."

"Well, I would not wish Lady Palmering's guests to lack any attention that lies within my power to show them," he replied.

"A very commendable sentiment," agreed Brookston, studying Palmering with interest. This was, indeed, a far cry, he thought, from what the young man had said the night of his father's death.

Rags, however, seemed to have his own doubts about Palmering's motives, for the terrier attached himself firmly to the tassel of one of his shining Hessians and shook it back and forth ferociously, growling all the while.

Before Lily could move to detach her pet, Palmering lifted the foot under attack and swung it violently. If the terrier's grip had been less tenacious, he would have gone flying against the wall. As it was, however, he returned to the floor with a jarring jolt, his teeth still anchored to the tassel.

It was Brookston who reached them first. Rags appeared slightly stunned by his fall, so a little firm pressure served to disengage him from the Hessian. Brookston noted gleefully that the boot would never be the same and that Palmering's face was livid.

"He is a high-spirited little animal, isn't he? Such determination!" Brookston said in a voice filled with enthusiastic admiration, watching Palmering's expression.

To his amazement, Palmering managed a thin smile, and he even forced himself to give Rags a single brief pat.

"Yes," he responded. "Amazing. I do apologize for my instinctive reaction. I trust he has taken no harm from my thoughtlessness."

Lily scooped up her pet and apologized profusely, but

he assured her smoothly that she was not to give it a thought.

Brookston watched him with consternation, wondering what Palmering had on his mind. This was not the behavior of the man he knew, and he could not imagine the reason for the transformation.

The butler appeared in the doorway and cleared his throat. "I beg your pardon, my lady, but there is a—a person at the door who wishes to speak to you."

His tone and outraged expression conveyed volumes. Obviously, he did not feel that the person in question should be calling upon a lady.

"Yes, Briggs?" inquired Lord Palmering. "And does the person have a name?"

"It is possible," responded Briggs, in a voice that indicated miracles might still occur.

"If you will excuse me," said Palmering, bowing to Lily, "I will look into this for you, ma'am. You should not be obliged to receive mysterious callers at a time such as this."

"Thank you," Lily responded gratefully.

Palmering bowed briefly to the others and strode firmly from the room, his walk conveying the message that he could handle any difficult situation that the stranger on the doorstep might present.

"How very good he is being to me!" exclaimed Lily, turning to Rose after the door had closed behind her stepson. "I must confess that I thought he held me in dislike, but since my husband's death, he has been kindness itself. I don't know how I shall be able to thank him."

Rose and Brookston maintained a thoughtful silence upon that subject, and Rags chewed his hard-won tassel with intensity. Brookston lingered for only a brief time; then, promising Lily that he would call again the next morning, he took his leave before Palmering returned to the drawing room. He regretted that he had had no opportunity to enjoy a real conversation with Miss Dayton—now, of course, Miss

Battinger—but he had hope of that for tomorrow. Also, he had been comforted to notice that she had not echoed her sister's heartfelt appreciation of the new Lord Palmering and his behavior.

Having had his dinner in lonely splendor at home in order to avoid further gossip at his club, he was just preparing for bed, promising himself a well-earned rest after several uncomfortable days on the road to Darrowby and back, when he was informed that he had a caller.

"A caller?" he repeated blankly, and the footman nodded without expression. "Who is it? Is there no card?"

"The caller is a young lady, sir."

"A young lady?" echoed Brookston, who appeared to be able to do nothing save repeat what was said to him. Taking himself in hand, he tried to regain control of the situation. "What is her name?"

"The young lady appears to be quite upset, sir, but I believe that she said her name is Miss Dayman," said the footman.

"Miss Dayton!" Brookston exclaimed.

The footman nodded once again. "I believe that could be what she said. I showed her to the library, sir."

"Thank you, Devon. That will do nicely," Brookston responded. "Please tell her that I will be down immediately and take in some—some ratafia. No! Take in some claret and biscuits!"

The footman bowed and went to execute his orders. It was not his affair, as he later told the upstairs maid that he was walking out with, to determine what the quality should and should not do, but it did seem to him that a young lady should never call upon a gentleman, even if there had been a death in the family.

The upstairs maid had agreed with him emphatically, and added that being considered forward was a reputation that would blight the prospects even of a member of the quality. "A lady must be respected," she added knowingly.

Devon had nodded. "You cannot be too careful about your reputation," he agreed. "Without that, a young woman has nothing."

Rose, although she was well aware of the dictum that stated a young woman was never to call upon a gentleman, had chosen to disregard it without the slightest consideration for her own position.

"I had to speak to you tonight, Lord Brookston. I hope you will forgive my intrusion," she told him, rising from the sofa where she had been awaiting him.

He discovered that he was delighted to have her awaiting him in his library, whatever the reason for it, so he simply nodded. She could have been dressed as a washerwoman, and he would have been ready to chat. Looking at her expression, however, he could see that something had distressed her greatly.

"What is it, Miss Battinger?" he asked. "What has happened to upset you so?"

Rose was nothing if not direct. "The person that came to see Lord Palmering this afternoon was from Bow Street," she informed him. "Someone has reported to them that his father died under suspicious circumstances, and they are inquiring into the matter!"

Taking her hand, he led her to a sofa. "Come sit down, Miss Battinger, and tell me all about it."

Rose sank down onto the sofa, and he seated himself beside her, still holding her hand—to comfort her, of course.

"Someone believes that Lily is responsible for her husband's death, Lord Brookston!" she told him, her voice shaking slightly in spite of her obvious effort to hold it in check. "I can't believe that anyone could believe her capable of such a coldhearted, calculating action."

He patted her hand. "They don't know her, of course. If they did, they would not suspect it for an instant."

Pulling her hand from his, she rose from the sofa and began to pace. "But that's just it, sir! They don't know her, and they do think that she might be capable of—" she said, scarcely able to bring herself to say the word, "of murder!"

Before he could reply, she turned upon him. "And you, sir!" she continued, waving a finger in his direction. "You did not tell me what Lord Palmering said that night!"

Startled by the sudden attack, he turned his mind back to that evening. When he did not reply immediately, she said, " 'Poison!' That's what he said, Lord Brookston— 'Poison!' Only you did not see fit to tell me about it!"

"Well, it isn't as though I was trying to keep it a secret!" he exclaimed, irritated. "After all, Lady Palmering was sitting right there, and she heard him, too!"

Rose blanched, and he suddenly felt terrible. "You're right," she whispered, sitting back down beside him. "Lily did know, and she said nothing to me about it."

"Don't be disheartened by that, Miss Battinger!" he begged her, eager to ease her sudden fear. "Consider the fact that your sister was clearly suffering from shock that evening. I daresay that she can scarcely recall the events at all."

Rose brightened at this. "That is true, sir," she responded. "She has told me little enough, and I have not pressed her to remember so unhappy a time; but her comment has been that it all seemed like a waking nightmare to her."

Here she turned to him, and he absently took her hand once more, and, intent upon what she was saying, Rose absently allowed him to do so.

"But we must protect her, Lord Brookston!" she continued. "She will not be able to take care of herself—we will have to do so! When Lord Palmering told us what the man from Bow Street had said, Lily crumpled to the floor. Aunt Elvira is with her now, and she had not opened her eyes when I left. I don't believe that she can face the truth of the matter at all."

"And there you have the heart of it," Brookston said,

musing over her words and gently patting her hand. "We don't know what that is."

"Precisely!" she agreed, her mind running along the same track as his. "And the truth of the matter is exactly what we must discover! That is why I have come to ask for your help, Lord Brookston!"

Brookston looked startled. "My help?" he asked.

She nodded firmly. "I cannot do this alone. I am a nobody in London, and my sister does not rank much above me, despite the fact she is Lady Palmering. I need the help of someone who is a part of the *ton.*"

Before he could stop himself, Brookston said, "What about Lord Palmering?"

He regretted his words immediately, for Rose stared at him in disbelief and promptly withdrew her hand from his.

"What about him?" she asked coldly. "Are you suggesting that I would be wiser to turn to him for help rather than to you?" Here she rose abruptly. "You must forgive me for intruding upon you, Lord Brookston. I shall not take any more of your time."

Guilt washed over him as he thought of his own suspicions about Palmering. Naturally a perceptive young woman like Miss Battinger would not place her trust in such a man. He also rose hastily and reclaimed her hand.

"Forgive my thoughtless comment, ma'am," he said. "Rest assured that I shall do everything within my power to help Lady Palmering."

Her look was reward enough. Indeed, he almost forgot what he had just promised and what they were discussing as he looked into her sea-green eyes. It had never occurred to him before that eyes could be quite so dangerous. He had the distinct feeling that he was drowning, but he had no wish to save himself.

Not even her next words shook him, although just moments ago they would have caused him to freeze in his tracks.

"Then, the first thing that I should like you to do, dear

sir, is to acquire a stranger's voucher for me so that I may attend Almack's tomorrow evening," she told him briskly. "I wish to see where this happened, and I should very much like to talk with any of the people who witnessed Lord Palmering's death."

If Brookston felt that he had suddenly taken an icy plunge into matters far over his head, those waters grew warm when he looked into her eyes. Nodding, he assured her that he would do so, and dismissed the thought of Lady Jersey's expression when he explained to her that he wished a voucher for his guest and explained to her the reasons for it. Upon brief reflection, he decided that approaching Lady Cowper would be wiser, and he hoped that she would be readily agreeable to his request.

"I shall expect you tomorrow morning, then, Lord Brookston," Rose announced briskly, again withdrawing her hand. "I do hope that you forgive my forwardness in coming to you with this matter. I know that this is not considered proper behavior for a young woman."

Although in truth he had been taken aback by her unexpected appearance, he shook his head firmly. "Your concern for your sister does you honor, ma'am," he said staunchly. "And I shall be honored to be of service to you."

This time it was Rose who took his hand. "Thank you, sir," she said warmly. "I do not know why it is so, but I am certain that I may trust you. I shall look forward to seeing you tomorrow morning."

Her fingers lingered a moment in his, and even as she turned toward the door, he could still feel their warmth.

"Please allow me to see you home, Miss Battinger," he said, suddenly remembering that she had come alone.

She smiled and shook her head, looking back at him for a moment. "There is no need, Lord Brookston. My carriage is waiting for me."

Brookston did not go early to bed that night. Instead, he sat long before his fire, thinking carefully through the events of the last ball at Almack's, all of his thoughts punctuated by the memory of laughing green eyes and the warmth of a small white hand.

He astonished his valet by arising before dawn and announcing that he was in need of a ride through the Park to clear his head. In all his years of service to Brookston, his valet had never known his master to express such a need. He later confided to the butler that it had given him a severe turn.

"I knew immediately that something was different about him," said the valet. "And just what could it be, I asked myself, to cause such a change. Then I thought of the young lady who had come to call and I had it—the master had fallen top over tail in love!"

Brookston laid his plan of action during his ride that morning. He did not wish for Miss Battinger to be refused admittance to Almack's, so he determined to call upon Lady Cowper before he did anything else. If anyone could—and would—help him, it would be the kind Lady Cowper. If he could win her over, then Lady Jersey could not refuse Miss Battinger entrance. Assuredly, Lady Jersey wanted to forget all mention of a murder, and she would welcome nothing—and no one—that endangered Almack's.

Accordingly, he startled Lady Cowper and her household by putting in an appearance far before the time for conventional calls. The lady was still in her bed, sipping her chocolate and reading her invitations, when his presence was announced.

"Brookston?" she demanded of her butler, who had brought her the news. "At this hour?"

The butler nodded. He, too, was shocked, but it was not suitable for him to speak of it, of course. "He said it was urgent, my lady."

"How very odd!" exclaimed Lady Cowper. Here, too, the butler agreed, but again he maintained his silence while his mistress considered the matter.

"This is most unlike Brookston," she said, appearing to have reached a decision. "I shall receive him here, Davis.

Show him up directly." Turning to her astonished maid, she called, "Constance! Bring me the blue dressing gown and a glass so that I may see if I am quite decent."

By the time Brookston reached her boudoir, Lady Cowper was seated by the fire, looking calm and well-groomed. She extended a hand to him, and he bent over it gratefully.

"You are all kindness to see me so early, ma'am," he told her. "And that is why I have come to you—because of your kindness and your quick understanding."

"I am filled with misgivings in the face of such flattery, Brookston," she told him gravely, but her expression was amused. He had always been a favorite of hers, or she would never have allowed him this private audience. "What is it that you want of me?"

Appreciating her directness, Brookston told her, explaining the situation as clearly as he could, and emphasizing Rose's concern for her sister.

Lady Cowper nodded when he had finished. "I have great sympathy for Lady Palmering," she assured him, "and I understand her sister's concern. However, Brookston," she added, looking at him speculatively, "there are two things you have not told me. One is why Miss Battinger did not turn to Lady Palmering's stepson for help."

Brookston met her gaze squarely. "I feel that I can speak to you in confidence, ma'am," he said, and she nodded. "Although she did not say so, I am certain that Miss Battinger does not feel that she can trust the new Lord Palmering to have her sister's best interests at heart."

Lady Cowper shook her head slowly. "I hate to speak ill of others," she said, "but I believe that she may well have a point. But she does feel that she can trust you?"

Brookston nodded.

"Then, she must be a quite sensible girl," she responded. "There is one other matter I would like to ask you about. Why did you come to me rather than to Lady Jersey, who is your good friend?"

"Because I know that Lady Jersey is very concerned

about the fate of Almack's. She fears that having had a
murder there will decrease its popularity, and so she does
not wish to do anything that would call attention to that
murder."

"Her fear is justified," observed Lady Cowper.

"Yes, it is," he returned, "but matters might go just the
opposite way."

"What do you mean?" she asked curiously.

"Merely that having had a murder there—and talking
about it—might make the club more fashionable rather
than less. People might flock there just to see what happens next."

"You could be correct, Brookston," she admitted.
"Given the fickleness of the *ton*, it is a possibility."

And so it was that Brookston emerged in triumph from
Lady Cowper's, guaranteed a stranger's voucher and her
support when he presented Miss Battinger at Almack's that
evening. He proceeded briskly to Lady Palmering's, confident that he had put the wheels of their plan in motion.

Although he had already paid one morning call, he was
still extraordinarily early in calling at Lady Palmering's.
Fortunately, Rose had also risen early and had anticipated
his arrival with instructions to the butler that she would be
waiting in the drawing room when Lord Brookston arrived. Rags, who was also an early riser, had joined her.

When he told her what he had accomplished thus far,
Rose applauded his efforts warmly, and for a moment he
felt that all was going well. Then she explained her plans
for the evening.

"Before we attend the ball this evening, Lord Brookston, I think it is very important to speak with the people
that were close to Lord Palmering at the time of his death
and ask them just what they saw."

Brookston's warm glow began to fade perceptibly. "Do
you mean that you actually wish to speak with each of
them?" he asked.

Rose nodded, a little impatiently. "Yes, naturally I need

to speak with them in order to learn just what they observed last week. I was hoping that you could give me your account of his death, and also identify the people that you know were close to him at the time."

Brookston swallowed hard and prepared to give her his account, while she, in a very official manner, picked up the paper and pen she had arranged on the table next to her. He had a sinking feeling that he no longer had a clear picture of their plan of action.

"Miss Battinger, what do you envision happening after you record all the accounts of his death?" he inquired.

"Why, I shall look at them as the pieces of a puzzle, Lord Brookston," she remarked, apparently surprised that he would have to ask. "And tonight we shall ask those who were there to reenact his death scene."

Once again Brookston saw Lady Jersey's reproachful face hovering before him, but again he dismissed it, trying not to think just what sort of stir this charade would cause at Almack's, that monument to propriety.

"Lady Palmering will not be attending, of course," he said. "Since she is so newly in mourning, it would scarcely be proper for her to go out."

"In this case, I feel that truth should take precedence over respectability and fashion, Lord Brookston. Sensible people will understand why she is there. And, although my aunt is a very sensitive person and is dressed in mourning for the late Lord Palmering, you will notice that I am not."

"Yes, I did notice that," he replied faintly, bracing himself for whatever was coming next.

"Lord Palmering was not a blood relation, nor did I actually know the man—and what I did know of him, I heartily disliked," she said frankly. "Therefore, it would be nonsensical for me to mourn for him."

"I see," said Brookston, more faintly still.

"You see, but you disapprove?" she commented, looking at him questioningly. It was clear that it did not matter a fig whether he approved or not. She appeared to be disappointed in him, and even the dog was looking at him questioningly.

"Of course not!" he asserted manfully. After all, what did such proprieties really matter when weighed against discovering the truth about a man's death and removing suspicion from his unfortunate widow? He would deal with Lady Jersey later.

Together they settled down to the serious business at hand. Brookston offered as clear and detailed a picture of the events surrounding Palmering's death as he was able to muster while Rose took careful notes, pausing to blot her work carefully. When he had finished, they sat in silence for a while as she reread what she had written.

"No one appears to have liked him," she commented, rubbing her writing fingers thoughtfully. "Was he really as arrogant a care-for-nobody as he appears to have been?"

Brookston shrugged. "My view of him has been colored by my own experience with him. You might wish to ask someone who has a clearer, more objective view."

"May I ask you why you disliked him so?" she asked slowly, watching his face.

"Because of my young cousin Arabella Clayton," he responded. "She is little more than a babe in the woods, but last year Palmering took advantage of the fact that he was part of a large house party at my uncle's to single her out and make advances to her when she was alone in a walled garden. He had apparently followed her there and realized how isolated they would be."

"And what happened?" she asked, still watching him.

"He surprised her in a corner of the garden and pressed his hand over her mouth. He had loosened his cravat and I think he believed he would gag her, but Arabella bit his hand and screamed. A gardener heard her and rushed in. He was a little man, but he and Arabella appeared to have been a match for Palmering. He left the garden immediately, and the gardener put his coat over Arabella, for her gown had been virtually ripped from her, and helped her to the house."

He stopped and looked at Rose. "My uncle is not a well man, and Arabella has no brothers. I was present at that party, and I challenged Palmering to a duel. I would have killed him without a thought. However, he left the house secretly that night and refused ever to face me. I could have gladly flogged him myself! Arabella should have had her first Season this year, but she is still fearful of being in a large party again. It will take a little more time, the doctors say, before she is herself again. So you see, Miss Battinger, I am not an unbiased source of information."

She nodded gravely. "But your grievance is an understandable one—and one that certainly fits with the picture I have of Palmering as a cruel coward."

"There we are in full agreement, ma'am," he assured her, bowing his head. "And there are many who would side with us."

"Which means, I fear, that there are many people who had very strong reasons for murdering Lord Palmering. I myself would have to be listed among them."

He looked at her in surprise, and she nodded. "Yes, indeed, for I had good reason to believe that he was beating my sister. At the very least, he was treating her with a cruel disregard for her happiness and well-being." She shrugged. "So you see, I, too, could have thought—and in fact, did think—of murdering the man. My difficulty was that there were no gypsies readily available to place a curse upon him."

Brookston smiled grimly. "I, on the other hand, could have made good use of my nearness to Palmering and eliminated him so that Arabella would not have to face him when she finally comes to Town."

Rose shook her head. "That is not what I was trying to point out, sir."

"But it is true, nonetheless." He paused a moment, then added, "Unfortunately, what you said about your reason for wishing to rid the world of Lord Palmering could also be read as a reason for your sister to feel the same way."

"Surely you don't believe that!" exclaimed Rose, her voice rising.

"You know that I do not, Miss Battinger," he returned, "but what I am saying is that someone else who does not know your sister and her situation might misread the situation and use your comment as evidence against her."

"Then, I shall not repeat it to anyone!" exclaimed Rose. "If I hear about this again, sir, I will know that the information came from you, so I trust you will be discreet."

"You know that I wish your sister no ill!" he protested.

"Yes, I do know that," Rose sighed, as the quick anger seeped away. "I am sorry. It simply terrifies me that I might do something that would cause greater difficulty for her than she is already facing, and I have no wish to do so. I just want to bring her home again safely."

Without a thought, Brookston took Rose in his arms and placed her head against his shoulder, stroking her dark hair soothingly and wiping away a tear that trickled down her smooth cheek. He had never before felt such a strong urge to protect another human being, and he was astonished by the strength of the emotion that washed over him. He kissed her forehead gently, then her eyelids, and finally her lips, blotting out the world for at least one blissful minute.

"What a touching scene!" exclaimed Lord Palmering, pausing in the doorway and looking at them as though to appreciate a painting. "I am undecided, Brookston, as to whether I should wish you happy or call you out for dishonoring a young woman who is both my relative and a guest in my home."

Brookston colored angrily, but Rose spoke before he could regain his composure. "I fear I am the one at fault. I had turned into a watering pot, and Lord Brookston was merely comforting me."

"Comforting you?" repeated Palmering, regarding them with his eyebrows arched. "I have never heard it called just that before."

Before Brookston could respond in kind, Rose once

again took charge, ignoring his comment and continuing her own investigation into the murder. She sat down with her pen and paper at hand and said crisply, "Now, Lord Palmering, since you told me of the investigation into your father's death, I have decided that I would also look into the matter."

Palmering looked at her blankly. "You?" he asked.

"Yes. Since my sister is so nearly connected to all of this, it seemed to me that I would examine the situation more closely so that I am certain Bow Street has all the facts at their disposal."

Palmering sat down rather suddenly. "Indeed?" he said. "Just who are you planning to interview?"

"Those that were close to your father at last week's ball, as well as any, like yourself, who have a very near interest in his death."

Palmering's pale cheeks flamed, and he looked at her with distaste. This, thought Brookston with some satisfaction, was the man that he knew, and he waited for Palmering to reveal himself further.

"Just what do you mean by that, Miss Battinger?" he asked, his tone ominous.

Rose, although she recognized the tone, blithely chose to disregard it, and spread her papers on the table and prepared the nib of her pen. Rags, however, also recognized the tone and chose to comment upon it. He glared at Palmering and began a low, throaty growl. Palmering stepped hastily to one side to remove his boots from harm's way.

"Merely, Lord Palmering, that it would be helpful to me to know your account of what happened at home that night, before your father and my sister left to attend Almack's."

To Brookston's surprise, Palmering managed to swallow his indignation and replied in an even, thoughtful tone.

"Well, the very fact that they were attending Almack's was unusual," he said slowly. "My father went there only rarely during the Season, and even then he normally went alone."

Rose nodded grimly as she recorded his comment. "I am aware that he rarely took my sister with him anywhere," she said, trying to keep from sounding as bitter as she felt. "Do you have any idea just why he chose to take Lady Palmering on that particular evening? Or is there anything unusual that happened during that day?"

Palmering, having thought about it for a moment, shook his head. "The only thing that I can think of is that he had two callers that afternoon."

"Who were they?" she inquired, and Brookston watched, amazed by Palmering's willingness to answer her questions.

"One was Jack Sterling," he replied. "He looked angry as he left, but that was not particularly surprising, since everyone knows that his young wife had been the subject of my father's attentions for several weeks."

Here he glanced at Rose apologetically. "I'm sorry to point that out, but you did ask me for what I knew."

Rose nodded, unperturbed. "And I appreciate your candor, Lord Palmering. What of the other man?"

Palmering shook his head. "I did not recognize him, but he appeared to be a gentleman, both in manner and dress."

"And did he also look angry?"

He nodded. "That was often the way after talking with my father. He had that effect upon almost everyone."

"Did he have that effect upon you, sir?" she asked.

"Indeed, he did, Miss Battinger—almost every day of my life."

She looked at him for a moment, and then she said slowly, "We are attending Almack's tonight, Lord Palmering, because I wish to reenact the scene just as it was at the time of your father's death. Even though you were not there on that evening, I thought perhaps you might also wish to attend."

Palmering stared at her in astonishment, and then directed his gaze toward Brookston, who nodded.

"That is what we plan to do, Palmering. Lady Cowper will provide a stranger's voucher for Miss Battinger so that she may attend, and as many of the others as we can manage will also be there."

"And what do you hope to accomplish by this, Miss Battinger?" he asked.

"To prove my sister's innocence," she responded frankly. "At the very least, I will have a clearer picture of what happened that evening so that I may attempt to solve the problem."

"So that *we* may attempt to solve the problem," Brookston reminded her, and she smiled up at him.

"I see," said Palmering, staring at the two of them. "I do see."

After a few moments of silence, he rose and bowed to Rose. "If you will excuse me, ma'am, I have one or two matters to attend to, but rest assured that I shall avail myself of your invitation. I will be at Almack's tonight."

The others involved appeared to be in complete agreement with him. Together, Rose and Brookston called upon Alistair Fitzgerald, the Chestertons, Lady Jersey, and three others who had been close enough to see and hear what had transpired. When they spoke with Lady Jersey, who was fully as horrified as Brookston had expected her to be, Rose also asked that the servants that were present at last week's ball be in the same positions that they had occupied at that time.

Brookston made it his business to call upon Jack Sterling privately since his business with Palmering had been of such a highly personal nature. He was deeply grateful that he had not taken Rose, for Sterling told him that when he had called upon Palmering the afternoon before his death, Palmering had only laughed over his outrage and his demands that he stay away from Sterling's wife.

"To be plain, sir," Sterling said to Brookston, "he told me to come to Almack's that night and have a look at Lady Palmering. He said that her favors could be had for the right price and suggested that she might take my mind off of my problems with my own wife."

Brookston stared at Sterling in disbelief. "Do you mean to say that he took her there to display her?"

Sterling nodded. "Palmering said she would go to the highest bidder. He told me that I would not be the only one there."

"But you weren't there, were you?" asked Brookston, for he was quite certain that Sterling had not put in an appearance.

"Naturally not! I went to Palmering to protest his behavior, not to lower myself to his level. I could only pity his poor wife. I'm certain she had no idea what Palmering was playing at."

Brookston knew that he would have to tell Rose the truth about Palmering's intention of selling Lily's favors to the highest bidder, for she would not rest until she knew just why he had decided to take his wife with him that night. Actually telling her, however, was fully as difficult as he had feared it would be.

When the worst of her anger had passed, he once again took her in his arms to comfort her, saying, "At least he died before he could further mistreat Lady Palmering."

Rose's hands were clenched into small fists. "Yes, I am grateful for that," she returned, "but he is still making her life miserable, even from the grave. She cannot even be left in peace because of the nature of his death. We cannot let him have the last word."

"We won't," he assured her. "I have known you only a few days, Miss Battinger, but I would place my money on your being able to do whatever you set out to accomplish." He embraced her again, brushing her dark curls back from her face.

"And do think about the things that you have already accomplished," he pointed out, hoping to keep her focused on more positive points. "Everyone will be there tonight, and you have already interviewed everyone, although we have ruled out a few possibilities, like Jack Sterling. Since he did not attend, he could not be the guilty party."

"However," commented Rose thoughtfully, "you told me that Lord Palmering poured himself a drink from his own flask, so there is always the possibility that something was placed in that."

"Yes, that had occurred to me earlier," he agreed, "although I confess that I had forgotten about that aspect of it." He frowned. "If we take that into account, his son also becomes a possibility."

Rose nodded, her face pale. "And we know that Lily would also have had that opportunity, although we know that she would not have taken it."

"Naturally she would not have," Brookston assured her, patting her hand. "All we can do now is to have your reenactment tonight and to keep a sharp lookout for any new indications about the identity of the guilty party, for we know it is not your sister."

Rose looked up into his eyes and smiled, causing his heart to leap into his throat. "Thank you, Lord Brookston," she said softly. "I know that this has been a great imposition upon you, but you have been very gracious to us—not at all selfish as I had expected a peer of the realm to be. I fear you have destroyed my illusions."

"Miss Dayton, you take my breath away," he replied, leaning closer.

"Do you think, sir, that you could come to like the country?" she asked, her tone growing deliberately lighter as she glanced down at Rags, who had arranged himself neatly across Brookston's boots. He had noticed that she seldom remained either gloomy or overly serious, which was, he felt, a part of her charm.

"Only certain parts of it," responded Brookston, sliding away from the terrier. "Perhaps the woods—and the vegetable gardens. There will be no dogs, however—definitely, no dogs."

Rags rolled over and regarded him seriously. "Yes, I did say it," Brookston assured him. "And I meant every syllable of it."

* * *

When Brookston came to call for the sisters and their aunt that evening, he was once again overcome by Rose, who, true to her declaration that she would wear no black for Palmering, was dressed in a gown of sea-foam green that matched her eyes precisely. He knew that Lady Palmering, even though she was dressed plainly in black, was by far the more beautiful woman, but it was Miss Battinger—or Miss Dayton—that made his pulse race, that made him laugh, that made him feel at home.

Rose and her aunt, both new to Almack's, scrutinized it closely upon their arrival.

"The lustres in the chandeliers are really quite lovely," observed Elvira, enraptured by their glow, which was reflected in countless large mirrors. "They make everything and everyone look quite festive."

"If that is their duty, perhaps a few more lustres should be added," said Rose, glancing about her. "This is quite a bare room, despite the gilt columns and the chandeliers, and many of us need a little more of the glow offered by their light."

"Hush, Rose!" whispered her scandalized aunt. "You cannot come in as a guest and then criticize the place and the people!"

Rose looked at her aunt in amused surprise. "You know very well that I can do that, Aunt. I just did so."

Seeing that everything was normal in the small family flock he was shepherding, Brookston took time to look around the room. He saw in a glance that there were more people here tonight than usual.

Almost immediately he felt someone grip his arm, and Sally Jersey whispered into his ear, "Have you ever seen anything like it, Brookston? They all want to know what is going to happen tonight and who Palmering's murderer is! Why, we may exceed our largest crowd!"

"You see, ma'am, you were worried for nothing," he replied.

"We shall see how this goes," Lady Jersey returned. "Let us know when you are ready and I will have everything arranged."

He nodded, and returned to his party. Lily looked almost ill from the strain of having to come back to this place, and Elvira and Rose were hovering about her protectively. Brookston went to fetch her something to drink and encountered Lord Palmering on the way.

"When will the little charade begin?" he asked.

"Very soon," replied Brookston briefly. "Lady Palmering needs a a few minutes to adjust to being here again."

He noticed that Palmering did not appear particularly sympathetic, and he was regarding Brookston with a quizzical expression. "You know, Brookston, I had no notion that you were quite a clever fellow. I never would have guessed it."

"What are you talking about?" inquired Brookston, puzzled.

"Why, marrying an heiress, of course," Palmering replied. "That's what you're after, isn't it?"

He continued without waiting for Brookston to reply. "I had the notion to do the same thing myself," he confided. "I had read the letter she sent my father, offering him ten thousand pounds to allow Lady Palmering to come home to live. I thought to myself when I read it that there was no need to let all that money go to waste—but I see that you were quicker than I."

Here he clapped Brookston on the shoulder in a familiar way, preparing to continue through the crowd. "I'm not in a pelter about losing her to you, though. After all, I've still got Lady Palmering's fortune. I'm not a greedy man."

Before he could stop to think, Brookston had twisted Palmering around and struck a sharp right to his chin, sending him tumbling to the floor like a rag doll and causing a scattering and scuttling among the guests.

"Brookston!" He heard Lady Jersey call his name indignantly, but he ignored her as he walked on to get a drink for Lady Palmering.

By the time he threaded his way back through the crowd, Lady Jersey had disappeared, and Lord Palmering had been borne away to have plaster of paris affixed to his chin and to have a fresh cravat arranged for him.

"Whatever happened?" demanded Rose when he returned.

He looked away and shrugged. "Lord Palmering and I had a brief disagreement."

She smiled. "Yes, we could see that much. I believe that you must have had the last word, however, so you must find that satisfying."

He smiled back at her, his anger subsiding. "Yes," he replied. "Very satisfying."

He looked at Lily, who had regained a little of her color, and then at Elvira. "Do you feel ready to go through with this?" he asked, and Lily nodded.

Brookston sought out Lady Jersey, who buttonholed him with vigor. "Brookston! Whatever were you thinking of to indulge in such vulgar behavior?" she demanded. "This is no gin mill down in Covent Garden!"

"Thank you, Sally, for reminding me of that," he commented calmly. "I shall try to remember that for the rest of the evening—unless Lord Palmering forgets himself again."

"Well, then I suppose we must prepare for the worst," she replied. "It is much more likely that he will be rude than not—but perhaps the reenactment will hold his attention for long enough to prevent another brawl."

In very short order, the scene was much as it had been the week before—with the exception of Rose sitting in Lord Palmering's place and a much larger crowd of onlookers studying every move.

Rose lifted her glass of orgeat to her lips, just as Brookston spoiled the performance by turning back and calling her name. She paused with the cup at her lips, and he hurried back and took it from her, turning to Lord Palmering, who was watching with a freshly patched lip and a cravat without bloodstains. Striding toward him, Brookston handed him the cup.

"Drink this!" he commanded, as Palmering lifted his arm to protect himself from a fresh onslaught.

"Are you mad?" he demanded of Brookston. "I can't drink anything with this lip! And why should I?"

Brookston was clearly about to force him to do so when Rose called out.

"No, not Lord Palmering! Lord Brookston, give the cup to him!"

He looked up to see her pointing at the waiter who had suffered the near collision with Palmering on the night of the murder.

"The waiter?" he asked, staring at her for a moment.

She nodded. "Have him drink it. After all, it is only orgeat."

The waiter backed away as Brookston approached with the cup and turned to run, but several men among the crowd stopped him. Lord Palmering approached them, staring at the waiter.

"I saw you in my home the afternoon before my father died," he said slowly. "Why were you there?"

The man made a brief show of bravado, but at the sight of several of the Bow Street Runners making their way through the crowd—to the horror of Lady Jersey and the delight of the crowd—he gave way.

"My name is Desmond Murray," he said in a low voice.

"Desmond Murray," echoed Lord Palmering, sudden understanding coming to him. "You are the one that will inherit should anything happen to me!"

Murray nodded, then smiled gently. "And it would have, you know. It would all have been quite easy. Your father gone, his widow accused. The widow's sister, who has been doing far too much asking of questions, out of the way. It would have required no skill at all to have sent you on your way as well—and then I would have been Lord Palmering and inherited the widow's very considerable fortune."

The Runners led him away, leaving behind an astonished crowd. There was a murmur of approval among the watchers and a brief scattering of applause, quite as though they were attending the theater.

Lord Palmering turned to Rose and Lord Brookston. "It appears that I owe you my life," he said, disbelief still evident in his expression. "I must thank you."

Brookston bowed, and Rose turned to him. "And I would have drunk that punch, had you not stopped me, sir. Why did you?"

"I confess that I thought Lord Palmering might have done something to tamper with it. When he went back to have his lip and his wardrobe repaired, he was very close to the table where your drink was."

"Well, even though he was not the guilty party, you save me nonetheless, sir—and I am afraid that I must tell you that I am now your responsibility."

"My responsibility?" he inquired, looking down at her.

She nodded emphatically. "It is a custom in the country that if you save the life of a person, you must marry that individual."

"That could be very inconvenient," he observed. "What if one were to save several people?"

"It would not be allowed," she assured him. "In time, Mr. Jamison, you will come to know and appreciate country ways."

He leaned toward her and kissed her, ignoring the comments from the interested onlookers.

"I think that I will, ma'am," he murmured. "I think that I will."

A Rare Blade

Valerie King

One

London, 1815

Lydia Sherborne tried very hard to ignore her aunt, but the task was proving impossible. "Yes, yes, I see Lord Kingslade, and, yes, he does seem to be looking in *our* direction."

"My dear, I do believe he is tumbled in love with you. How else can you account for his staring at you so frequently as he does?"

"Undoubtedly to find fault with me, something I promise you he delights in doing."

"Stuff and nonsense!" she cried in response. "Oh, but he is that handsome. Michaelangelo would have made use of that figure, I have little doubt, in a sculpture or two."

"Aunt!" she cried. "What a scandalous thing to say! I am greatly shocked."

"Well, you must admit he is something of an Adonis, and those shoulders! No military man could be more beautifully athletic in appearance."

Lydia could not help but agree. There were few gentlemen among the *haut ton* who equaled his lordship. The Earl of Kingslade was accounted the finest matrimonial prize of this Season, as he had been for the past twelve Seasons when he first appeared in London so many years ago ready to acquire a little town-bronze. He had been the object of any number of matchmaking mamas but had thus far succeeded in repulsing every battle-ready effort launched to secure him.

"You make far too much of his attentions to me, I am sure."

"I am persuaded I do not."

Kingslade at that moment met her gaze fully and offered his familiar smile, a trifle crooked and knowing as though reminding her that were he to converse with her, he would strive to set up her back if he could. Wretched man!

She offered a faint smile in return, wondering if her aunt's suspicions were in any way correct. When his gaze held, and he narrowed his eyes slightly, a very peculiar sensation came over her, as though she were suddenly standing up in a boat upon a slightly rolling sea. She had trouble balancing her sensibilities and could only wonder as she had time and again how it was that the mere exchanging of a smile with Lord Kingslade would cause her to feel so dizzy.

"See how he smiles even now?" Mrs. Morestead whispered, leaning close. "My dear niece, are you very certain he is not in love with you?"

"How could he be when we brangle so?"

"I suppose you are right, but what a great thing it would be were you to become the next Countess Kingslade."

"But we do not suit!" Lydia protested.

"I vow your generation is a great deal too fastidious. I should have poked my eye out had I the chance to get a handle to my name! Ah, here is Mr. Ellis. How do you go on, Mr. Ellis? Are you enjoying the assemblies this evening?"

"Prodigiously," he answered in his warm manner. "And I shall do so even more if your niece will permit me to lead her down the next set."

"I should be delighted, as well you know," Lydia returned in a like manner.

Mr. Ellis was an excellent sort of man, gentlemanly, kind and of an open temper, a quality she valued above all others. He was in possession of a fine property in Wiltshire, was invested in "the funds," and had numerous business interests in Europe, all of which most certainly made him an excellent match for any hopeful young lady. She had oftened wondered just why he was not yet married, for she had little doubt he would make an agreeable husband. He was tall, though perhaps not so powerfully built as Lord Kingslade. His hair was a light brown and his eyes an unusual pale blue.

As he led her out, he stated, "You are doing quite well this evening, Miss Sherborne. I have seen you yawn but twice."

"Oh, dear," she returned, laughing. "I am become quite hopeless."

"I am convinced you are not suited to our London festivities."

"As am I," Lydia concurred. "I should have enjoyed a profession were it allowed to young ladies of quality."

"You could always write novels," he whispered.

At that she trilled her laughter and took up her place opposite him. When the dance commenced and the steps brought them together, she said, "Were I to do so, my heroine would not waste a single moment painting in watercolors and learning to dance."

The steps separated them. Upon coming together, his eyes were bright with laughter. "What would constitute their studies, I wonder?"

"Swordplay," she responded, once more laughing heartily, which he did as well.

The remainder of the set was conducted in this manner, exchanging any number of ridiculous ideas about just what adventures her heroines would enjoy, from traveling to all the Americas, to China, the Spice Islands, India, and of course a lengthy stay in the Levant. He teased her endlessly, and she rather thought, by the time the music drew to a close, that she had not been so well entertained in a fortnight.

"You would do better, I think, to have been married by now," he said, leading her off the floor. "I believe your time would have been engaged quite delightfully in raising a hopeful brood of children and tending to the demands of a husband."

She could not help it. She yawned quite deeply, which set Mr. Ellis to laughing rather loudly yet again. Such an expression of merriment on his part could not help but draw notice. Even Kingslade turned to look in her direction again. She met his gaze and saw the curious expression on his face. She curtseyed faintly and flashed him a brilliant if facetious smile. He rolled his eyes and looked away.

"Are you still at war with him?" Mr. Ellis queried.

"Yes, most happily. It is one of the great pleasures of my existence. At least in all our brangling I find I am rarely bored."

"As you are in my company?"

"No, no you much mistake the matter, Mr. Ellis, as well you know. I take great enjoyment in your society. Were it not for you and a few others, I should perish from *ennui.* Which puts me in mind of something I have been attempting to forget—you are leaving me for a time, and that quite soon. Do I have the right of it?"

Mr. Ellis took an active involvement in his investments abroad and traveled frequently to tend to them, unlike most gentlemen with whom she was acquainted. He had done so during much of the troublesome war with France so that his fortunes had increased while many others had diminished.

He smiled. "I expect to have word from my partner in Belgium any day now, though I do not anticipate departing England sooner than a fortnight. Therefore you will have my unflagging support until that time."

"You are very kind," she murmured, but her thoughts had drifted elsewhere. "How very much I envy all these journeys you make. Do you never grow weary of them?"

"A little, perhaps, and there are always many things for me to miss in London. Your company for one."

"Why, how very gallant, and yet I believe I am hearing a great deal of humbug. Admit it is so, Mr. Ellis, that you go to Europe as much for the adventure as anything else."

"I believe you have come to know me far better than is at all good for me." He glanced about the assemblies, and to her surprise she watched his expression grow rather dark. "I am as fatigued with these superficialities as you are. My abilities are wasted here."

"I have never heard you speak thusly. You do not find the management of your numerous investments sufficient to satisfy you?"

He glanced at her, his eyes unusually sharp. "They are adequate in their way. I suppose I always hoped for a place in grander schemes."

"I understand quite *grand* schemes occur frequently in India."

A smile touched his lips. "So it is said."

He seemed secretive suddenly, and she found herself curious. He gave himself a shake, however, and said, "I vow the conversation has become far more serious than I had wished for you. Do you care for a little lemonade or one of those stale cakes I think quite abominable?"

She chuckled. How nice it was to have such good friends. "Well, perhaps a glass of lemonade, but the cake? Never!"

With that, he offered her his arm and guided her toward the refreshments.

"So you are to desert me."

"I fear it is true, and had Boney not escaped from Elba, I should be in Paris by now!"

Lord Kingslade glanced at Miss Sherborne yet again. Ellis was escorting her in the opposite direction, and it had

not been lost to him how frequently she had made him
laugh. Envy pierced him, for there was nothing he liked
better than to have Miss Sherborne teasing his sense of the
absurd. Indeed, he felt the strongest impulse to cross the
room and beg her to go down a second set with him. However, he had promised himself that tonight he would resist
any such impulse since he was always careful to keep his
attentions to any young lady wholly undistinguished. He
knew all too well how quickly a woman's mind leapt to
love and matrimony, neither of which applied in the least
to Miss Sherborne.

No, he was not in love with her, and he had no desire to
wed her. In truth, he did not know quite what it was that
drew him to her, particularly since they brangled so frequently as they did, and yet in one respect his interest was
not in the least incomprehensible since she was quite the
most beautiful woman he had ever before seen. Her complexion was as pure as ivory, her eyes were a large,
cornflower blue and seemed to sparkle when she smiled,
and her hair was the color of honey, which she wore spun
into myriad curls, giving her a deceptively fragile appearance. He chuckled. Her curls and the creamy delicacy of
her beauty had fooled many a heedless fellow in the past.
There was nothing inherently fragile about Miss Sherborne.

"Robert," Mary whispered, nudging him. "You are staring at Miss Sherborne . . . again. Are you certain you have
not tumbled in love with her?"

Mary was quite young, having just arrived at the ad-
vanced age of one and twenty. She was eleven years his
junior and was not entirely discreet. He would have re-
proved her in this moment, but there was such an
expression of sweetness and challenge in her eyes that he
found he could do little more than scowl and shake his
head. Since she immediately wrapped her arm about his
and gave it a squeeze, he knew she was not in the least
overawed by her eldest brother.

"I look at her, Mary, because she is so beautiful. Even you must admit there is not a lady present to equal her."

Mary sighed. "I only wish I had half her beauty, and she is so amusing! Have you never conversed with her and found yourself caught over the merest trifle?"

Indeed, Kingslade had, but he did not feel he should say as much. All of his sisters, Mary included, were already far too determined to believe him in love with her. Instead, he sipped his champagne and steadfastly avoided looking at Miss Sherborne again.

His thoughts were not so easily governed, particularly when Mary began prattling about a recent ball she had attended at the Vauxhall Pleasure Gardens. He had met Miss Sherborne for the first time at a masquerade at Vauxhall nearly two years past. She had been admiring a grotto along with her friend, Miss Sparshott. Mr. Weyhill, who was his own particular friend and with whom he had attended the masquerade, had offered to make the introductions. Weyhill's interest in Miss Sparshott had been a large portion of his desire to introduce him to Miss Sherborne, particularly since once the deed had been done, he quickly took Miss Sparshott away, leading her in the direction of the Thames where the fireworks would soon be displayed.

He had, therefore, found himself quite alone with the lovely beauty who had so recently entered some of the First Circles through her aunt's efforts. She had been gowned in a ravishing red velvet Elizabethan costume and appeared utterly magnificent. He, himself, wore the costume of a famous explorer of the era. The odd serendipitous occurrence of their sporting fashions that undoubtedly held a historic connection was not lost to him and was perhaps the reason he had behaved so scandalously toward her in that moment.

"Your Majesty, I presume?" He had bowed in some irony to her. He had seen the amused twinkle in her eye, and his attention had been caught.

"Are you *exploring* this evening, my lord?" There had been at least one man of the sail who had captured Elizabeth Regina's fancy. "Or are you perchance a poet?"

"Both, if it pleases you," he had responded. He doubted he would ever forget the rather piercing sensation that twisted through him in that moment, of a profound desire to take the lady before him quite rakishly in his arms. Oddly, he had not hesitated, but acted upon this impulse. He had taken a single long step toward her, gathered her up quite forcefully in his arms, and kissed her.

He had expected her to struggle, but instead, she had responded first as one stunned, then her entire body had become limp and she had leaned into him. She had kissed him in return in a manner that might have led him to believe she had been kissed before, but instinctively he knew she had not. He had plied his lips over hers, and every touch was met with a responding shift of her mouth or sliding of her hand into his hair or the tenderest little moan issuing from her throat. He had been ignited as never before, feeling with every rocket now bursting in the sky into a shower of white sparkling light that he, too, was being propelled high into the air.

The quite wicked encounter had not ended until the fireworks had ceased. Then she had drawn back, exclaimed her horror, and struck him with her open hand hard across his cheek, clearly frightened at what had happened. Thus had his entire acquaintance with her been defined.

Now, with the smoky smell of the fireworks remembered as though it were yesterday, he turned once more to look at her and to observe her in her conversation with Mr. Ellis. His sister, Mary, nudged him again. "Caught again, Robert?" Before he could protest, she added, "Mr. Bentham is waving to you. Do you not see him?"

He searched the room and found his good friend on the other side of the chamber sitting in a chair. His age had caught up with him of late, and Kingslade realized Bentham rarely stood in a drawing room or ballroom, but rather sought out the nearest chair and remained there most of the evening. Such was the case tonight. He waved and smiled in return. Bentham was undoubtedly the finest man of his acquaintance and a great patriot.

Later that evening, Lydia had just gone down a second set with Mr. Ellis and was being escorted from the floor by him, when he leaned close. "Here is Kingslade. I told you he would ask you next. I do believe he is grown jealous of my attentions to you."

"How nonsensical you can be, Mr. Ellis," she returned with a disbelieving laugh. Although, when Kingslade immediately approached her and asked her for the waltz, she wondered if there might be some truth to it. He rarely asked a lady for a second set, unwilling to set the Tabbies to gossiping about his possible intentions. That he so frequently asked her to do so was the greatest wonder. She could only suppose he felt comfortable in doing so because there was little of the romantic in their prickly relationship.

As he led her onto the floor, she glanced up at him, struck as always by how very handsome he was. He was quite tall which accented to a nicety her own height, for she had been described by some as rather queenly in stature. His hair was thick and dark, a very rich brown which he wore cropped *a la Brutus* and which she believed suited his rather strong temper. His eyes were also quite dark, a coffee brown which could appear quite fierce when he was angered, which happened to be quite often in her company. His features appeared sculpted, which she rather thought was due to the fact that he was an athletic man, giving the angles of his face a lean sharpness not usual in other men.

When he took her into his arms in preparation for the dance often referred to as *an excuse for hugging*, she wondered why it was whenever she danced the waltz with him that she simply could not feel her feet. She could not deny that she felt a very strong attraction to him, but then, what lady did not when he was so very handsome. However, from the first she had detected a reserve in him which she did not in the least like. In the past two years, though she had conversed with him numerous times, she knew very little about him. He was adept at evading her questions, and she rarely felt anything but disgust at what she felt was a haughty secretiveness.

Regardless, she spent the next several minutes delighting in his superior ability on the dance floor. Around and around he whirled her, up and back, up and back. She gave herself to the pleasure of the dizzying sensation, smiling nearly the whole while and only occasionally engaging him in conversation.

"You do enjoy the waltz," he stated, once the dance was concluded.

She chuckled. "Is it that obvious?" She knew it was.

"The entire *ton* remarks on it after every assembly or ball. I suppose that is why, though we detest one another, I ask you so often for a second dance. You are lovely when you smile."

She gave him an arch look. "Trying to turn me up sweet?" she inquired. "Only to what purpose, I cannot imagine, unless, of course, it is merely a ruse since you have not insulted me yet this evening, a circumstance I find quite suspect."

He merely laughed at her. "Do you know how absurd you can be?"

"Yes. Now, offer me some lemonade. I am grown thirsty again after so much dancing."

He did as he was bid and extended his arm to her. She wrapped hers readily about his own.

As he weaved a path for her among the many guests, she looked up at him, curious as always about who he really was.

"So why do you attend the assemblies?" she asked. His shirt points were crisp and white against the strong line of his jaw.

He shrugged faintly. "Habit, perhaps, and I do enjoy some of the society present." He cast his gaze over the assembled dancers. She realized there was something shrewd in the manner in which he watched everyone, as though always looking for something to criticize.

"How magnanimous of you," she responded facetiously.

He met her gaze with a lifted brow. "What have I said to send you in the boughs, and that so quickly?"

Lydia met his gaze boldly. "You have given me no answer except the most prosaic of responses and at the same time appear to be above your company! I must say, Kingslade, I am out of patience with you!"

He appeared bemused. "I was being polite."

"I had much rather you be excessively rude but reveal something, *anything,* of yourself of some degree of merit. You are always horridly reserved with me, and for some reason, in this moment, I wish that I might plant you a facer!"

A familiar smile, quite crooked in nature, played at the edges of his mouth. "I can well believe it since both your cheeks have turned bright pink."

She stopped in her tracks and withdrew her arm from his. Turning in to him, she said, "Even now, the only response you will give me is a comment on my complexion."

His lips twitched. "Miss Sherborne, I beg you will lower your voice, or someone will think you have tumbled in love with me!"

She gasped. "Oh," she growled. "If I were a man, I should call you out for that."

"Hardly a dueling offense," he returned. He leaned close. "Although, if I had kissed you, that might have warranted a gauntlet across my cheek, but then it would not have been the first time."

"I knew how it would be!" she countered strongly. "You

must speak of that . . . that wretched masquerade at Vaux-hall!"

"Why wouldn't I speak of it. *Observing the grotto* that evening is one of my favorite memories."

She ground her teeth. She felt her temper rising in quick stages and only by a powerful effort restrained herself from coming the crab with him. He could provoke her so easily, more than any other gentleman of her acquaintance.

"Gently," he murmured, leaning close to her. "I do apologize, for I can see that you are ready to eat me. Only, there is something I have wondered for a very long time—is that why you always brangle with me? Have you never forgiven me for having kissed you that night?"

Lydia looked into eyes that had grown quite sincere. She was surprised, but then, she knew so little of Kingslade that what else would she be but surprised. "No," she responded, lowering her voice as Lady Cowper passed behind them. "Not the kiss. I have long since forgiven you that."

"What then?"

"That afterward, nearly every day since when we have met, you have never really allowed me to know you. That, I do not hesitate to say, is frustrating beyond permission."

"Is that what you really think, that you do not know me?"

"Of course, and I shall give you an example of precisely what I mean. Do you recall Michaelmas last when I chanced upon you in Bond Street?"

He seemed conscious suddenly. "Yes, I do."

"You were peering into the windows of Berry Brothers, and when I asked you, 'What are you looking at,' which I must say is the most innocuous question possible, you completely avoided giving me an answer. I expected you to say a tin of biscuits or an umbrella, but you replied, 'Nothing in particular.' You were fortunate it had begun in that moment to rain or I would have struck you down with *my* umbrella!"

"And I truly said, 'nothing in particular'?"

"You know you did, so now I can only wonder why you are pretending otherwise. No, no, I beg you will say nothing more on the subject. You are a man who will not be known, and for that I am quite put out, more often than not!"

"I see."

She was just about to offer a small, sarcastic curtsey and move away, when a thought struck her. "Is there no one in whom you confide?" she asked.

"My family," he said. "My brothers and sisters know me well."

"None of your acquaintance?"

He shook his head. "I suppose not."

Lydia glanced around the chamber and said, "I imagine there is one person, however, who knows you better than anyone. I often see you in the company of Mr. Bentham, and you always seem completely engaged by his discourse." Mr. Bentham sat far across the room, slumped over a trifle, his head in one hand, his elbow propped up on the arm of his chair. He wore a kerchief over his broad stomach and appeared to be asleep.

Kingslade smiled. "I believe you are right on both counts. I do not share my thoughts, my opinions, readily, except with Bentham."

"Perhaps you would give him leave to answer any questions I might have about you, then? Indeed, I am so much taken with the idea that I believe I shall go to him now and find out all that he will tell me of you."

"Do you know how beautiful your eyes are when filled with determination as they are now?"

"What do you say?" she retorted, ignoring his attempt to deflect her request. "Shall I apply to him?

Once more his smile was crooked and odiously charming. "Go to him," he said. "Ask what you will. I am not afraid of you."

"Excellent," she responded, turning abruptly on her heel.

Lydia turned about immediately and crossed the chamber to Mr. Bentham. She was smiling, hoping to catch his eye; but he continued to stare at the floor, and now she was certain he was asleep. He had chosen his resting place quite well, the very corner of the chamber. However, the closer she drew to him, she began to feel uneasy. He was so very pale. Perhaps he was not feeling well.

She called his name gently as she drew near. Crumbs from the dry little cakes served at the assemblies were sprinkled about his lapel. "Mr. Bentham?"

His eyes opened, and he blinked several times. He shifted his gaze to her, which appeared rather panic-stricken. "Miss Sherborne. Yes . . . You will do." His breathing was labored.

"You are not well. Let me call someone for you." Even Mr. Ellis was close enough to be of use, but before she could move or turn to summon anyone, Mr. Bentham caught her wrist in a tight grip.

"No, I beg you," he whispered urgently. "You must help me. Take this from me now."

She heard an odd gurgling sound, and with what appeared to be a painfully slow movement, he drew aside the napkin that covered his chest.

Lydia did not know how she remained standing, for planted in his chest was a dagger. "Oh, God," she whispered hoarsely.

He still had hold of her wrist. "You must be brave. Remove it now. Give it immediately to . . . to . . . Kingslade. Tell him . . . *Rufus*. Now, child. So much depends on your being brave and on your discretion. Please. But do it quickly!"

His expression was so desperate that she took hold of the handle and in a brisk movement withdrew the knife. A suppressed groan accompanied this movement.

"Now . . . give it . . . to me," he said. Each word spoken was a struggle. He wrapped the blade slowly in his kerchief and handed it back to her. "Hide this . . . and remember . . .

Rufus." He struggled to draw breath. "Go now, I am done for."

Tears stung her eyes. "Please, do not die," she murmured. The words seemed silly, for life was ebbing from him even as she spoke.

A smile touched his lips. "I . . . have had a . . . good life. Go now. Be . . . a good girl. Do as I have bid. Kingslade . . . will know what to do."

He returned his head to his hand. She did not wait to see the remainder of his life slip from his old, portly body. She turned as one in a nightmare, at the same time tucking the small, thin deadly weapon into the pocket of her gown.

She walked toward Kingslade, who was conversing with his sister Mary, an affectionate expression on his lips. He turned to watch her move toward him, and a frown overtook his features. A moment later, he was hurrying toward her. "What is amiss?" he asked.

"Bentham," she murmured, then promptly swooned into his arms.

Rufus watched the lovely Miss Sherborne drop into a faint. He could not keep from smiling. How easy it would be to retrieve the dagger from her, a great deal easier than from another man unless. . . . He watched Kingslade scoop up the young woman in his arms. He had never cared for Lord Kingslade, not by half, and he had always suspected that he was one of Bentham's pawns. Now he was certain of it. He understood then that Bentham had foiled him in the end, somehow persuading Miss Sherborne to draw the blade from his chest and to secrete it, or so it would seem, for the dagger was not to be seen in her hands. She had more pluck than he had at first imagined.

He had to have the dagger back, however, before he left England. Only, how to get it without arousing her or Kingslade's suspicions.

Two

Lydia emerged from the blackness of having fainted to a roar in her ears. There seemed to be a thousand people running about, to and fro across the wood floor. Ladies were screaming; men shouted from one of the assembly rooms to the other, "Bentham is dead! Bentham! A wound to the chest! Murdered!"

She looked up and saw that Kingslade was very close to her. Only then did she realize he was carrying her in his arms, pushing his way through the crowd. Her aunt was beside her, and every once in a while a waft of her strong vinaigrette would pass below Lydia's nose.

"Enough," she cried weakly.

"She speaks!" her aunt squealed.

Kingslade looked down at her. "I am accompanying you and your aunt to Upper Brook Street," he said.

"He told me something."

"Hush. You will feel better in a moment."

"But—"

"Hush," he reiterated, only this time smiling. "All will be well. You must trust me a little."

"I do," she murmured. Immediately afterward, she could not credit she had said any such thing to him. She hardly knew Kingslade well enough to trust him on any score, and yet she had spoken what she believed was her truest opinion of him. How was it possible she trusted the man when he was so wretchedly reserved?

There was a great deal of shoving as they made their

way to the entrance. Panic had seized the assemblage, and more than once she heard nonsensical statements about radicals having broken into the assembly rooms intent on murdering everyone.

Before long she was sitting within the protective confines of her coach. Though her aunt expressed her concerns several times and more than once offered her the use of her vinaigrette, Lydia made it clear that she wished only to be quiet for a time. The remainder of the journey to Upper Brook Street, therefore, was spent in silence. She had only one desire, to speak with Kingslade as soon as possible . . . alone!

As the coach rolled through the darkened street, she stared out the window, watching the deep shadows of the night creep by. Bentham had been murdered, but by whom. And what was Kingslade's connection to him that he had asked that the weapon be given into his hands? She had so very many questions, only would he be willing to give her a proper answer to each one? And how was she to be rid of her aunt once they arrived at the town house?

Kingslade, however, settled the matter nicely. Once arrived before her aunt's town house in Upper Brook Street, he addressed Mrs. Morestead, requesting a private audience with her niece. He wore such a smile that Mrs. Morestead's eyes grew quite large, his expressed desire to see Lydia *alone* being interpreted just as he apparently hoped it would, that an offer of marriage would be forthcoming.

"Yes, yes, of course. At once, if you wish for it, my lord. That is, of course, if my dear Lydia is equal to just such a conversation?"

Lydia did not hesitate, but smiled in what she hoped was a rather shy manner that might support her aunt's mistaken beliefs. Mrs. Morestead did not fail her, but responded with a quick fluttering of her arms, ushering the pair into the office on the first floor, closing the door behind them, then racing up the creaking stairs to the first floor.

Once certain that her aunt was happily employed pacing

the drawing room abovestairs, Lydia collapsed into a chair. Kingslade, in turn, took up a seat on an ottoman before her and possessed himself of her hands. "You were very brave tonight. Good God, when I think what you must have endured! Are you certain you are well enough to speak with me?"

She smiled half-heartedly. "Only if you *don't* make me an offer of marriage."

At that he laughed, but gave her hands a squeeze, his expression all troubled concern. "Are you certain you are well?"

His obvious compassion in this moment brought the experience with Mr. Bentham flooding back to her. "I shall not be well for quite some time, I fear," she said. Though she wished it otherwise, she began to weep. He released her hands and offered his kerchief to her. "Thank you. Oh, Kingslade, he . . . he . . . begged me to remove the dagger."

"What!" he cried. "Good God! I had no notion!"

She began to sob in earnest. He did not hesitate, but quickly gathered her up in his arms, pulling her gently onto his lap.

"My dear child," he murmured. He cradled her for a very long time, indeed, until the tears had ceased and she had blown her nose at least three times.

"I am so sorry," she said at last, drawing deep, ragged breaths.

"Do not be nonsensical, Miss Sherborne. I would have been more concerned had you remained calm and composed."

"It was so small," she said, her mind still engaged in the recent experience at Almack's, "to have actually taken a life."

"The dagger, you mean?"

She nodded. "Yes, I have it with me." She disentangled herself from his warm, comforting embrace and retrieved the dagger from within the deep pocket of her gown. It was still wrapped in Mr. Bentham's kerchief. Dark stains now marred the white cambric. More tears flooded her eyes at the thought that so dear a man was now gone from the earth, forever. She sat down on the edge of the chair opposite him and gave him the weapon.

He carefully unwrapped the knife. Lydia stared at it, remembering the feel of pulling it from Mr. Bentham. She wiped at more tears. Blood had dried on the thin, pointed blade. The hilt was wide, giving it the appearance of a cross.

She glanced at Kingslade. His expression was cold and assessing. He rose and carried it to a branch of candles by the door. Slowly he turned the blade over, examining every part of it.

"Do you know to whom the dagger belongs?" she queried.

He shook his head. "It is a rare blade. I do not recall ever having seen one like it. It was made smaller than most, perhaps for the purpose of concealment. The actual blade is but seven inches in length, albeit deadly. The owner will not like being parted from it for very long."

"What do you mean to do?"

He turned his gaze to her. "Do you mean, shall I attempt to find Bentham's murderer?"

She nodded.

"Of course. The sooner the better." Once more he set to examining the knife.

"Kingslade," she said. "There is more."

At that he straightened and turned to her. "Tell me everything," he commanded, a frown between his brows as he recrossed the chamber and once more took up his seat on the ottoman.

"Bentham spoke to me before he died. He told me to find you, to give you the blade, and to tell you . . . *Rufus*, though I do not know at all what he meant by it."

His brow grew pinched, and if possible the dark of his eyes grew darker still. "Are you certain he said 'Rufus'?"

"I could not have been mistaken in that, I promise you."

"I see," he murmured.

"But what does it mean? Who is this Rufus? Do I apprehend he was the one who killed Mr. Bentham?"

He remained silent. He did not look at her.

"Kingslade, will you not answer me?"

He glanced at her, his expression cloaked. "I should not trespass further on you, Miss Sherborne. These difficulties are mine to bear, not yours." Wrapping the blade back up in the kerchief, he slid it into an inside pocket of his coat.

She gasped. "How dare you say such a thing to me!" she cried.

He seemed perplexed. "I did not intend to give offense."

"But you most certainly have. I could not be more deeply involved than had I plunged the dagger myself. I believe I deserve a little candor from you, even if you are wont to be so secretive. You owe me at least that much."

"You do not know what you ask."

"You do not wish to tell me, that much is clear. That much I have always understood quite to perfection."

"Are we at that? Now?"

"Is there a difference? Whether you choose to keep your thoughts and feelings hidden or whether you withhold information from me now, there cannot be a significant difference."

"You misunderstand my intent. If I am restrained in offering information about whom I believe it is that killed my friend . . ." He got no further, but suddenly covered his face with his hands. "It is as though I am losing my father all over again. Bentham was a very great friend, a very dear, cherished soul."

This time, she went to him, moving behind him and surrounding him with her arms. "Kingslade, I am so sorry." He gripped her arm very hard. Her arm grew wet with his tears.

Lydia now felt that she had been foolish to have pressed him so.

After a time, he said, "You are right. You deserve some

answers. Will you permit, however, a few days' grace? There will be many matters to sort out in the forthcoming days."

"Yes, of course."

He rose to his feet. "I must go."

She accompanied him to the entrance hall, wishing he was not leaving so soon. Of course, he had no reason to stay, but his presence had been such a comfort.

"I beg you will speak of this to no one," he added.

"Of course not."

He held her gaze steadfastly. "It is a great compliment to you that Bentham entrusted you to help him at such a terrible moment. I wish you to know that. He is . . . was a very great man, greater than anyone knows."

She nodded, feeling overcome by what he was saying. When he continued to look at her, but did not speak, she began feeling quite strange, as though he were speaking to her, yet his lips remained still.

"I should not," he murmured.

She would have asked him what he meant, but his meaning became clear when suddenly he slung an arm about her waist and dragged her roughly against him. He slanted his lips over hers and kissed her so forcefully she felt near to swooning all over again.

He was kissing her! Why? For what reason? Yet, what did it matter? There was so much comfort in his strong embrace, and for this moment she could forget about the horrid events of the evening. She was back at Vauxhall, at the grotto, alone with Kingslade, her heart rising to the stars above as the fireworks exploded into the night sky. His lips became a soft poem against hers, searching, speaking so very tenderly of ancient things. She left the earth as she had two years ago when held so tightly in his arms. Everything was forgotten, the odd boredom of her existence, the pain of Bentham's death, Kingslade's reserve that so often set her against him.

Instead, she was lost to things so wondrous, she doubted

she would ever comprehend what was happening to her in this moment. At long last he released her, and as one falling gently from a cloud, she drifted back to earth. She looked up at him, her arm still resting over his shoulder. Again, she thought he was speaking, but once more his lips did not move. She felt like weeping anew.

He drew back farther, but caught her hand in his as her arm slid from his shoulder. He kissed her fingers. "Good night, Miss Sherborne."

"Good night." She closed the door as he walked out into the night, his commanding voice calling out an order to her aunt's coachman.

She turned slowly, exhaustion suddenly pouring over her in heavy streams. She glanced up at the elegant stairwell, wondering how she was to manage climbing so many steps. She moved forward and began plodding upward one step at a time. How strange that one moment she had felt as though she were flying and the next moment as though her feet had become encased in the thickest mud.

When she reached the landing, her aunt called to her. "Is it settled, then?" she asked on an excited whisper.

Lydia squinted, for the hallway was very dark. "What? Oh, yes, it is settled." She had agreed to say nothing of her experience with Mr. Bentham, and she would await Kingslade. "I told him I would speak to no one of . . . of poor Mr. Bentham."

"Yes, yes, of course. That dear, dear, excellent Mr. Bentham. He will be greatly missed."

Lydia glanced back at the door. "Kingslade was very devoted to him. I believe he thought of him as a father."

"It is all quite shocking, and you are very right. Nothing more should be said on the subject for the present. Well, well, you must be longing for your bed. Your maid awaits you, and I sent up a glass of warm milk with a little nutmeg to help you sleep."

Lydia parted from her aunt at the top of the stairs, then gratefully gave herself to the ministrations of her maid.

Within half an hour she was tucked between the sheets. Though she fell asleep quickly, her dreams were troubled, and more than once she awakened with a start only to drift off again.

Later than night, Kingslade sat in the study of his home in Grosvenor Square. He was bent forward, his elbows on his knees, his hands clasped loosely. His gaze was fixed on the blade that had taken the life of one of the best men he had ever known. He reached for his snifter of brandy, and tossed a hearty gulp. No way to drink brandy, but tonight he was certain this was no way to live. Bentham should not have died, and what the devil had he been thinking to have actually kissed Miss Sherborne . . . again?

Except that he had wanted more than life itself to kiss her, to feel if but for a moment the comfort of her soft body pressed to his, her lips soothing beneath his own, her arms wrapped about his shoulders. He smiled, albeit sadly. By God, there was something in a woman's embrace that was more soothing than anything else on earth.

Not for the first time did he wonder if he had inadvertently become attached, and that quite seriously, to Miss Sherborne. Examining his conduct throughout the evening in as rational a light as possible, there was sufficient evidence to suggest that he had come to desire her society. There could be no doubt he admired her. He had always believed she was a strong, capable woman, and her actions tonight had proven his opinion of her. She had managed to remove a dagger from Bentham's chest, to secret the bloodied weapon in the pocket of her gown, to cross a ballroom floor and not swoon until she had reached the relative safety of his arms. He did not believe there were many ladies of his acquaintance capable of so much courage and presence of mind in the face of a truly great horror.

On the other hand, he did not wholly trust Lydia Sherborne. She had set herself against him nearly from the moment he had kissed her two years ago, and last year she had broken off her engagement to a young gentleman, Harry Leckford, without warning or provocation, or so he had been told. She was a puzzle to him, he did not wholly understand her, and he did not completely trust her.

He set the snifter back on the table and picked up the dagger once more. Again, and for perhaps the twentieth time, he turned the small, fiendish weapon over and over in his hands. He had since wiped the polished steel clean of the blood, of Bentham's blood, but he could almost sense the dividing of the flesh as Rufus killed his prey.

Only why had Rufus killed Bentham tonight, in so conspicuous a place as Almack's? There was only one reason—Bentham had learned his identity. How? Rufus had been the craftiest of spies. Bentham had given him his name after William the II, who was known to torture his enemies. Rufus's spying had tortured a nation. The secrets he had unearthed over the years and sold to Bonaparte had prolonged the war by months, perhaps years, and now, with Boney back in France, the information he had somehow managed to cull from his sources detailed Wellington's combined forces. Could a value be placed on such incredible information? What would Napoleon be willing to pay for such a treasure?

Bentham had wanted him to have the knife, but why? He searched every inch of it looking for a hidden message, but the spiraling of wire about the handle and the clean lines of the blade left little room for transporting secrets. The only other explanation, therefore, was that Bentham believed the dagger could be used as leverage, to somehow force Rufus into the open. Surely, Rufus would want his blade back.

At two and thirty, Kingslade had been in service to the crown for seven years. Bentham had brought him in, and he had been glad to do his part in England while thousands of troops were killed each year battling the French on the Continent. There were several traitors operating in England, all Englishmen, impoverished gentlemen of little conscience and no patriotism, eager to earn a fortune through treachery. Several had been known to Bentham and therefore Kingslade, but they were allowed to move about, their movements watched closely in order to gain some idea of what particular kind of information was being sought after by Bonaparte.

Rufus was the exception, and the only clue to his identity was the dagger.

Sometime well past midnight, Lydia awoke from a dreadful nightmare. She was being chased through crowded rooms by a man without a face. In his hand, he held a dagger, the same dagger that had killed Mr. Bentham.

She sat up, breathing hard, her heart racing, her nightdress soaked with perspiration. She crawled from her bed and traded the damp gown for a fresh one, shivering as she slid the clean gown over her head. She quickly buried herself in her covers, rolling up on her side and forcing her heart to grow calm. She doubted this would be the last of such horrible dreams. She did not know what to think, or which thought to summon first—Kingslade's extraordinary conduct in having kissed her or the murder at Almack's for reasons that seemed to go far beyond a vengeful act. What could Mr. Bentham have meant by saying, *"So much depends on your being brave,"* which led her to ponder Kingslade again.

She could not imagine who would want such a dear old man dead. Why had Bentham wanted Kingslade to have the dagger? She simply did not understand what had happened. She thought of the moment it was the greatest irony that she had been thinking earlier that evening how so very little of interest ever happened to her. A moment later and she was drawing a dagger from a man's chest.

She shuddered anew and began to weep, as much for herself as for Mr. Bentham. After a time, she again thought over the extraordinary events that had taken place at the *haut ton's* most prestigious of assemblies. Afterward, Kingslade had been restrained in sharing what information he knew of the possible causes for the murder. What was his connection to Mr. Bentham, and what precisely had they been involved in of so suspicious a nature that someone had wanted Bentham dead? And who or what was Rufus?

Her stormy thoughts were disrupted suddenly by a gentle clattering on her window. She slipped from bed and glanced down into the garden below. There, barely discernible in a patch of moonlight, was Mr. Ellis waving to her and weaving about slightly.

Good God! He was completely foxed, and he had come to her house! She donned a warm robe and crept quickly down the stairs.

"What are you doing?" she whispered, crossing the garden to him. "It is nearly three in the morning."

"You must marry me," he whispered in a slurred voice, barely able to lift his lids.

"You wish me to marry you?" she asked, stunned.

"Y-yes," he stammered, weaving again. "I have l-loved you"—here he hiccoughed—"for . . . forever! Marry me, my dear, sw-weet, Miss Sherborne."

"Hush! You will awaken the servants and my aunt!"

"I will only be quiet if . . . if you say you will marry me."

"Perhaps I shall," she responded, giggling. "But not tonight!"

He pressed a hand to his chest and sighed heavily. "What hope you have given me! I do not wish to leave England alone. I want you to come with . . . with me. Oh . . . dear." He began to groan and weave a little more. "I feel very bad." He stumbled toward the door and was inside her aunt's house before she could prevent him.

"This is most scandalous, Mr. Ellis," she whispered urgently. "Indeed, you should not be here."

"I must be where my heart is." He was hunched over and could barely walk.

She guided him in the direction of the entrance hall, intending to usher him onto the street to find his own way back to his lodgings in Half Moon Street; but he turned toward the drawing room, espied a sofa, aimed himself in that particular direction, and before she knew what had happened, he fell down on it, unconscious.

She stared down at him in complete astonishment. She had never known Mr. Ellis to behave so strangely, and yet, he, too, had been at Almack's last night. Was there a one of them who would not suffer in some manner or other because of Rufus's terrible deed?

She felt sad all over again. She removed her robe and covered him against the night chill. She picked up his hat, which had fallen to the floor, and settled it on a small table near the fireplace. She patted him on the shoulder, wished him a good night's sleep, and made her way back to her bed.

Oddly enough, Mr. Ellis's unexpected arrival somehow comforted her, and she fell into a deep sleep.

Sometime later, though just how much she could not say, she awoke rather abruptly, thinking something had fallen. She sat up. "Is someone there?" Had she had another dream? She could not say. Only silence returned to her.

After a moment, she sighed deeply, thinking she must have awakened from another dream, and lay back down. Once more she slipped into sleep.

She awoke past dawn with a start. Another nightmare had chased her awake. She sat on the side of the bed and covered her face with her hands. Fear gripped her for a long, long moment. Mr. Bentham had been in this dream calling to her to help him. She had followed after the sound of his voice, but she could not find him. She gave herself a shake. It was, after all, only a dream.

This would not do, however. She left her bed, rang for her maid, Annie, and began her morning ablutions. As she sat at her dressing table, she reached for her brush and

found that it was not in its usual place but was on the opposite side, askew. Her maid never left her personal
articles in anything but the strictest order, for she was fastidious in the extreme.

Lydia could not help but smile. Everything was askew
this morning. How could it be anything else? Undoubtedly,
she had disturbed her dressing table before climbing between the sheets last night.

When Annie arrived, she queried, "Was my aunt much
shocked to find Mr. Ellis on her sofa?"

"I beg your pardon, miss?"

"Mr. Ellis. Has he gone?"

"I do not take your meaning, miss. No one has called
this morning, although there is a missive for you. Do you
wish me to fetch it?"

"Yes, please."

When Annie returned, she quickly discovered what she
already suspected. The note was from Mr. Ellis, which
read, "I was able to steal from your aunt's home before the
servants began stirring. I beg you will forgive me for my
truly wretched conduct of last night, and if I have disturbed a few things on your writing desk, I humbly ask for
your pardon. I could not see at all in the dark and cannot
even answer for the quality of this note. I shall call soon to
continue my abject apologies. Your servant, Ellis."

She could not help but smile. Poor Mr. Ellis. However
strongly his conscience might be bitten this morning, she
had no doubt his head was suffering grievously because of
his drunkenness. Punishment enough, she thought.

Thursday passed mournfully for Lydia. The entire *beau
monde* seemed to be in a state of shock so that her aunt's
house—indeed, all of Upper Brook Street—was quiet
throughout the day. Dear Mr. Bentham had died. And Almack's, that sanctuary of every good thing, had been
violated in a horrible, extreme, and violent manner. She

wondered just how long it would be before their days returned to a normal rhythm.

On Friday, Lydia awoke yet again with fearful nightmares chasing her into the morning. She felt desperate in a way she could not quite comprehend, as though the only way she would ever know any peace was if she solved the murder herself. There was little hope of that, however, though she did wonder if Kingslade would call on her. Perhaps she may not be able to be of much use in discovering Mr. Bentham's murderer, but she might be able to grow calmer in her spirit and find rest at night if she had at least some of her questions answered.

In truth, she had been thinking of little else since she last saw Kingslade than his promise he would speak to her of Rufus and what he knew of Mr. Bentham's murder. He did not come to her, however, and with Mr. Bentham's funeral conducted that morning on his estate outside of London for a small contingency of friends and family, she did not feel she should disturb him with her own sufferings.

That night, however, Mr. Bentham invaded her dreams yet again, this time appearing to her while at the same time begging for her help; but she could not reach him, she could not make him hear her, and then she was being chased, hunted like a frightened rabbit pursued by a pack of hounds. She wished she could speak with Kingslade. Perhaps there was something in her dreams that might speak to the situation, that might offer some clue as to the solution of the identity of Rufus. Her suffering was acute.

Off and on, throughout the night, she strove with images of Mr. Bentham until at last she awoke in the morning, again haunted by him. By now, she was in such a state of panic that she wondered if she would ever feel normal again.

Though she did not wish to intrude on Kingslade's grieving, particularly with Mr. Bentham's funeral having taken place but the day before, she felt she had to address the questions about his murder that were afflicting her so sorely in her dreams.

She rang for her carriage, and a half hour later she was standing before the door of his town house in Grosvenor Square. She was admitted by an extremely proper butler who regarded her with a faint and quite disapproving lift of his brow. She ignored this evidence of the social solecism she was committing and told that good retainer that she had come to see his lordship on a matter of the utmost urgency and would he please be so good as to inform him that Miss Sherborne had arrived.

He was about to protest when Kingslade was heard on the landing above.

"I thought I recognized your voice, Miss Sherborne." He turned to smile at his butler. "You may go, Stephens. I will see to my guest."

"Very good, m'lord," he responded. The faint sniff Lydia heard as he turned away from her and began a stately progress down the hall in the direction of the nether regions could be heard echoing to the spiraling second floor above.

Lydia cast her gaze up the stairwell, which was lined with several exquisite paintings. In the midst of battling Stephens, she had not been able to notice the elegance of her surroundings. She did so now in a quick sweep of her gaze. Marble, a very fine wood banister and wainscoting, the smell of beeswax, an extraordinary bouquet of hothouse flowers. She approved of the elegant arrangements.

In a second sweep, her gaze flowed over Kingslade, who was dressed as he always was in fine attire. He wore a dark blue tail coat, buff pantaloons, a subtly patterned waistcoat, and a neckcloth arranged in but the simplest of folds. With his short hair brushed *a la Brutus*, he gave all the appearance of a dashing Corinthian. He was as handsome as ever, but there were etched into his face lines of grief and worry.

"What brings you here?" he inquired, the smile which

he had offered to Stephens diminishing steadily. He began descending the staircase, a frown creasing his brow. "You do not look well . . . lovely, as usual, but not in your usual bloom of health."

"I have not been sleeping, Kingslade, hardly a wink in three days, and I have come to ask for your help."

Reaching the bottom of the stairs, he guided her into a large receiving room and begged her to take a seat. She felt reluctant to do so. Clasping her hands together quite tightly, she shook her head. "I hope you do not mind if I remain standing. I feel as though I am about to fly apart from within." She drew near him and lowered her voice. "I awake every morning with the worst nightmares about hunting for Bentham, hearing his voice, sometimes seeing him, but never being able to reach him. I know it is because of the nature of his death, but I was hoping that we might talk over the matter—all that happened once more—in hopes of giving my mind the relief it is obviously seeking. I could hardly discuss such things with my aunt, and you have asked me otherwise to remain silent on the subject."

"I see," he murmured.

"Before that, however, I wish to know how you fare?"

He laughed harshly. "How do I fare? Like the devil. Bentham's funeral was hard to bear. His wife never ceased weeping the entire duration."

Lydia shook her head. She felt ill and dizzy of a sudden. "I think I should sit down now."

"Yes, yes, of course. I would feel better if you did. Otherwise, I will always have the impression you did not feel welcome here, and you are, very much so. Would you care for some tea?"

"Yes, thank you."

The next few minutes were spent quietly, ordering the tea and awaiting its arrival. There seemed to exist between herself and Kingslade an understanding that for the moment made conversation unnecessary. A thick coal fire burned in the grate, and Lydia's gaze became quite fixed to the red, steady glow.

Sometime later, with teacup in hand, Kingslade queried, "Nightmares?"

"Indeed, quite vicious ones and always Bentham is in them asking for my help, only I cannot give it to him, I cannot reach him, and then I am chased for what seems like hours on end."

"I am so very sorry," he said.

"Kingslade, you must tell me what is going on here. I have pondered the extraordinary events of Wednesday night a hundred times, but I cannot quite understand what happened. I feel if I am ever to sleep again, I must know what is going forward and what, if anything, I might do to help bring the evil perpetrator of this crime to justice."

"I do not wish to involve you, Miss Sherborne. These matters are best left to me."

She felt all her former pique return to her. Why must he be so evasive, so secretive? "I will not permit you to be self-serving in this moment, Kingslade. It is not fair to me. I would not presume to take you to task for this under other circumstances, but you cannot possibly mean to be reserved in this moment, not when I am suffering as I am, not when I was the one who—"

"I beg you will not say it," he cried, rising abruptly to his feet. He hushed her with both hands and glanced toward the doorway. When he moved to lean over her, she was properly startled by his odd conduct and nearly spilled her tea. "Not another word, not here," he whispered. "You deserve the answers you are seeking, but I cannot give them to you now."

He drew back, and she stared up at him. "You are frightening me," she whispered.

"As well you should be," he returned quietly, his expression deadly serious. In a louder voice, he continued, "Will you be so good as to drive out with me this afternoon at Hyde Park?"

"Of course."

"Four o'clock?"

"Yes." She nodded.

"Very good. Will you take another cup of tea?"

Lydia shook her head. Her cup was empty and her nerves sorely rattled. "No, I thank you. I believe I shall be going."

"Very well. Allow me." He then most kindly escorted her to her carriage.

"Four o'clock, Upper Brook Street?" he queried, handing her up into her aunt's coach.

"Yes. I shall see you then."

She bid him farewell and with a heavy sigh leaned back against the squabs. She began to feel that she had inadvertently stumbled upon something quite beyond her comprehension. She could not imagine what it was Kingslade meant to tell her of so secretive a nature that he could not speak of it within his own house.

Three

Kingslade closed the door and listened as the carriage rolled up the street, Miss Sherborne's coachman calling to his teams. When he had first heard her voice, he had been astonished that she would have called on him. Young ladies, particularly those unwed, did not visit bachelors, and that unaccompanied by even a maid, nonetheless a proper chaperon like Mrs. Morestead. After his initial shock, however, as he guided her into the drawing room, his surprise gave way to a profound sense of relief, even contentment, that completely took him aback. He was thrilled that she had come to him, regardless the purpose of her scandalous visit.

When he had moved to the landing and looked down at her, he had been bowled over as he always was by the mere sight of her. She had been gowned in the prettiest pale yellow, looking like a daffodil in the midst of his darkened entrance hall. He had been in the doldrums, feeling so sad about Bentham's demise, that her appearance had worked like a balm on his soul. When he had spoken, and she had looked up at him, his heart had constricted almost painfully. Would he ever become accustomed to her beauty? How long had it been? Two years since he had first made her acquaintance and yet he was seeing her as he always did—as if for the very first time. She was so beautiful, she took his breath away, particularly in that moment when her expression had been so imploring. She had come for his help, and something in that worked in his heart strongly.

He had not wanted to speak of anything that had happened on Wednesday, in part because he was still not certain just what he should tell her and in part because he was convinced she would be overheard, however innocently, and her tale repeated as such tales were along the extensive network of servants in Mayfair.

The funeral had been difficult as he had said, but beyond that, his reasons for requesting her silence were important, even critical to national security. In his opinion, the less people who knew of her part in Bentham's death, the better. Now he had but to decide precisely what he could tell her and whether or not he should warn her that her life might be in jeopardy.

Later that afternoon, during her aunt's at home, Lydia found herself seated beside Mr. Ellis in the drawing room, sipping tea and listening to his amused recounting of a silly wager at Boodle's last night. "The mouse, which Egerton refused to allow any of the servants to capture, scampered from one table to the next. I bet ten pounds he would reach the south wall first and Egerton the north. We were all half-foxed, and even the more conservative fellows were soon intrigued by the little fellow's progress."

"How did it end?"

He smiled broadly. "I am ten pounds the richer!"

She laughed heartily, grateful for a moment's reprieve from the sadness and distress she had been feeling since Wednesday night. Who did not enjoy an excellent wager, or even a rather ridiculous one?

She glanced about the drawing room, and though Mr. Bentham's death was close to the surface of nearly every conversation, there seemed to be a general accepting of fate that had occurred in the intervening days. Her own conversation earlier with Kingslade had eased her heart immensely.

Mr. Ellis leaned close to her. "And have you recovered from Wednesday night?" he asked.

His expression was so sympathetic she did not hesitate to speak the truth. "Not by half, I am afraid. Though I must say I am doing better now. I find I am having some difficulty sleeping."

"I am so very sorry that I importuned you late that night. I cannot conceive of how I came to your house and in such a state! Will you forgive me?"

"Of course. We were all so overset. I am not surprised your own conduct was a trifle bizarre. Nothing has seemed the same since Wednesday night."

"You swooned," he said. "I only wish that I could have been there to help you, but at least Kingslade was able to look after you."

"He was more than solicitous. He saw my aunt and myself home, you know."

"I suspected as much. He is a good man."

"Indeed, I believe he is."

"I must say, however, that I was horrified that you fainted as you did. I know you to be of a strong constitution and not much given to the vapors. I only wonder . . . That is, I suppose it would be best not to speak of it."

Lydia frowned slightly. She felt a powerful impulse to recount the whole of it to him, but given the chattering presence of so many guests, she hardly thought the moment propitious. A little discussion, however, might suffice. "Oh, I do not know," she responded, forcing a smile. "I believe that confiding in a good friend can be quite beneficial."

He drew her to one of the windows overlooking the street. "You were brave that night," he murmured, almost urgently. "I believe I know what you did, and how can I express my admiration for you? You took the implement that caused the wound, did you not?"

She gasped. "How did you guess?"

"You were the last to speak with him before he died, and then you swooned, which was not at all like you."

"It was all too horrible," she confided. "I awake with nightmares several times throughout the night."

She watched an expression of frustration cross his features. He shook his head. "Good God, this must have affected you more deeply than I had supposed, but why? Miss Sherborne, there is something you are not telling me, and I have long observed that when one speaks of these things, the monsters depart."

She looked into his concerned pale blue eyes. "I have been asked not to speak of this, and for the present I believe I should keep my promise. You are such an excellent friend, though. You cannot know how much I value and appreciate your concern."

"I can only hope that at least Bow Street has been consulted in the matter."

"As to that, I cannot say, but I hope to know more by this evening."

"Indeed?"

She nodded. "I am riding to Hyde with Kingslade this afternoon. He has promised to tell me what he knows, which I have reason to believe is considerable."

"He was a very great friend of Bentham's, as I recall."

"Indeed, he was."

"Then, perhaps, you will know some peace of mind, and that will make me very happy."

He smiled down at her with such tenderness in his eyes that Lydia could not help but wonder yet again how it was she had not long since tumbled in love with Geoffrey Ellis. He was many things she desired in a gentleman. He was kind, very considerate in everything he said, and so very open in demeanor and discourse. She doubted there was very little she did not know of him. She could only wonder, then, why she did not love him, yet she did not. He may have been in his cups when he proposed matrimony to her, a subject he had not broached with her since that dreadful night, but she knew of his love for her. If only she returned his regard, how quickly would she have given hints that his suit would be acceptable to her! How odd, then, that her heart remained untouched. It seemed a great mystery.

An hour after the last of the guests had departed from her aunt's home, Lydia accepted Kingslade's assistance as he handed her up into his curricle. A brisk April wind beneath gathering clouds pushed and tugged at her bonnet. The earl popped his hat farther down about his ears as he took up his seat beside her and picked up the reins. He gave his tiger, a small lad with a broad smile and sharp gray eyes, the command to release the horses. Once in motion, the curricle moved briskly.

Lydia turned to watch the tiger swing himself up behind with perfect ease, even though the carriage by then had begun moving rapidly. He wore the dark blue livery of the Kingslade household, a gray wig tied at the back with a black ribbon, and a hat which he, too, pressed more firmly down about his ears. His nose was pink from the chilly afternoon.

"A very charming bonnet," Kingslade said, glancing at her. "You wear that shade of green quite well, I think."

Lydia thanked him. She had suffered acutely over just which particular gown, pelisse and bonnet to wear, a circumstance that had taken her by surprise. She could not comprehend in the least why she was so concerned about what she wore to Hyde this afternoon, but so she had been. She had chosen a carriage dress and matching pelisse of Pomona green silk, nearly the shade of apples, and ruched, puckered, and flounced quite prettily. Of course, to be traveling alongside the Earl of Kingslade would naturally require a certain degree of elegance, but she rather thought her motivation was entirely different. In dressing for the excursion, however dark in nature, she had desired to please him and so, apparently, she had. "You are very kind to have said as much," she responded.

When a roll of thunder could be heard far to the west, he frowned slightly. "And perfectly suited for such a lovely day," he murmured facetiously.

Lydia chuckled. "What do we do if it should begin to rain?" she asked, her heart fluttering oddly as she glanced up at him. The curricle was not equipped with a hood.

"There is an umbrella stowed beneath the seat, but that is for my use. You, I fear, will have to merely endure the elements as best you might."

She shook her head at him, enjoying the teasing light in his eye.

"If you become chilled, there is a carriage rug," he added.

"I would not dream of making use of it, my lord, you being of such a fragile constitution. There is another gust of wind! Shall I wrap the rug about your knees?"

He smiled broadly, maneuvering the curricle and pair around a wagon that had stopped just at the end of the street in front of Mr. Ellis's house.

She glanced in the direction of the trunks being moved. "My good friend is journeying to Brussels in a fortnight, I think. It would seem he is sending his baggage on ahead of him."

"Indeed?" he queried. "Mr. Ellis, you say?"

"Yes, you know him a little, I think. Geoffrey Ellis."

"Why is he leaving England at such a time?"

"He has many business interests on the Continent, which, unlike many gentlemen, he prefers to see to himself, though I have long suspected he goes because he enjoys the adventure of traveling."

"I envy him a little, I think. I should prefer to be in Belgium myself at present. Bentham had meant to go there in two days' time."

Lydia glanced up at him. There was so much she wanted to say, nonetheless several questions she wished to ask, that she found herself struggling to remain silent. However, she could hardly address the matter at hand with his tiger's ears cocked forward as they undoubtedly were. She wondered just how much conversation she would have today on important matters given the proximity of one of his servants.

She was soon enlightened. For the remainder of the trip to Hyde, which was not far, Kingslade kept his remarks limited strictly to quite mundane events and ideas, like her bonnet, or the Prince Regent's most recent weight since he was known to have weighed himself again at Berry Brothers in Bond Street, or Mrs. Price's shockingly red hair. Once at Hyde Park Corner, however, he drew to a stop and bade his tiger alight, promising to retrieve him when they were ready to depart the Park.

"I was not certain how you were to manage it," she said, a new and stiffer breeze buffeting her bonnet. She reached up and held tightly to the single white ostrich feather, fearing it might fly away. The Park, for reasons of an approaching thunderstorm, was rather thin of company. Perfect, she thought, for just the conversation they were in need of. "We could hardly have spoken of Rufus in front of your tiger."

He glanced sharply at her. "No, that we could not."

"Kingslade, I hope you mean to open your budget. I fear I have been in the worst suspense and believe that unless I receive some relief, I shall continue in my nightmares."

"For that I am so very sorry, Miss Sherborne. I would not have embroiled you in my troubles, nor would Bentham, for the world. You must forgive us both."

"That I can easily do, but what, pray tell, am I forgiving you for?"

He became very silent, a state far too familiar to her to be of the least comfort. She felt suddenly quite discouraged. He was always reserved, except when speaking of bonnets or the like. Had he been of a different temper. . . . Well, she would not think of that, or the way she felt a little dizzy just being seated beside him. In this moment, he put her so forcibly in mind of Harry Leckford that she felt close to tears. She almost begged him to return her at once to Upper Brook Street. Instead, she pursed her lips in her frustration, fuming at his reticence and wondering whether or not to take him to task for what she considered to be a terrible flaw in his character.

She could not think of Harry without being cast into the dismals. She had loved him, or thought she did. She had believed he loved her as well. But when she had decided to surprise him at the Vauxhall masquerade, which he had said he was attending against his will to do the pretty with his sister and that he meant to remain only an hour or so, she had searched the gardens for him and had finally discovered him locked in the embrace of a lady entirely unknown to her.

To have believed herself loved and to have been so betrayed was not something she had yet risen above, either in her thinking or in her heart. Her confidence in her ability to judge between one man and the next had been seriously compromised. In retrospect, she had come to see that though she had enjoyed an easy camaraderie with Harry, she had never truly known him. As she glanced up at Kingslade, whose expression had grown rather fierce, she was painfully aware that she knew equally as little of him. How, then, could she ever trust him?

"Do you intend to tell me nothing, then?" she asked stiffly, after the coach had passed by yet another carriage. She waved to Miss Smith and her mother.

"The matter is an extremely difficult one," he responded.

"Is this to be your excuse, then, for withholding information from me? That you think I am incapable of either comprehending or managing the difficult nature of the subject? If so, I wish to remind you that I took the dagger from Mr. Bentham . . . I alone!"

"I know," he responded quietly. "Which is why you are seated beside me in this moment. Had Bentham not spoken with you, had he not given you a message for me, had you not been so nearly involved, this conversation would have ended earlier at my town house. I would have told you nothing."

She opened her eyes very wide. What did he mean, she wondered, and what was it he was now debating whether or not to tell her? As though sensing that something enormous was coming, her heart began to pound in her chest.

"What I am about to tell you, Miss Sherborne, must remain a secret between you and myself, and believe me when I reiterate that were you not already so nearly involved, I would say nothing to you." He drew in a deep breath and began speaking in a low, even tone. "Bentham managed a network of British spies, operating here and abroad. One of his primary tasks was to keep detailed records of those Englishmen who traded in matters of state for the purpose of gain. Rufus, who killed Bentham on Wednesday night, is just such a man. Until that night, however, no one, not even Bentham, knew his identity. His operations here have been as discreet as they have been covert."

Lydia stared straight ahead. She was so stunned she could not speak.

"Miss Sherborne," he murmured, giving her a slight nudge. "Lady Jersey is waving to you and even frowning."

"Oh, I am sorry." She glanced about and found her. She smiled and waved. Once the carriage passed on, she shifted toward Kingslade slightly and said, "Does this mean that you, too, are a spy?"

He chuckled. "Of sorts, I suppose. I help, or I used to help, Bentham now and again. Do I need to caution you further about discretion? May I request that you vow not to speak of this to anyone?"

"Of course I will not!" she cried. "You have my most solemn promise." She was silent apace, then added, "So, Bentham learned Rufus's identity that night."

"So it would seem."

"Why did he not tell me himself so that I in turn could tell you? This makes no sense whatsoever."

"I have no doubt he did so for the strict purpose of protecting you. The more you know at this juncture, the less safe you are. Do you understand?"

"Do you think I am in danger?" she asked, startled.

"To a degree . . . yes. I am sorry to say it, but because you were so nearly involved, and I have every certainty Rufus saw your part in it, he will not rest until he knows if you are a threat. For that reason, I have not sought you out, and even now I feel I am placing you in jeopardy by riding out with you. Rufus knows who I am and of my involvement with Bentham, but now he may turn his attention to you, particularly if he thinks you have the dagger."

Lydia turned this over in her mind. Rufus, on every count, was a vile man, a traitor to his country, a murderer. "If I could be of the least use in bringing this wicked man to justice, then I do not give a fig for whether he means to harm me or not!"

"You ought to care, Miss Sherborne, since his intention will likely be to kill in order to protect his identity."

She met his hard gaze by straightening her shoulders, even against the mounting wind. "I did not mean to sound flippant," she replied. "However, I do wish you to know that given the circumstances, I hope I might love my country sufficiently to be willing to be in jeopardy, if but this once."

At that, he turned to her, his smile warm and perhaps even a little affectionate. "I remember now. You are the lady who longs for adventure, or so you have told me time and again. Well, I believe to a degree you are in the middle of one now." His smile faded as his gaze drifted past her shoulder.

"What is it?"

"Your friend Ellis. Do you see that lady with whom he is conversing?"

"In the scarlet riding habit?"

"Yes."

"Is she—?"

"A cyprian of the first order. I hope I do not offend you in speaking so openly."

"Not in the least." She was, after all, five and twenty. Hardly a chit just emerged from the schoolroom. She rather thought she could bear having one of the *haut ton's* courtesans pointed out to her at Hyde Park.

"She is more, however. She is known to pass secrets since she is so well connected in military circles."

Lydia looked away, but could not repress a gasp. "And yet she is allowed to continue?"

"Of course, for she passes many along to good English spies."

"I see, so that you know what is being discussed up and down the ranks."

"Precisely, and I must say, very astute of you."

Lydia wondered that her good friend was chatting in so lively a manner, also astride a horse, with such a notorious female, who held on to the ribbons of her bonnet against the wind as well. Another glance explained the whole of it—the lady was quite beautiful. Even she could scarcely keep from staring.

As Kingslade continued driving the curricle about the Park, he spoke of his efforts, thus far, in comprising a list of everyone who was at Almack's on Wednesday night. "I believe it is complete. The patronesses, as well as the servants, were able to help me greatly. But that is all I know at present. I only wonder if my revelations today will be of any real use to you. After all, what I have told you can hardly be of comfort."

"Sometimes I think it is easier for the mind to know the very worst than to be given only bits and pieces of a tragedy. I suppose I will not know exactly how I have been affected until I climb between the sheets tonight. Only tell me, how are you faring through all of this? Are you able to sleep?"

"A little," he said, chuckling. "Better after the funeral, but not by much. Thank you for inquiring, though. I take it kindly in you."

"I suppose you would, since I am not usually kind to you."

'No, you are not," he responded stridently. "Really, I find myself of the moment quite shocked at so much excessive civility. But now it is your turn, I believe, to tell me something of yourself. Are you enjoying the Season?"

"Shall I be polite? Or do you have sufficient fortitude to bear the truth?"

"Always the truth," he returned.

"Very well, if you must know, I am heartily bored and can scarcely bear going from one engagement to the next. *Our* brangling is the only amusement I find I can tolerate with even a degree of equanimity!"

Kingslade glanced at the beautiful young woman seated beside him and laughed outright. "Do you know how dangerous these words are? Were I to repeat them, you would be banned from all polite society. Indeed, I cannot think of a greater solecism you could commit than denouncing the general run of events as boring."

"Then, I believe my fate is in your hands."

He smiled and was thoughtful for the present. "Do you not have any siblings, Miss Sherborne? In all our conversation, I do not recall your having mentioned anyone."

She sighed. "I do not," she responded. "And I do not believe a day has passed that I have not felt the lack of it. Yes, I know that there is always a great deal of grief and squabbling that goes on amongst brothers and sisters, but you cannot know the loneliness of a schoolroom in which there is but a rather indifferent governess seated opposite you the duration of your childhood."

"I am sorry," he responded, quite sincerely.

"You, on the other hand, were blessed with family."

"Indeed, I was. Three brothers, three sisters, and a growing host of nieces and nephews. I love them all."

"Will you tell me of them? Mary, I know, of course, and Louisa."

He glanced at her, a curious expression on his face. "If you truly wish for it."

"I would not have asked otherwise."

"Very well." He then launched into a review of his family, of his next brother, Colonel James Russell, not yet married, of the Reverend Stephen Russell, who was married with three children, and of Captain George Russell, not yet wed but betrothed to a lovely young woman from Buckinghamshire. "Sophia is the eldest of my sisters and rarely comes to Town. She also has three children and is increasing. She resides in Kent, not too far. I try to visit as often as I am able."

"You are fortunate, indeed! And your mother?"

"She is infirmed and lives not far from London so that we may all visit her in our turns. During the Season, I am there often. She has a villa on the Thames."

"How delightful. You are a good son, then, I see."

"I try to be. I think it important, only why do you stare at me as though you do not believe me? I see what it is—your ill opinion of me is rearing its head once more."

"You mistake me. It is just that, well, you have never confided in me before. I did not know of your family, though I believe my aunt told me that your mother was ill and could not partake of the London festivities. So you may not wonder at my surprise since generally you keep me quite ignorant of anything pertaining to you."

"I suppose I do." Another roll of thunder, this time closer, caused him to laugh. "What a day to be exchanging histories."

"And to be speaking of spies in England."

He said nothing for a long moment. His thoughts had drawn him inward and to Lady Violet whom he had loved so very dearly many years ago. With her, he had been completely open, restraining nothing. How blind he had been to her, not seeing the truth of her feelings that she had jilted him and he not having even the smallest notion she meant to do so. Of course he was reserved with Miss Sherborne, and with all the ladies of his acquaintance, for he had promised himself never to be so wretchedly exposed again.

Today, it would seem, he had begun breaking that promise. He could not recall the last time he had told a

young lady of his family. He felt drawn to her rather inexplicably. He turned to her slightly, adjusting the reins,
intending to ask her where she grew up, but when she met
his gaze, he found himself bereft of all speech, all thought.
He heard a small sigh pass her lips, which then remained
parted almost invitingly, except that he knew she was not
aware of just how kissable she appeared in this moment in
her pretty green bonnet. He wondered, not for the first
time, if perhaps he was falling in love with her.

He heard his name called out cheerfully and reverted his
attention to the drive. Seeing Lady Cowper, he drew rein,
bringing the carriage to a stop beside hers. She was a lovely
woman, with cropped brown hair and a warm countenance.
"How do you go on, Miss Sherborne, Kingslade?"

Miss Sherborne inclined her head. "Quite well, thank
you," she said. "Still a little sad, I think."

"Of course, we all are," she returned gently. "But I was
glad to see you out today, both of you, even if we will all
need to race for shelter soon." As if by design, a rain-laden
gust blew over them both. "I think it is time to put the top
up! Before I go, however, may I congratulate you,
Kingslade, and wish you every joy, Miss Sherborne? Oh,
dear. I felt the first drop!" She then called to her servants,
and a general bustling began.

Kingslade did not wait but withdrew a carriage rug, an
umbrella, and a light cape from the floor of the curricle.
Within a trice, he had Miss Sherborne bundled up in the
cape and the rug and gave the unfurled umbrella into her
hand. He then slapped the reins hard and, with an accompanying score of pleasure-seekers, made a dash to the
various gates, returning to the one at which he had left his
tiger. To his surprise, Miss Sherborne moved quite close to
him and held the umbrella over both their heads as the rain
began in earnest.

"What do you think Lady Cowper meant?" she cried.
"Did I hear her correctly? Was she congratulating you and
wishing me joy?"

"Evidently, almost as though—"

"Oh, dear God!" she cried. "I am the greatest simpleton! My aunt—Kingslade, I fear you will be very angry, but I believe my aunt believes we are engaged to be married. I now realize that I said something in response to a question of hers on Wednesday, after you had gone, which I believe she has interpreted to mean that we are betrothed! And now Lady Cowper . . . oh, dear!"

She explained how the night of Bentham's murder, she had been so exhausted that when her aunt had asked if all was settled, she had nodded, but she had not thought her aunt was referring to a betrothal, but rather that the pair of them had agreed for that moment as to what should be done about the horrid events of the evening. "Are you very angry with me?" she asked.

He shook his head. "As I recall, we both misled her that night, but good God, could you imagine you and I wed?"

She trilled her laughter. By that time, the curricle drew before the gate where his tiger waited. Without the vehicle actually stopping, the small lad jumped quickly up behind.

He glanced at Miss Sherborne and saw the laughter, even the joy, in her eyes. "We will correct my aunt's unfortunate misapprehension," she said, "the moment we arrive in Upper Brook Street. In the meantime"—and here, a crack of thunder split the air, nearly sending his cattle bolting—"I strongly suggest you spring 'em, my lord!"

A half hour later, Lydia entered her aunt's town house, laughing all the while. She was only a little soaked about the hem. Kingslade had cared for her well, while he, once stripping off his greatcoat, was none the worse for the storm either.

He escorted her up the stairs, and if Lydia had been uncertain as to her aunt's beliefs, her worries were confirmed instantly. Mrs. Morestead welcomed them both in just such a fashion as left neither in doubt of her convictions. Lydia at once explained the error, thinking that her aunt would have a good laugh as well. On this score she was quite wrong, however, since an expression of horror overtook Mrs. Morestead's face.

"But, my dears!" she cried. "This is dreadful! I have . . . I fear you will be very angry, Lydia . . . but I have told everyone that you are betrothed to Kingslade!"

Lydia glanced at Kingslade and saw a thoughtful expression cross his features. She rather thought he was pondering what to do next. To her aunt, she said, "I am sorry, but we will simply have to make the truth known. I have no intention of wedding Kingslade, and he certainly has no desire to marry me. In all the confusion, I do apologize."

"Well, that is easy for you to say; but you do not know how badly this will reflect on me, and I have strived so hard . . ." She burst into tears, whisked a kerchief from her pocket and her vinaigrette from her reticule in quick succession, then retired to her chaise lounge in what Lydia felt was a marked theatrical manner. She began to suspect her aunt of some mischief.

"Certainly we should not have deceived you that first night, and I did err when I told you all was settled; but you should have asked me later, and certainly nothing should have been said, even if it were true, until a notice might have been sent."

"A notice?" she queried, sitting up quite abruptly. "Then, you are to be married?"

Her aunt was generally not so dull-witted, and she now understood quite to perfection that the whole of her conduct had been deceptive. "No, Aunt," she responded firmly. "No notice, no betrothal, no marriage, no 'Did you hear, my niece is to be the next Countess Kingslade.'"

Mrs. Morestead began to pout. "Well, I must say, I have been very badly used."

"I daresay you will get over it, Aunt."

Kingslade stepped forward. "On the other hand . . . ," he ventured.

Lydia glanced at him sharply. She could not imagine what he meant to say. "What?" she queried.

"You and I should speak privately, I think. Will you allow it, Mrs. Morestead?"

The brightening of her expression left Lydia in little doubt of what her response would be even before she cried out, "Yes, of course!"

Lydia would have protested, for she did not wish to give Mrs. Morestead even a particle of hope on so hopeless a subject. However, Kingslade took her arm and gently guided her from the chamber. "Shall we make use of the office again?" he inquired.

"As you wish," she returned, looking up at him doubtfully.

He said nothing more until they had descended the stairs and were alone in her office. A fine blaze of coals had kept the afternoon's storm from casting a chill over the chamber. Even so, she drew close to the fire and warmed her hands.

"We should pretend an engagement," he said, shutting the door. "Later we can quarrel, you can put a notice in the post dissolving your intentions of wedding me, and we can resume our lives. I believe this would satisfy your aunt, at least a little."

"But this makes no sense," she cried. "To what possible purpose would you propose such a course? I promise if you are thinking we need to salve my aunt's wounded pride, it is nothing of the sort. She will recover from her disappointment."

"Actually," he said, drawing close to the fire as well. "I was not being so kind. In truth, I was thinking of how such an arrangement would allow me the freedom to come and go at Upper Brook Street with, hopefully, Rufus none the wiser as to my real design. If I do not miss my mark, Rufus will attempt to get his dagger back as quickly as possible. If he believes you have it . . . Well, my presence in your home would allow me to protect you better should it become necessary."

Lydia opened her eyes wide. "Oh, I see!" she cried.

"By now, I believe he would be growing desperate, the blade being the link to the murder."

"You think he will come here?" she queried. "And you believe I am in such danger?"

"You know I do."

"And you would not find it troubling to be feigning an engagement?"

"Only a very little, but these are difficult times."

Though she was not certain, she thought she could sense his reserve again. However, she felt she had to agree. "Then, of course I will acquiesce."

She once more extended her hand to the coals. "This certainly is an unexpected turn of events."

"Has anything been expected since Wednesday night?"

"No," she responded, giving her curls a shake. She glanced at him. "So, we are betrothed, you and I?"

"So it would seem." He drew next to her and looked down into the fire. Once more his smile was crooked.

A flash of lightning lit the muslin drapes in a glow, a rumbling of thunder encircled the house, and Lydia drew in a deep breath. She could not credit all that had happened which had culminated in a pretend betrothal to the man next to her. She was astonished and something more . . . excited.

She turned toward him. "I wish you to know, Kingslade, that you may rely on me. I am not missish, and though I fainted at Almack's, I am usually not so henhearted. Whatever happens, I will not disappoint you."

He turned toward her as well. His gaze caught and held. "You have never disappointed me," he said, searching her eyes. "Aggravated me, disturbed me, made me as mad as fire, but never disappointed."

The look in his eye was fierce and had the oddest effect of weakening her knees. She felt suddenly dizzy and strange, and still his gaze pierced her. She knew she was staring at him, but why, she could not say, as though she was waiting for him to say something further.

She watched a scowl deepen over his features. "I should go," he whispered.

"No," she murmured quite without thinking. "Not yet."

"The devil take it!" he cried. "You must be a vixen or perhaps of gypsy descent!" Before he could elaborate on this theme, he closed the gap between them, slid his arm about her waist, and as he had done but three nights past, he kissed her quite thoroughly.

Lydia received his kiss as though she had been waiting for it her entire life. She quickly and quite without ceremony snaked her arm about his neck and held him tightly, leaning into him until she could feel the entire length of him. Though she was vaguely aware that her conduct could be construed as utterly wanton, for the moment she did not care.

She became lost again in the most incomprehensible manner.

Kingslade had not meant to kiss her. Indeed, such conduct had been as far from his mind as it could be. But the moment she turned toward him, he felt as though he had been swept into the strong current of a river from which he had no desire to escape. Now, as she leaned into him and he gathered her closer still, the desire to kiss her swelled into a passionate feeling that completely stunned him. What was this feeling he shared with her that could not be given a name? With no other young lady of his acquaintance was he so indiscreet, so willing to cast caution to the wind. But why Lydia Sherborne?

After what must have been several minutes, he drew back and looked into eyes that seemed utterly lost. He had the feeling she was not wholly conscious. "Oh, Kingslade," she murmured softly.

He had hoped for a rebuke, something to break the spell, not an enchanting invitation. There was nothing for it. He kissed her again, only this time he touched his tongue to her lips, which parted beneath the soft pressure. He plumbed the depths of her mouth and, after a few seconds, felt her knees give way. He held her firmly, caressing her face, supporting her head against him, and kissing her until soft moans escaped her throat. Every sense of propriety rebelled, and yet he kissed her again and again, more intensely still when her fingers slid up the back of his neck and drifted into his hair.

After another prolonged passage of time, he drew back more fully, though supporting her still with an arm about her waist. "Lydia," he whispered, urging her to come back from that world which had held them both captive for so long. "Miss Sherborne."

She blinked and sighed. "Kingslade."

He stroked her cheek. "Lydia . . . come back."

She smiled softly, her eyes closing. "So magical . . . ," she murmured. She blinked anew, and he could feel the strength return to her legs. She stood upright and planted a hand against his chest. "You should not . . . We should not . . . Whatever were you, was I, thinking?"

He released her a little more.

She gave her head a shake and balanced herself over her feet. "I feel so dizzy, so completely shatterbrained. You kissed me again! Oh!" She looked up at him, and he took a step away from her.

"Do you mean to strike me as you did at Vauxhall two years ago?" he asked, smiling.

"No, but . . ." She thrust a hand toward the door. "You must go. Immediately." She paused and swallowed quite visibly. "Yes, you should go. We should never have . . . You should never have. Good heavens, how do you do this to me?"

Her expression was bemused and accusing all at once. At the same time there was this adorable smile on her lovely lips. "I asked the same thing of you before I kissed you." Almost, he stepped toward her. "I shall go now." He summoned his strength and strode quickly through the doorway and equally as quickly across the entrance hall. He was gone, into what was now a light rain, his greatcoat slung about his shoulders, and his damp hat pressed down about his ears.

Lydia moved slowly into the hall, her senses finally regaining their equilibrium, and stared at the door. She listened as the carriage clattered up the street and found that she was unable to credit that Kingslade had kissed her again and that she had permitted him, yet again, to do so. Worse still was the truly incomprehensible way in which the embrace berefted her of all ability to reason. She could not help but wonder at what had led her to give herself again to him in such a way, though as she turned and began to slowly mount the stairs, she rather thought that having shared a little of their histories, she had been lulled into an odd complacency.

Yet, the kiss had been such a wondrous joy. How easy it would be to be completely fooled by such a sensation, to stake her entire future on the false hopes and promises the miracle of his embrace had afforded.

Now that the moment was cooling, and she could once more actually feel her feet touching the stairs, one after the other, she was able to be more rational. There could be no question that for some reason she enjoyed a truly remarkable rapport with Kingslade, but it did not necessarily follow that her heart ought to be given to him. What, after all, did she know of him except that he enjoyed a large family, was apparently quite devoted to his mother, and that he engaged on occasion in espionage activities on behalf of his country? Other than these interesting facts, she still knew very little of him. Such had been his reserve over the past two years whenever he was in her company, or any other lady's. He had a reputation as being a rather cold fish, not easily known and certainly not easily pleased, and throughout the duration of her acquaintance with him, he had proven his reputation time and again.

She shook her head in utter bewilderment. What, for instance, did such an encounter possibly mean to Kingslade? Worse still, however, was the truly horrible thought that she was falling in love with a man made very much in the mold of Harry Leckford!

With these thoughts ruling her mind, she made her way up the stairs to the drawing room where her aunt sat chewing on the corner of her kerchief.

"Well?" she asked, her face brightening at the sight of her niece.

Lydia kept her explanation for their decision to continue misleading the *ton* about their supposed betrothal succinct. "For your sake, Aunt, we have agreed to pretend to be *informally* engaged for a few days more, possibly a sennight. But you must understand, we are planning to stage a quarrel after which we will *end* the betrothal."

Her aunt stared at her for a very long time, her brow pinched as though trying to comprehend what Lydia had just told her. After a minute, however, the frown disappeared, and Mrs. Morestead smiled. "As you wish," was all she said.

Lydia thought so calm a response was not in keeping with her aunt's temper, but of the moment she felt her aunt's disappointment once she and Kingslade made it clear to the *beau monde* that they were no longer engaged was the least of her concerns.

Kingslade drove his team a little faster than he ought, but, damn, he was far too overset to be entirely careful. The rain was barely a drizzle now, but when his leader slipped a trifle, he reined the horses in and fairly walked them home. He still could not understand what had prompted him to kiss Miss Sherborne, nor precisely what had urged him most strenuously to continue kissing her as he had, and that rather scandalously. Had she not been a maiden, by God, he would not have left that house for a very long time, indeed!

Which was more troubling than anything, he thought. Given that he would undoubtedly be seeing much more of her over the next several days, if his plan proved effective, he wondered just how he was to keep from kissing her again. He might have suggested pretending an engagement, but not for a moment had the kiss he had given her been in any manner connected to that pretense. What, then, had the kiss meant, or perhaps, more to the point, what was she to think of his desire to keep dragging her into his arms?

He knew he needed to be careful or she would very soon have the right to demand a betrothal whether he wished for it or not. Yet, she had been heavenly to hold in his arms, feeling as precious wrapped up in his embrace as the finest gem. He had not wanted to let her go . . . ever! What the deuce could this possibly mean? Was he falling in love with Lydia Sherborne, or did she merely hold some inexplicable, gypsylike power over him?

Whenever he contemplated the mysteries of eros, his thoughts drifted as they always did to Lady Violet and her betrayal of what he had believed was a profound love. Miss Sherborne had already proven her character in this regard, that she was not to be trusted, so why, then, must there be any discussion at all? He did not believe her heart was faithful and that if he was not careful, he would end up losing his own heart again merely because for some incomprehensible reason, he thoroughly enjoyed taking her in his arms and kissing her!

Perhaps it was for this reason that he steeled himself against her, reminding himself that at present his first duty was to his country. He knew the damaging papers Rufus carried with him, and should he leave England with them, the entire position and strength of the combined armies to the last man would be made known to Bonaparte. The very thought of it sickened him, for with such information, Boney could easily decide to advance his army against Wellington before Blucher could arrive in time with his Prussian forces. How many decades of war would then follow? How many English lives lost? How many more European countries decimated of their young men all for one man's vaunted ambition?

He had already formed a tentative plan for exposing Rufus, the sooner, the better. He meant to tempt him with the dagger and with Miss Sherborne. For a brief moment he debated telling her of his plan, but again and again as he reviewed the details, he thought it would serve his purposes much better to keep her ignorant. The less she knew, the better, for her, for everyone. At the same time, he felt a bell of warning clanging within his mind that to do so would be most imprudent.

Regardless, it was time to flush out a spy!

Four

On Sunday morning, Lydia walked beside Kingslade following church services.

"You were tugging at your curls, again," he murmured, leaning close to her. "You do so quite often, you know."

"A dreadful habit. I beg you will say nothing to my aunt. She is forever slapping at my wrist when I forget myself, which, I believe, is all too frequent."

"Yes, I quite agree," he said, nodding and smiling. "And the expression on your face while pulling at your curls is generally exceedingly solemn, even distressed. Were you distressed this morning?"

She glanced up at him and quickly looked away. She could hardly tell him that she had been thinking, quite inappropriately during an excellent sermon, about the kiss he had placed on her lips yesterday after their ride to Hyde Park. Of course, that was not the only disturbing thought in her head. Throughout the entire morning, her mind had been unruly, rarely obeying her commands to be peaceful and circumspect as befitted attendance at church. Instead, she had thought of poor Bentham and, in contrast, how she had awakened that morning free from the distress of nightmares for the first time since Wednesday. She worried if her aunt was continuing to speak of the supposed betrothal to her friends and what sort of danger Kingslade believed her to be in that they must continue the ruse. But worse, however, was that she had broken a promise to herself earlier in the week that she would never permit Kingslade to kiss her again, only to not resist even in the slightest the kiss he gave her last night!

At this point in her ruminations, just as the good priest was expounding on the need for the strictest morals in society, her thoughts had run amuck. She had recalled in detail just how Kingslade had looked yesterday evening at the precise moment he had taken her in his arms, how she had submitted without scarcely a protest or any very clear idea that she was being kissed at all, and how the natural progression of the kiss seemed to involve her disappearing from the earth for a time. She had frowned at this, she had wrapped a curl about her finger, and she had begun to tug at it quite distractedly. How could a man's mere kiss cause her to feel so wondrous?

To Kingslade now, she said, "I was thinking of Bentham, of course." Which was at least true, in part.

"Of course," he returned. "I must confess he is rarely far from my thoughts as well."

They had walked along the street and were very near her aunt's carriage. Mrs. Morestead, however, was nowhere to be seen, probably still within the church gossiping further about her niece's forthcoming marriage. She could not imagine what her aunt would do once she and Kingslade broke formally with one another, although she suspected that after exhibiting a fit of hysterics, she would take to a darkened room for several days.

"You are not thinking of putting a notice in the *Morning Post* about our engagement?" she queried.

"As long as possible, I think, we should keep it just as it is, as a form of gabblemongering. Once Rufus is apprehended, we can dispel the rumors."

She looked up at him and smiled. "And how do you enjoy being betrothed, my lord?"

He smiled, and her breath caught. She could see that he was genuinely amused, and in his delight, he was more handsome than ever. She gave herself a small inward shake. This would not do, to encourage even in the slightest a *tendre* which was based only on a man's smile. Still, he was a delight to gaze upon.

"I am enjoying being betrothed to you prodigiously," he responded in kind. "Particularly in the office yesterday."

She gasped aloud. "Kingslade! How could you say that to me when you know we should not have . . . that is . . . You should not have . . . and I should most certainly have not encouraged . . ." She could think of nothing more to say.

He chuckled. "I do owe you an apology, but seeing your discomfiture in this moment, and how prettily you stammer and blush, I vow it was worth it to bring the subject forward so indelicately!"

"Beast," she responded, lifting her chin haughtily.

He drew closer. "Why did you not slap my face as you did at Vauxhall?" he queried.

"Must we now discuss what happened? I think we would do far better to forget it entirely. I promise you, I have done so already."

"The devil you have!"

"You would speak to me thus, within the shadows of this fine church?"

"I would speak to you thus, always! You are far too pretty to be yet unwed. And who would have thought the elegant, proper Miss Sherborne would be such a delight to kiss?"

At that, she became offended and glared at him. "You go far beyond the pale, Kingslade! How dare you say such a thing to me!"

In truth, Kingslade did not know why he was pressing her as he was except that she was, indeed, quite beautiful this morning in a dark blue silk pelisse and matching bonnet. Having begun a conversation about the kiss of yesterday, he had opened a Pandora's box, for he had suddenly become full of the experience as though it had just happened and he swore that had they been alone, he would have kissed her again. This would hardly do, and yet he could not seem to prevent more words from escaping his lips. "I would kiss you again, in the space of a heartbeat, were we not surrounded by a hundred gapeseeds."

She could only laugh. "You exasperate me so completely, you can have no notion." She glanced toward the church. "Only, where is my aunt, I wonder, for I long to return to Upper Brook Street."

"What? And quit my delightful company? You would miss me dreadfully."

"You are being absurd as well as reprehensible. You should be drawn and quartered."

"I vow I would risk it for another kiss like last night, or the one on Wednesday night, or the one from two years past at Vauxhall. Speaking of which, I want you to come with me to the masquerade tomorrow night."

"Have you lost your senses? Why on earth would I agree to go with you when you are being so very wicked!"

"Because I wish to apologize in this way to you for my conduct of last night."

"By taking me to a masquerade?"

"Why not?"

"You mean to kiss me again," she stated, confronting him in her direct manner that appealed to him mightily.

"With your aunt as chaperon, I think that hardly unlikely."

"Oh, I see. My aunt is to come, then?"

"You did not think we would go alone, did you, or is that what you were *hoping?*"

She drew in her breath sharply. "Oh, you are making me as mad as fire!"

"Why are you scowling at Kingslade, dearest!"

"Aunt Morestead!" Lydia cried. "I did not see you."

"Well, I think you ought to apologize to your betrothed for having raised more than one eyebrow this morning. I was watching you the whole time." She turned to Kingslade. "Has my niece been coming the crab?"

He smiled. "Not more so than I deserve," he said.

"I vow the pair of you are quite vexing. Will you join us this evening, Kingslade? We are always quiet on Sunday, but your dining with us would be seen as unexceptionable I am sure."

"Thank you, but I am engaged elsewhere. I am taking my sisters to my mother's house for dinner."

"And how is your mother, such a dear lady?"

"She is doing as well as can be expected. She is always cheerful, of course." He then added, "I was hoping that you and your niece would join me tomorrow night at a masquerade at Vauxhall."

Mrs. Morestead's eyes began to glow. "I can think of nothing that would give me greater pleasure," she responded.

"Eight o'clock?"

"We shall be ready. Come, Lydia, I daresay you have set up his lordship's back sufficiently for one morning! And, Kingslade, do send our warmest wishes to your mother for her renewed health."

"I shall."

He watched her hook her niece by the elbow and guide her the remaining distance to the carriage. Watching them go, his conscience struck him badly. He had teased Miss Sherborne, taunted her, and essentially tricked her into attending a masquerade at which he was, by her presence, hoping to flush Rufus into the open. He was convinced that by being seen with the lady who had extracted the blade from Bentham, the spy would have little choice but to attend the masquerade as well, and hopefully to at last make himself known to Kingslade. He was using Miss Sherborne, and though he felt he had to continue on this course with so much at stake, he was likely to suffer for it. There was nothing for it, however, for he had already submitted a notice of sorts into the *Times* designed to capture Rufus's attention, and all he had to do now was prepare an appropriate costume, appear at Vauxhall with Miss Sherborne on his arm, and . . . wait.

* * *

On the following morning, Rufus read the advertisement in the *Times* and thought either Kingslade was a trifle cow-handed, or he had discounted the intelligence of his enemy. The brief, almost poetic message was beyond obvious.

The Rufus Stone, blood on the hands of a king, masquerading as a good man, all weaponry worn to a purpose, a lady in distress, Monday. How he despised Kingslade, who had so much and who even had the woman he might have had in other circumstances. There could be only one interpretation to the message—Kingslade would be wearing the dagger at a masquerade, Vauxhall no doubt, on Monday night, and Miss Sherborne would be with him.

Well, at least he would be able to retrieve his dagger, and then he could leave for the Continent with an easy mind!

On Monday morning, Lydia laid out her Elizabethan costume carefully. She had a serious case of butterflies which so danced about in her stomach she rather thought she might swoon. Kingslade had asked her to go to the masquerade, and even though he had been teasing her quite sorely, she had begun to entertain certain ideas about him that the butterflies reflected in their extraordinary acrobatics.

She had debated several times just how wise it would be to wear the same costume she had been wearing when she first met him . . . and kissed him . . . but in the end she had justified the decision by the fact that she really had had only one day to prepare for the fete. How could she then manage a suitable costume in so short a time? If she chose to forget that in the very depths of her wardrobe there existed a very nice milkmaid ensemble that she had worn last year, she ignored it.

Hearing the front bell, her heart leapt. Had Kingslade

come to call despite the fact that she would be seeing him this evening? Oh, dear, when was it she had come to anticipate his arrival as though a series of fireworks had just lit a dark night sky? Standing in the middle of her bedchamber, she gave herself a strong shake. She could not allow herself to be overcome with the most ridiculous of thoughts where Kingslade was concerned merely because he had suggested she and her aunt attend a masquerade with him.

Her aunt's footman scratched on the door. When she opened it, he informed her that Mr. Ellis had come to call and was she wishful of receiving him.

Mr. Ellis! She could not have asked for a better diversion.

A few minutes later, she entered the drawing room. He smiled in that way of his, knowing and amused all at once. "I would ask you to marry me if I thought you would say yes," he said.

"You did ask me," she countered.

He frowned slightly. "No, I do not think so. I would have remembered such a momentous occasion."

At that, Lydia laughed. "The night you came to my house quite foxed, you cried out, *Marry me!* in the most piercing manner. I had feared the whole house might have been awakened by your declaration."

He laughed. "I was completely in my cups and cannot be held accountable for anything I said that night." For a moment, however, he grew quite serious. "I would, you know . . . ask you, if I thought you would wed me."

Lydia drew in a deep breath, knowing that he was hoping for permission to pay his addresses to her. However, she had known for a very long time that though he was the best of friends, she simply did not love him. "We have been friends for too long a time for any such nonsense as that. But how glad I am you have come. I did not see you in church yesterday. Do sit down. I trust you are well?"

He paused only a trifle before taking up a seat opposite her and responding. "Quite well. I had just taken an early ride through Hyde Park and thought I would call, to a purpose, however. If you are planning to attend Lady Jersey's ball this evening, I was hoping to secure a waltz before any of your other numerous beaus were before me."

"I had completely forgotten about her ball!" she cried. She realized that her aunt would never have forgotten Lady Jersey's ball, and her quick agreement yesterday to Kingslade's invitation to join him at the masquerade now held a rather shrewd meaning. She was in little doubt that regardless of her insistence that the betrothal would come to an end, Mrs. Morestead had other hopes and plans.

"You are not to attend?" he queried.

"I am promised elsewhere."

"How can this be? When I spoke with you on Wednesday, I remember distinctly that you said nothing would keep you from that particular ball."

She suddenly felt very conscious. "Kingslade asked me to attend the masquerade at Vauxhall tonight, and I felt under some obligation to go with him."

"Ah, so it is true," he mused, nodding. "I have heard through the usual gabblemongering that you are betrothed to him."

"No . . . yes . . . That is, I know there have been rumors, but it is not completely settled."

He crossed an easy leg over his knee. "Are you in love with him, my dear Miss Sherborne? Has cupid struck at last?"

"No, of course not. The whole thing was a mistake, something my aunt misunderstood, and unfortunately, before I could quell her enthusiasm, she had let it be known that we were betrothed. For the present, for her sake, we are continuing a pretense. I have little doubt that but within the next fortnight, we shall stage a dramatic quarrel after which the ending of our supposed betrothal will come as no great shock to anyone."

"All this merely to soothe your aunt's pride?"

Lydia smiled. Even though there were other circumstances involved which, of course, she could not reveal to Mr. Ellis, she still replied quite sincerely, "I can think of no better reason. She has been as a mother to me, and the fault was mine. Kingslade has been very much the gentleman in allowing the sham to continue."

"As I have said before, he is a good man."

"Kingslade is not so bad a fellow as I once thought. If you must know, he is quite dedicated to catching the man who killed Bentham."

Mr. Ellis shook his head and compressed his lips. "The deuced fellow should see Tyburn Tree, the sooner, the better!"

"Indeed! I could not agree more!"

"And just how is he proposing to capture this terrible man?"

"I do not know all the particulars, but what I do know I have promised to keep secret."

"Then, of course, I will not press you."

Lydia looked at him for a long moment, wondering yet again why love had not entered into her relationship with Mr. Ellis. He was so completely unreserved. She felt there was nothing she could not discuss with him, and had she been at liberty to do so, she most certainly would have told him everything about Mr. Bentham and his network of British spies. She only wished that Kingslade could follow Mr. Ellis's lead and engage her in so open and ingenuous a fashion. What would happen then? she wondered.

At eight o'clock that evening, Lydia frowned at her aunt. "But do you think it at all wise that I attend the masquerade with Lord Kingslade *alone?*"

"Why are you being so missish!" Mrs. Morestead cried. "You are hardly a chit just out of the schoolroom, which would of course prevent me from allowing you to go. But at *five and twenty*—! Really, you are being quite absurd!"

Lydia lifted a hand. "Very well, Aunt!' she cried, unwilling to listen to her complaints that her niece had grown into a spinster.

A few minutes later, Lydia watched Kingslade enter the drawing room sporting the very same costume he had worn at Vauxhall some two years past. She wondered if he had worn it to a purpose and was not surprised when a crooked smile graced his lips as with a sweep of his eyes he took in her own costume. She stood up to greet him, as did Mrs. Morestead, and swayed a little unsteadily on her feet. She supposed the weight of the heavy velvet gown had been the cause of it, but as she looked at Kingslade, and felt her heart begin to beat rapidly, she rather wondered if it was not the odd *tendre* he evoked in her whenever she but looked at him.

He offered a pleasant greeting to them both, and when presented with the news that Mrs. Morestead would not be attending since she had the headache, he responded politely. "I hope you are otherwise in good health?" he inquired.

"Oh, yes, yes, indeed I am. It is only a trifling pain in my head which will pass as soon as I rest for a time. I beg, however, you will not put off your evening's amusements on my account. I fear Lydia would be grievously disappointed."

Lydia barely restrained rolling her eyes, but somehow managed to keep her countenance. Kingslade promised he would take good care of her and, after offering his arm to her, escorted her from the house.

An hour later, while strolling along one of the darkened pathways, Kingslade glanced down at the lady on his arm. She wore a small, beaded mask of white silk and every now and then lifted her gaze to him, a playful smile on her lips. Though the purpose of their venturing forth this evening was rarely far from his thoughts, still the very sight of Lydia Sherborne seemed to cause everything else to pale in significance.

"What are you thinking?" he asked.

"I believe you know. Rufus, of course."

"With that smile on your lips? I would think you addled if I believed you."

"Oh, very well. I was thinking of . . . the grotto."

He chuckled. "You should not be, you know."

He heard her sigh. "I suppose I should not, but it was quite singular. Whatever possessed you to kiss me as you did . . . and that when we had just met?"

"Need you ask?"

"I should like to know."

"Very well. I doubt I had ever seen so beautiful a lady as you, Miss Sherborne."

He glanced at her and saw that she had lowered her gaze. When they passed by the dim light of a Chinese lantern, he could see she was blushing. He added, "You do know how pretty you are."

She looked up at him. "Even if a lady is pretty, does that always prompt you to steal a kiss?"

"There you have me. I suppose not."

"Then, why?"

"Because of what you said to me that night as well as the teasing expression on your face. *Are you exploring?* But you smiled in that way of yours that I have come to know so well, and I swear it was nothing short of an invitation."

"An invitation!" she cried. "I vow it was no such thing. I merely thought it ironic that we were costumed as personages from history who had known one another."

"And that so scandalously."

He heard her gasp and could not keep from chuckling in response.

He realized in this moment he was exceedingly content, and the thought occurred to him that he could spend many such evenings just in this manner, walking beside Lydia Sherborne and teasing her in a manner that shocked her a trifle, made her gasp on occasion, and brought a blush to her cheeks particularly when, among all these varied protests, she still smiled in that charming manner of hers.

"Is that a waltz I hear?" he queried, stopping their progress and glancing back up the path.

"I believe it is."

"Would you honor me with the next dance, Miss Sherborne?"

"I should be delighted."

He escorted her the short distance to the dance floor and guided her with a measure of skill into the melee, for the numerous partners were making a riotous progress about the dance floor. She laughed joyously as together they entered the fray.

"What a hand you are!" she cried, as he began waltzing her about the crowded floor.

"I would only attempt something of this sort at a masquerade where I would not be known."

"You are always known wherever you go, Kingslade," she countered. "You are too tall, and far too handsome even sporting your black mask, to not be quickly recognized, or do you not know how good-looking you are?"

"Serving me with my own sauce, eh?"

"The very least you deserve!"

The dance was spent in just this manner, he taunting her and she offering a rejoinder that could only serve to delight him. He found himself forgetting one minute out of three the dastardly nature of his true purpose in bringing her to Vauxhall. If once in a while his conscience called to him, that he was using her quite ill in presenting her as bait to Rufus, he quelled such unhappy thoughts. The dagger he was wearing, however, reminded him frequently, since he sported it but partially concealed on an embroidered belt about his waist.

At the end of the waltz the fireworks were announced, at which time a general rush in the direction of the Thames nearly resulted in Miss Sherborne being knocked down. Just as he was gathering her arm more tightly about his and asking if she had suffered an injury, he was jostled severely from behind by a party of foxed young men. Miss

Sherborne was as well. She tripped slightly, but caught hold of his doublet to balance herself.

"The dagger," she murmured.

When she lifted an inquiring gaze to him, he said, "Yes, I wore it to a purpose. I thought—" Again, they were bumped and rammed. She was thrown into him, then away from him as a large party fairly bowled them over. She was laughing, however, which greatly relieved his mind of any concern that she might have been hurt.

When at last he returned to her, he was about to ask her if she had in any manner suffered harm when his hand slid instinctively to his waist. The dagger was gone.

"Good God!" he cried.

"What is it?"

"I . . . I have lost the dagger." He scanned the various scurrying masqueraders as the fireworks began lighting up the night sky, but because of the costumes, no one appeared in the least suspicious. He would, however, have trailed after them, but at that moment a servant approached them and offered a missive to Miss Sherborne.

"Thank you," she murmured. The servant bowed and hurried away. "What do you suppose it is?" She turned the letter over.

Kingslade looked down at the wax seal and saw that a prominent, quite bold *R* was imprinted in the wax. "Rufus," he murmured.

For her part, Lydia glanced at Kingslade, whose brow was deeply furrowed. If Rufus had sent her a missive, and that at Vauxhall, she could not imagine why he would have done so or even how he knew where she would be tonight. She broke the seal and silently read the note quickly: "Do you know yet what a fool your beau is, Miss Sherborne? Or do you care that Kingslade has used you tonight in attempting to get to me. Rufus."

For her part, Lydia felt the blood drain from her face. The man who had killed Bentham had written this missive and had meant for several hours to see that she was informed of Kingslade's purposes. She dropped the note as though it were on fire.

"It is from Rufus," she whispered.

Kingslade retrieved it.

Lydia could not keep her gaze from his face. She watched his complexion pale as he in turn read the brief note.

"What does he mean by this?" she inquired. "Did you know Rufus would be here?"

Kingslade met her gaze fully. "Yes," he responded. "I invited him."

"What?" she cried. "I do not take your meaning?"

"I placed a notice, a sort of riddle, in the *Times*. It is a favorite method of communication."

"What did it say?"

He recited it to her, word for word.

"Then, Rufus did not lie. You used me. I was a sort of bait for your trap. And to think somehow I thought we had come here to support the rumors of our betrothal for my aunt's sake."

He remained silent, confirmation enough of his conduct.

Lydia shook her head and cast her gaze to the walk below. She could not credit he had been so cold in his dealings with her. "But, Kingslade, do you not understand that had you asked me, I would have acquiesced readily? Did I not tell you I would do everything I could to be of assistance to you?"

"Yes," he responded. "But I had to act quickly, and I could not risk your refusal."

"I was that necessary, then?"

"I was certain from the first that Rufus had seen you take the dagger, that he believed you might still be in possession of it."

"Why not advertise that you were in possession of it?"

She saw that his color had become more heightened. "I thought there was a greater likelihood that were you present, he would be easier to identify and to manage. I was mistaken."

Lydia felt ill. She realized she had been behaving like a schoolgirl nearly the entire evening, feeling dizzy and excited to be with Kingslade. Yet she had always known who he was, that he was not a man easily known. But this, to have deceived her within the context of his reserve, made her physically ill. "Take me home at once. And I beg you will never, never speak to me again!"

"Miss Sherborne," he cried. "You are being ridiculous in this moment."

At that, she rounded on him. "From the first I saw what you were, your reserve and how you watch with great care every word that comes from your mouth. You hold this power over all your friends in doing so, for you will not allow anyone to know you. But tonight, you have taken your reserve and used it against me. How will I ever forgive you for that!"

"What of you?" he countered. "Why should I have honored you with my trust when I cannot trust you?"

"What?" she cried in response. "What have I ever done to have proven myself unworthy of your trust?"

"What man of sense could trust a lady who jilted Harry Leckford as you did, without cause."

Lydia stared at him. She was beyond angry that he would compare her conduct with his and somehow use her ending of her betrothal to Harry against her in this moment. "Is this truly your opinion of me, that somehow I used Harry badly?"

"It is," he responded coldly.

She laughed bitterly, unable to believe that because she had promised herself for Harry's sake never to speak of what he had done, his misdeeds had returned to haunt her in this manner. "I am convinced you deserve no particular explanation, but for reasons I cannot explain, I want you to know the truth. Come! I shall show you why I broke off my engagement to him."

He frowned slightly. "How can you possibly *show* me?"

"I suppose you will simply have to *trust* me to show you."

"Very well."

She led him to the precise place where she had found Harry embracing another woman. She pointed at a darkened pathway at the end of which was a stone bench.

"There," she said. "We had not been betrothed but a fortnight when he said he had promised several of his friends to attend the masquerade here with them. I decided, perhaps foolishly and yet, in the end, wisely, to surprise him. I found him near that bench, kissing a lovely young shepherdess. Later, I confronted him with his conduct, and though he promised me it would never happen again, I could not continue in the engagement." She turned to Kingslade. "Now that you know, I hope you realize how ridiculous your arguments are, and I beg you will take me home. If you are unwilling to do so, I shall summon a hackney." She did not wait for an answer, but hurried away.

He caught up with her, but did not speak. Only once they were within his coach, did he say, "I was mistaken in you, and I am sorry for it."

"I loved him, Kingslade, and he betrayed me."

Kingslade did not look at Miss Sherborne. Instead, his gaze was fixed out the window. There arose a strange sensation within his chest of wonder and release. His heart beat as if for the first time. So Harry Leckford had betrayed Lydia. Dear, sweet, trusting Lydia. He should be desperately worried that he had lost all hope of stopping Rufus from leaving England, now that the spy had retrieved his dagger, but all he could think was that he was in love, quite extraordinarily, with the woman opposite him, who would not meet his gaze and with whom he wondered if he could ever heal so terrible a breach as the one he had created between them.

He finally understood that for several years, Lady Violet's ending of his betrothal had kept his heart concealed behind a careful fortress where he never allowed himself to trust. He recalled Lydia's earlier question: Why had he kissed her upon first meeting her? He knew the answer now. He had fallen in love with her the moment he first saw her and she had teased him so charmingly, but he had not allowed himself to believe in that love. Over the ensuing year, prior to her betrothal to Mr. Leckford, he had purposely taunted her whenever he would meet her in society in order to keep his heart safe. A year past, when he read of her engagement in the *Morning Post*, he had known a moment of panic, as though he had made the greatest mistake of his life. A fortnight later, however, when she had jilted Mr. Leckford for no apparent reason, he had believed her character to be of a similar mold as the woman he had loved and lost, causing him to further insulate his heart against her.

Now, however, with the breaking of her engagement explained, the fortress about his heart had come crashing down and with it the sure knowledge that he would do whatever he could to win the darling girl seated across from him.

Lydia awoke wondering why the birds outside her windows were chirping so loudly. As sleep deserted her brain, she realized they were not so loud, but that her head was fairly aching. She sighed heavily as recollections of the night before swelled within her mind. She was still so angry with Kingslade that she could hardly keep her thoughts in order. He had judged her severely, which to some extent then accounted for how he seemed to enjoy setting up her back so often as he did. With such a poor opinion of her, she now wondered how it had come about he had ever paid her even the smallest attention.

She sat up, struggling but failing to empty her mind of such wretched thoughts. Instead, she kept seeing Rufus's note before her and his words so succinct, "Kingslade has used you." Worse still, Kingslade did not even attempt to deny he had done so, wretched man. Of course, she would not have wanted him to prevaricate, but to have learned he thought her ending of her betrothal to Leckford to have been "whimsical!" Oh, she could barely think of it without shuddering anew.

For the next several minutes she wondered just how she could go about exacting some sort of retribution for his unhappy opinion of her. Then, as though dawn suddenly rose in her mind dispelling many of her thoughts, she wondered for the first time if this had been the cause of his reserve with her. Would he be different now that he knew the truth? Would he even believe her?

Her nerves frayed, she finally rose from her bed, summoned her maid, and began dressing for the day. Once gowned and her golden hair coifed in a pretty array of curls atop her head, she descended the stairs to enjoy her breakfast. Her aunt eyed her askance several times.

"How was the masquerade?" she queried.

"Not quite all that I had expected, but charming in its way."

"Of course, the last time you were there was a year ago . . . almost to the day."

Lydia nodded and took a quick sip of coffee. "Yes, so it was." Her hand began to tremble, and she quickly settled the delicate cup on its waiting saucer. "So, what are your plans this morning, Aunt? Do you mean to go to Hookham's?"

Mrs. Morestead opened her mouth to speak; but the front knocker was heard, and both ladies turned toward the hall leading to the foyer.

"I wonder who would be calling, and that so early, for it is just past ten o'clock? Kingslade?"

"I would be greatly surprised," Lydia responded.

A moment later and a serving maid appeared in the doorway. "Mr. Ellis to see Miss Sherborne. He said as to tell you, miss, that he wished to say good-bye. He is on his way to Dover. He is in the drawing room."

"Thank you," Lydia said, rising to her feet at the same time. "I shall go to him directly."

Lydia hurried to the drawing room. "Mr. Ellis!" she cried. "I cannot credit that you are to leave me just now. I thought you would not be going for a fortnight yet."

"I decided the time was propitious." His smile was warm, almost amused.

"Can you sit with me for a few minutes at least? And you must promise to correspond with me. Will you do that?"

He nodded. "Yes, on both accounts."

He took up a seat in a tall, winged chair near the fire-place, and she seated herself opposite him on the sofa. "Even though I cannot help but proclaim my disappointment, you must be very excited to be going."

"You can have no idea, but then, I believe you, above all my acquaintance, will understand when I say that I shall be glad to leave London behind if but for a time."

Lydia pondered all that had happened last night and thought these words had never been more true. She gave herself a shake and placed her full attention on Mr. Ellis. He seemed quite joyful this morning, as he ought to be. She had never seen him smile more.

"Did you enjoy the masquerade last night?"

She forced a smile. "It was tolerable, I suppose, but if you recall, I do not have the fondest associations with Vauxhall."

"Of course. I had forgot. Poor old Harry Leckford. What a fool he was! I should never have treated you so infamously. I do not suppose you would care to take my name and join me on the Continent?"

"Another proposal?" she returned, laughing. When he laughed with her, she leaned forward. "You will always be one of my dearest friends. I hope you do not mean to stay too long in Europe."

"With Boney about, I expect I shall be blockaded in Brussels with the rest of my fellow Englishmen. However, if I know you to be languishing for my company, I shall return instantly."

"I may hold you to your word."

His eyes narrowed slightly. "So, you did not have the most pleasant evening last night. Only tell me, did you find your, what was his name, Rufus last night?"

She frowned suddenly. "What do you mean?"

"Rufus, you spoke of him yesterday."

"If I did, I was being quite indiscreet. That name was to be kept a secret, and I honestly cannot recall having made mention of it."

He shook his head. "I forgot!" he cried. "You did not speak of Rufus; it was something I read in the newspaper of the day before, something very much like a riddle, involving a masquerade. Forgive me. I have grown quite confused."

"Something in the *Times*? Yesterday?"

"Yes, if you have the paper, you ought to see for yourself. I thought it was a riddle about you and Kingslade, who I supposed must be this Rufus fellow."

She shook her head. "I think it all very odd." She realized that Mr. Ellis was referring to the notice Kingslade had put in the *Times*.

"No Rufus then, just Kingslade?"

"Just Kingslade. But we quarreled. I do not think we will be accounted friends after last night."

"I am sorry to hear it. I had begun to think the pair of you would make a match of it. I see I am mistaken."

"Greatly so."

He glanced at the mantel. "But I see that I must be going."

Lydia saw that the hour was nearing eleven. "I suppose you must." She rose and extended her hand to him. He took it warmly and placed a kiss on the back of her hand.

"Good-bye, then, Miss Sherborne. Once I am settled in Brussels, I shall sit down at my writing desk and recount my passage to you and every other mundane detail I can recall of my journey across the Channel."

She smiled and led him from the chamber. "I shall await your correspondence eagerly."

He bowed to her and passed from her house. He appeared quite dashing in a black greatcoat and glossy beaver hat.

Closing the door, she returned to the morning room and completed her breakfast.

Sometime later, when her spirits were finally settling into the rhythms of the day, she was arranging a bouquet of pink roses when she remembered what Mr. Ellis had said about Rufus. She sent for a maid and bid her secure the *Times* from the day before. Once in hand, she carefully went through the pages and finally found the notice:

The Rufus Stone, blood on the hands of a king, masquerading as a good man, all weaponry worn to a purpose, a lady in distress, Monday.

Lydia read Kingslade's notice and agreed that it certainly had the feel of a riddle. She tried to remember what it was Mr. Ellis had said to her. *Have you found your Rufus?* She saw Kingslade's intent, but she could not comprehend how Mr. Ellis would have made any connection between the Rufus Stone and there actually being a Rufus. That she was the lady in distress was clear, that place where Kingslade had made use of her to bait the trap for Rufus. *All weaponry worn to a purpose* referred to Kingslade wearing the dagger at Vauxhall. She recalled that Ellis kept speaking about "this Rufus fellow."

She felt suddenly dizzy. A thought tried to work its way to the forefront of her mind, but it was too ridiculous, too horrible, to be contemplated.

She went to her aunt and queried, "Have you heard any particular gossip about Mr. Ellis of late?"

She shook her head. "Only that he is going to Brussels quite soon and that he is well-connected in diplomatic circles. Oh, yes, and Lady Jersey was saying something that I dismissed."

"What?"

"That he frequents the East End Hells."

The feeling of dizziness and betrayal increased. "Are you certain?"

"Well, it is only gossip after all, and he most certainly is not the first gentleman to frequent those wicked gambling halls, as they are known. Even Mr. Morestead did on occasion."

"Is Mr. Ellis in debt, do you think?"

"I cannot say. Why do you ask?"

Lydia shook her head. "No reason, I suppose." She left her aunt shortly afterward and returned to the drawing room. She felt quite ill, as though she knew the truth without being able to prove it. She remembered the night after Bentham's death when Mr. Ellis appeared in her garden, completely foxed, and fell asleep on her sofa. Or had he? She recalled how she had awakened later feeling as though someone was in her room. Could Ellis have stolen up the stairs and entered her bedchamber, searching for . . . the dagger?

"It is impossible!" she cried aloud, though the chamber was empty. "I do not believe it!"

On the other hand, she most certainly had said nothing to him of Rufus, yet he had asked her about him in the most offhand manner possible. Perhaps he had spoken to Bentham in the same way, exposing the truth of who he was.

Another circumstance occurred to her, that when he had called on her the day before, he had inquired after Kingslade's attempts to find Bentham's murderer, specifically, how he meant to go about the business.

There was only one way of knowing for certain, however, and as much as she disliked the notion of it, she felt certain she had but one recourse. Returning to her aunt, she said, "I know it will seem very odd in me, Aunt, but I must go away today, to Dover. Kingslade has invited me on an excursion to the seaside port, and I feel I ought to accept, given the ruse we are attempting to maintain. Would this be acceptable to you?" She became alarmed by the joy that so quickly suffused her aunt's face.

Mrs. Morestead rose with a flutter of her hands. "Of course you must go. He means to introduce you to his sister who I know to live in Kent, or is it his brother, the vicar. I cannot recall, but it hardly matters! Yes, yes, you must go! Of course. Were you not a spinster, I should certainly insist on attending you, but there can be no harm for engaged persons to travel together to a relative's home. I shall send for the carriage at once."

With all these rambling, inappropriate notions, Lydia had to be content. She wanted to assure her aunt that Kingslade would be doing no such thing, since they would very soon announce they were not betrothed after all, but she felt this would be in direct contradiction to her purposes. She hurried, therefore, to her bedchamber, donned a warm pelisse, settled a bonnet over her curls, and slipped her reticule over her wrist.

A half hour later she knocked on Kingslade's door.

Five

"Miss Sherborne is here? Again?" Kingslade asked, pausing in the midst of straightening the folds of his neckcloth.

His butler pursed his lips faintly. "Yes, my lord," he returned, in depressive accents.

Hope fired his mind. She had come to him. Whatever the reason, she had come to him. "Very good. Show her to the drawing room. I shall be down directly."

In some haste he continued adjusting his neckcloth. He could not credit the woman he loved, who had every reason to despise him, was presently in his house.

He frowned suddenly. She had been so out of patience with him last night that her visit could not possibly bode well. Certainly, if she had merely wanted to discuss the matter, she would have sent him a note requesting he call on her.

Last night, upon returning to Grosvenor Square, he had wondered just what the deuce he was going to do to bring about what had become a truly disastrous situation. At the very moment he realized not only was he in love with Miss Sherborne, but that he desired to make her his wife—the sooner, the better!—he realized he could have done nothing worse in using her as he had. He would never forget the look of betrayal and deep hurt that had crossed her countenance the moment he had proudly confessed to having baited his trap with her presence just as Rufus's note had indicated. He knew quite well what it was to be betrayed, and he had betrayed Miss Sherborne badly. How, then, was he to put things right with her? He could not say.

She had not been the subject of all this thoughts, however. He had been in a state of deep despair that he had somehow managed to bungle the trap he had laid carefully of the night before. It was almost as though Rufus knew his thoughts and his every movement, but how could that be possible?

As he descended the stairs, he steadied his thoughts, intent only on understanding what it was Miss Sherborne meant to say to him in this moment, whether it was to take him to task again for last night's debacle, or for some other purpose. Entering the drawing room, he saw at once that she had not come to discuss her sentiments about his own conduct. Her expression was far too distraught for that, and her complexion was greatly heightened.

She rushed forward and beckoned him close. "I believe I know who Rufus is," she whispered.

"Good God," he murmured. He led her quickly to the windows, as far from the entrance to the chamber as possible. He then listened as she quietly poured forth her suspicions.

"He was in your house? That night?"

"Yes, but I thought nothing of it at the time. He has been such a good friend, and gentlemen will get foxed on occasion and do things they ought not; but only after he said all that he said this morning did I begin to suspect why he had been in my house, possibly even in my room. I am convinced he left within the hour, for he was gone before the servants had arisen, and when I sat before my dressing table that morning, I noticed that not everything was in its usual place. My maid is most fastidious about such things. Oh, and that night I had awakened abruptly to the feeling that someone was in my room."

"Had he been so deeply in his cups as you have suggested, he would not have moved from that sofa until noon. Tell me again what he said about Rufus." He listened intently, then shook his head. "He must be the one. All the pieces fit. Was he nearby when you found Bentham . . . ?"

"Oh, dear God, he was. I even remember at the time thinking that I should summon him to help me, but Mr. Bentham had been so adamant about not asking anyone for assistance."

"And you say he is gone to Dover?"

"These two hours and more."

"The packet will not sail until the morn. Thank you for coming to me, Miss Sherborne. I am not certain at what hour the packets generally sail, but with a mere two hours before me, I feel confident we can reach him in time. You may rest assured that I shall go to Dover immediately and do what must be done."

"I am coming with you," she pronounced in such a manner he knew she would brook no opposition.

"Such a man is dangerous!" he cried. "You must know that. You could be hurt should he become desperate. I cannot allow it."

"I see," she returned, lifting her chin. He watched her begin pulling on her gloves in a rather purposeful manner.

"You mean to follow me," he responded, a certain joy at the thought of it piercing his heart, though at the same time he scowled at her.

"I do not intend to tell you what I mean to do, only Mr. Ellis has used me even more badly than you have. If he is, indeed, this Rufus, then I shan't rest until I see justice prevail."

He debated rather quickly just what he should do and in the end decided he would rather have her beside him than not knowing where or at what moment she would appear to jeopardize what must be done next. "Very well, will you come with me, then?"

He watched her countenance soften. "Thank you. Most happily, I will."

"What of your aunt?"

"I already told her we were traveling to Dover. She was

quite delighted with the notion, since she believes me to be going to visit one of your relatives in Kent."

He smiled. "Most excellent humbug. I am impressed."

"I would take credit for it, but the idea of being introduced to your family reflects the workings of her mind. I told her we were merely making an outing of visiting the ancient seaport."

A half hour later, Lydia sat opposite Kingslade in his large traveling coach. Having most happily achieved her object, she realized she might have erred, for now they must travel together for several hours on end, and she was still quite put out with him!

Having left London behind, the road gave way to verdant spring growth in a varied countryside of plowed fields, thick hedgerows, and village succeeding village.

"Miss Sherborne—Lydia . . ."

She turned to look at him, surprised that he would address her in so familiar a manner. "Miss Sherborne," she returned quietly.

"Very well. *Lydia,* I beg you will hear me out."

At that, she shifted toward him and frowned him down. "Did you not hear me, my lord? I beg you will not address me by my Christian name. We are not so nearly connected that it would be in the least appropriate for you to do so."

"But we are betrothed," he said, a smile touching the edges of his lips.

She gasped and looked away. How very much like him to be so provoking. She did not look at him when she said, "If you wish to address me, you must use my proper name."

"My dear Miss Lydia . . ."

She bit her lip. How very much like him to attempt to charm her in just that manner she liked so very much. She could think of no other man who knew just how to address her so that she felt all these bubbles of laughter forming in her chest.

"Is that a smile I see, Miss Lydia?"

"No, it is not," she responded firmly. "You have hurt me quite deeply, and do not think for a moment that these bamboozling ways of yours will cause my heart to soften toward you in the least."

"But I am in love with you."

At that, she glanced at him quite sharply. "Are you certain you know what it is to love, my lord? Your conduct last night certainly would have convinced even a simpleton otherwise."

"Will you marry me?"

"What?" she cried, unable to credit she had heard him properly. "You would declare yourself in this offhand manner, when you have used me so ill? You must be in need of a physician. You cannot be well!"

"You are so lovely, and I am never so happy as when I am with you. I believe I have been in love with you from the moment I met you at Vauxhall, two years past, and kissed you so wickedly."

Lydia felt her cheeks begin to burn, since the tone of his voice and the passionate nature of his discourse could not help but put her forcibly in mind of having permitted him to kiss her not just that night, but Wednesday night and Saturday evening! Good God, she most certainly had encouraged him, but now . . . "I beg you will not speak of such things. Though I am sensible of the honor you are paying me in giving voice to such warm sentiments, I . . . I do not return your regard. I will never be able to do so. How can I possibly trust a man who would make use of me as you did last night?"

He nodded. "You have every right to think ill of me in that regard. I can in no manner justify my conduct, particularly since it was based on my prejudice and not on your character. I hope I may never do so again, but I cannot for the life of me conceive just how I am to prove myself to you."

"You are not obligated to prove anything to me."

"Of course I am, since I mean to make you my wife, if I can."

She pursed her lips and glared at him. "Pray do not speak such fustian to me. I will not allow you to delude yourself. I shall never be your wife."

"I see," he murmured. "There is nothing for it, then. My brother's eldest son will inherit my home and title, for you are the only woman I want to bear my children. A sad loss for England I suppose, being bereft of our children."

"Gudgeon," she mumbled, turning her gaze out the window and refusing to listen to a jot more of his ridiculous ramblings. Foolish man!

To Lydia's relief, Kingslade let the subject drop entirely. Instead, he became a solicitous traveling partner in which her comfort and welfare became his object. She was grateful for the tea he procured for her at one village and the nuncheon he ordered at another. She wanted for nothing and yet did not in any way feel he was going out of his way to attend to her. His actions seemed to be perfectly natural in every sense, which only made her own predicament worse. It was very hard to continue thinking ill of a man when he was being polite and gentlemanly.

As the hours passed, and the coach drew ever closer to Dover, a gradual change overtook Kingslade. Lydia observed it with interest and admiration. His expression became increasingly determined, as though he knew well the difficult man with whom he was dealing and that at the very least he would need his wits about him once he was face-to-face with Ellis.

For her part, Lydia's heart began to beat more quickly, and a certain sensation of being very much alive began threading itself through her veins. She realized she was quite happy in this moment, as the coach reached the outskirts of Dover. For so long she had felt suffocated by the constraints of her society, but now, particularly in the company of a spy, she felt a measure of freedom that had never before come to her. She felt in this moment as though she might do anything.

"I should have been a soldier," she murmured.

"You would have made an admirable one," Kingslade responded.

She glanced at him and saw a sympathetic smile on his lips. "Yes, I would have. A pair of colors, a cavalry regiment, and service in India as Lord Wellesley has done."

"You would not have minded the hot climate?"

"Of course not," she returned with a toss of her head. "No good soldier would."

"I suppose not."

"To The Ship Inn?"

"Of course."

The coach rattled its way along the Marine Parade, Dover castle brooding over the small seaport like a hawk perched on a tall prominence, ever watchful of movement below. The salty smell of the ocean was heavily in the air. Dark clouds, shoved by a brisk wind, marched across the sky, setting a gloom over the town. A drop of rain struck the coach, and then another, until soon Lydia thought drums were beating rapidly on the top of the carriage.

"We are arrived," Kingslade said at last, peering out the window as the coach slowed and turned into the innyard.

"Do you think he is here?" she queried. "You do not think he would have attempted to make use of one of the other seaports?"

"He could not have been more taunting in the moment he asked you about Rufus. He believes you to be much less intelligent and discerning than you are and therefore believes himself safe. Oh, yes, he is in Dover. Of that I am utterly convinced."

"Perhaps he is merely bored, having been too successful." She could not help but recall her conversation with Mr. Ellis at Almack's the night he murdered Mr. Bentham. There had been a moment when he had seemed so bitter, but about what she had not quite understood. "Was he in debt to the cent-percenters?" she asked.

"I believe he was."

"I see. Then his motives are perfectly clear. And to think he spoke of investments in Europe—!"

The sudden shower ceased as quickly as it had begun. Once the coach stopped, Lydia waited within while Kingslade secured a private parlor and made inquiries about Mr. Ellis. Her thoughts were soon engulfed by her long friendship with Ellis, now the infamous Rufus, and her heart sank. She had always thought him the best of men, just as she had believed Harry Leckford was the most adoring and faithful of beaus. The sense that she had some difficulty in determining the character of the gentlemen she drew to her began to sink her spirits further. She wondered if she would ever be able to trust her instincts again! At least Kingslade betrayed her first before offering for her! That much, at least, was new!

How sad she was suddenly. Only this would not do. There was work to be done in Dover, and given how cunning and vile their adversary was, she would need all her wits about her once they found and confronted Ellis.

As though her thoughts had conjured him up, the very man emerged from the back entrance of the inn, a scowl on his face as he drew on his gloves. He lifted his gaze, which became fixed on the door, and therefore the coat of arms emblazoned on Kingslade's coach. His expression froze. A moment more, his gaze rose yet again and settled upon her.

Lydia forced a smile and waved, then quickly opened the door. "Hallo, my dear friend. You will never guess what I . . . that is, *we,* are about!"

"I cannot imagine," he responded warily. "But may I say how stunned but pleased I am to see you."

"And how happy I am to see you." She quickly descended the coach, crossed to him on a leaping run, splashing through puddles all the while, and took his arm in hers. "We are eloping, you see. I cannot believe it is true!"

"But this is all so sudden."

She stopped him and looked up. "Mr. Ellis, you heard the rumors and you must have seen how I looked at him. I vow, whenever he but entered a room, I could no longer feel my feet."

"Forgive me if I seem amazed, but what of your aunt? Miss Sherborne, this does not at all seem like you."

She laughed. "How can you say as much? Do you not recall our conversation at Almack's, how I was so utterly bored, indeed, quite beyond belief? Do but think. This morning when you called, I know I seemed out of sorts, but that was because Kingslade had kissed me again—"

"Again?"

"Yes, it is most scandalous, I know, and I should not be saying these things to you, but we were always most excellent friends. He kissed me and yet did not offer for me, and I was outraged. We quarreled, badly. However, after you left this morning, he arrived bearing an enormous bouquet of flowers and actually dropped on one knee and proclaimed his love for me." Here, unexpected tears welled up in her eyes. From whence such tears had come, she would never know, but it served the most admirable purpose of wiping all manner of disbelief from Rufus's countenance.

"Then, you are truly in love with him," he stated, searching her eyes.

"More than you will ever know, more, I believe, than he will ever comprehend. But come. Will you have a cup of tea with us? Kingslade is even now procuring a parlor for us."

"I should be delighted."

Lydia gave his arm a squeeze as together they entered the inn. By that time, Kingslade was just descending the stairs, having secured a parlor. "Look who I have found! I told you he would be here and so he is. He will be the first to wish us joy!"

Mr. Ellis said nothing, but turned to Kingslade and waited. As Lydia looked up at him, she saw so much arrogance in his countenance that a ripple of disgust passed through her mind. She also understood he was using his silence to force Kingslade to speak, perhaps to confirm what she had just said to him. She realized that were she to give Kingslade another hint, Rufus would understand she had been telling whiskers. She therefore let the earl guess at what she had done.

"It is scandalous, I know," he responded easily, completing his descent. "But if you are to wish us joy, then perhaps I will not feel so guilty about what we are about to do."

Mr. Ellis once more glanced at Lydia. She did not hesitate, but released his arm and took up Kingslade's, another effective tear escaping her eye. "I am so very happy," she murmured, giving his arm a squeeze. "Now, what about a cup of tea, or if you gentlemen prefer, sherry?"

"Why not champagne?" Kingslade said.

"Why not?" Mr. Ellis returned.

"We are at the top of the stairs and to the left. The parlor overlooks the harbor which is quite lovely. Ellis, would you escort my bride-to-be up the stairs? I will be only a moment."

Lydia thought it excellent that he did not give further explanation for what he intended to do. To have rattled on about ordering champagne or anything else would have seemed too much. Only, what was it he intended?

For herself, as she took Rufus's arm, she found she was trembling.

"Are you well?" he inquired.

"I suppose in seeing you the reality of what we are doing has just settled over my mind. I was so certain before, but now . . . my nerves seem a trifle overset."

"A glass of champagne will undoubtedly have a calming effect."

"I believe you are right about that. I did not expect to be so emotional." She wiped again at her cheek and had the pleasure of feeling Rufus pat her hand sympathetically.

Once the champagne was settled all round, Mr. Ellis made a toast. "To great love and to great adventures."

Lydia glanced at Kingslade and, with a lift of her chin and a warm smile, raised her glass to him, then took a hearty sip. She had not feigned the trembling, and the feeling of wanting to burst into a heavy bout of tears seemed to be lying just below the surface. More than once she forced herself to repress the thought that sitting so very near her was a man she had accounted a friend for so long, but who had proved himself a traitor.

A few minutes later, a scratching sounded on the door. "That must be the maid. I requested a light repast."

"How very thoughtful," Lydia said, once more imbibing the champagne.

The door opened when Kingslade gave the order, but instead of the maid, three rather tall and strongly built gentlemen entered the room. "He is the one," the earl said, quite simply.

Lydia watched in some surprise as the men descended on Mr. Ellis and, before he could so much as utter a surprised sound, drew him to his feet and bound his hands behind his back.

Mr. Ellis glared at Kingslade, then shifted his gaze quite suddenly to Lydia. "You knew about this," he cried. "Good God! I thought you were, indeed, eloping. The tears, your demeanor! I underestimated you completely."

"Rufus?" she asked.

He snorted his disgust. "To be undone by a woman!"

"I never knew you," she returned, more tears flooding her eyes. "How could you? I trusted you so implicitly. Never for a second would I have believed you could be so vile. Of course, it is quite lowering that you would think me so lacking in wit that I could not connect your blunder this morning or the riddle in the *Times* to your true identity, which leads me to wonder, Rufus, if perhaps you had desired to be caught. Will you at least tell us why you have done these heinous things?"

He was silent apace. All his former arrogance deserted him, and a grayish hue suffused his features. "It was a game," he said. "At least at first. Once I had sunk so far in debt, and came close to losing my lands, it became a necessity."

"You are not a patriot, then, in any sense?"

He merely shrugged. "Perhaps I am. After all, I allowed a mere female to trick me when I had succeeded for so many years in besting even Mr. Bentham, who I believe possessed one of the most brilliant minds of our time."

"The night of the murder, when you came to my aunt's home and were foxed, was it all a sham?"

"Of course. I had come looking for the dagger."

Lydia thought for a moment. "I awakened, in the middle of the night. Were you in my bedchamber?"

He nodded.

"Where is the dagger?"

"In my valise with the papers you are seeking."

Kingslade addressed the tallest of the men. "Did he speak with anyone since his arrival?"

The man shook his head. "Nay."

Ellis turned to stare at Kingslade. "You had me followed?" he asked, stunned.

"Miss Sherborne told me you meant to leave England quite soon. Though I had no reason to suspect you, I thought it prudent to watch your movements anyway. Bentham would have done so without hesitation."

Resignation now settled deeply into his features. "Then, I was done for regardless."

"Perhaps." Turning to the gentlemen. "You may remove Mr. Ellis now."

An hour later, Lydia stood beside Kingslade in Rufus's room. The documents had been found in a clever compartment in one of his trunks. The dagger had been folded inside them. "A rare blade, indeed," he murmured, turning the dagger once more in his hands.

"Indeed," Lydia responded, but she was not looking

at the weapon. Instead, her gaze was fixed on Kingslade. She then chuckled. "You know, I had expected a little more excitement and danger today. I must tell you I feel quite deflated that all I was required to do was to sip a little champagne before so villainous a spy was apprehended."

"It is lowering," he responded, glancing at her, a familiar crooked smile playing about the edges of his mouth.

"He will suffer a quite humiliating and public execution, though, will he not? I believe that will be punishment enough."

Kingslade shook his head. "It might be best if you did not know Rufus's fate. Let us just say that whatever happens to him will not be conducted in public."

Lydia saw the grim set of his chin and the working of his jaw. She felt she could read his thoughts and shuddered.

He tossed the dagger back into the trunk and turned toward her. "You were magnificent today. How did you manage to keep your wits about you and to fool him as you did?"

She shook her head, a sense of soberness descending on her. "I watched him emerge from the inn, and though I felt a bolt of fright, it was as though I knew what needed to be done. He already suspected that I had a *tendre* for you, so the rest played out quite easily."

"It was more than that," he said. "You seem to have a knack for the subtleties. Do you realize that had you rattled on about an elopement, he would have known immediately that he was suspect, and then we would have been in the basket, indeed!"

"Yes, I felt that to be true. Which leads me to say that you conducted yourself perfectly throughout as well. The moment I said, 'He has come to wish us joy,' I thought for certain you would stumble and fail to pick up the hint. All would have been lost in that moment as well."

"Not lost," he said, smiling. "But more adventurous, perhaps. He might even have fled, and then we could have engaged in an exhausting chase across several countries, even continents!"

"Then I did bungle it, for I was hoping for nothing less!" Suddenly, the tears came, unexpectedly. "He was my friend. I thought he was everything that a gentleman ought to be, so open and confiding. How could I have been so mistaken?"

He did not give answer, but gathered her up in his arms and held her tightly. She was trembling again. He kissed her forehead gently and told her how brave she had been, how proud he was of her, that she had done more for her country today than the average person did in a lifetime. He kissed her cheek and with a gentle hand wiped away her tears.

Lydia lifted her face slightly, and his lips found the corner of her mouth. She had but to turn, which she did, and his lips were suddenly fully on hers. Perhaps it was the extraordinary nature of the afternoon's adventure, or perhaps merely because she was feeling so vulnerable, but the most powerful, passionate feeling suddenly swelled over her like an enormous wave. He kissed her deeply, his tongue plumbing the soft depths of her mouth. She was put forcibly in mind of the marriage bed, and her knees buckled beneath her. He caught her about the waist, holding her roughly against him. She murmured his name against his lips. Why was it such an embrace could bring so much comfort?

After a time, she drew back and blinked. "I . . . oh, dear . . . I should not have done that!" She placed a hand against her cheek. "Forgive me."

She turned away and moved to the window. "I suppose we should be returning to London."

"I love you so very much, my dearest Lydia."

She looked back at him and knew the strongest desire to run back into his arms. She recalled, however, their quarrel of the night before and how little she knew of him. "It is your reserve, Kingslade. Perhaps I was mistaken in Mr.

Ellis, for I had believed I knew everything of him, but what do I truly know of you? Yes, you are brave and in many ways wonderful, but I can't bear the thought that I might be deceived in yet another man."

He nodded. "I see," he murmured. "Well, I daresay a new team has been hitched to the coach. Shall we away?"

"Yes, I would like that."

For the first hour of the return journey, Kingslade contemplated the lady opposite him. She was deeply saddened, and he found himself desiring more than anything to put his arms about her once more and to offer her what comfort he could. He knew, however, by the set of her countenance, that she would rebuff any such attempt. He understood her reticence, but he did not agree with it. He therefore set about pondering both her complaints about his reserve, which were his own fault since he had mistakenly believed her to be in the same mold as his own former betrothed, as well as just what he was to do to bring her about.

After a time, he began speaking, at first slowly and thoughtfully, about his life. He told her in some detail about his betrothal to Lady Violet, how he had loved her and how she had jilted him. "I had been so open with her, you cannot imagine. There was nothing I withheld from her. Later, she told me I frightened her, that I carried so much—what did she say—*lightning in my demeanor* which I have never quite understood, that she could not bear the thought of being wed to me. Believe me, I have had cause to restrain myself, fearing that such "lightning" would overset another female."

"She sounds like an oddity. I should think most women would enjoy a little lightning, now and again."

He chuckled. "The truth is, she is not an oddity. She is lovely and kind and married a very quiet man."

"Then, that is your answer. She required a different sort of husband and life."

"But you do not," he said.

"That is a very different matter, entirely," she responded, lifting her chin.

He smiled and cast his gaze out the window, but continued unveiling fact after fact about his life, his childhood, school, fighting with his brothers, the death of his father and the prolonged, painful illness his mother was enduring. He only ceased speaking when the journey was broken while taking a cup of tea or tankard of ale. Once he followed her into his coach, he began again.

Finally, she lifted a hand. "You have mistaken me, Kingslade, if you think such conduct will win my heart!"

"That is not what I think at all," he countered, "for I believe your heart to have been already won, else you would not fall so easily into my arms." He watched a delightful blush climb her cheeks. "No, my intention is for you to know me, as I am, or as I was before I was jilted and lost my voice." He leaned forward and took her hand. "I love you so desperately, and I promise you, dearest Lydia, that you must even now prepare yourself for a siege. There is nothing I will not do to win you, to make you my wife. You already know of me what not even my family knows—that I am a spy. Better still, I suspect this knowledge will in the end decide me in your favor."

She tried to protest, but he merely continued chatting away until Upper Brook Street was reached and he had returned her, albeit in a rather stunned state, to her aunt. Before he released her, however, and in the presence of her aunt, he begged her to dance the waltz with him at Almack's on the following night. When she had promised him she would do so, he left her to return in much haste to his house. If he hoped to accomplish all that he must and win her as swiftly as he could before she had much time to build her defenses, he would have to act quickly.

Once at his town house, he sat down and wrote several letters, each of which was sent by his own servants at a gallop to various parts of the kingdom. The final letter he wrote was to Lady Cowper, one of the patronesses of the

Almack Assembly Rooms, requesting several vouchers for tomorrow night's assembly.

"Aunt, I wish to go home!" Lydia cried, just as the coach drew before the assembly rooms.

"You have been as nervous as a cat's tail. Whatever is the matter with you?"

Lydia stared at her aunt, feeling panicky. How could she explain the desperation she was feeling at the mere thought of being in Kingslade's company tonight. "I . . . I have the headache!"

"Stuff and nonsense! I will hear no more, and if I might remind you, you promised to attend tonight. Should you fail to do so, you would be breaking your word!"

At that, Lydia's shoulders fell. "You are right, but what was I thinking to have made such a promise!"

Mrs. Morestead opened her mouth to protest anew, paused, then drew in a very deep breath. "Take my advice, Lydia, marry the man. You love him to the point of distraction. You are struggling against the current of a river so swollen with rain that unless you surrender, you risk drowning completely."

Lydia had never considered her aunt a very wise woman, but in this moment, she thought there might be a measure of truth in what she was saying. She was struggling as one caught in a swift-flowing stream; but in surrendering it did not mean she had to marry the man, merely to dance with him and that she felt she could accomplish tonight with at least a small degree of equanimity. "Very well."

"Much better. Now, let us go inside and see if we can discover what has set every gabblemonger in London to bandying your name about hours on end!"

With these less than encouraging words, Lydia descended her aunt's coach.

Once within, Lady Cowper approached Mrs. Morestead, greeting her kindly and suggesting she accompany them.

Lydia thought this quite odd, but even odder still when, as she followed behind the two ladies, the entire assemblage parted upon their approach and remained standing and gaping at her as she crossed the remainder of the chamber. Mrs. Morestead chatted happily with Lady Cowper as though nothing untoward were occurring, as though they did not notice how everyone was smiling at her and nodding and whispering.

She began to wonder just what Kingslade had done to have commanded the attention of the entire room.

As the assemblage parted even farther still, as Lady Cowper and her aunt drew farther apart so that she had a clear view in front of her, she was astonished to find not just Kingslade before her, but what she realized in her acquaintance with some and in the resemblance of others were all of his siblings. He stepped forward immediately, made his bow, and begged if he might make her known to his family.

"Of course," she murmured, dumbfounded. She glanced up at him and could not mistake the smile of delight on his face.

Each sibling greeted her in a warm, almost laughing manner. Lydia thought his next eldest brother spoke accurately when he said, "You must have captured his fancy, indeed, for I have never known him to make such a cake of himself before."

Lydia knew she had blushed, and that deeply, but this only served to cause him to laugh and to express his wish that she relieve Kingslade of his torment and marry him.

After that, Lydia might have perished entirely of embarrassment, had Lady Cowper not taken the assembly in hand and ordered the next dance to commence immediately. For the duration of the next set, she began conversing with his siblings until by the time the waltz was announced, she had begun to feel at least a little at ease.

Kingslade drew her onto the ballroom floor. Fortunately by now, their pairing evoked but only a smattering of gawking interest, and she was able to enter into the dance feeling relatively comfortable.

Kingslade was always an unexceptional partner, but she could not help but berate him a little for having made such a spectacle of her this evening. "And I particularly take it most unkindly in you that your family must be so congenial!"

He whirled her around and around. His smile, which seemed perpetually affixed to his face, grew broader still. "I knew you would like them. They are an excellent lot."

"I do like them. Very much. Mary's company, of course, I have always enjoyed."

Again and again, he turned her in dizzying circles.

"A thought has just occurred to me," he said. "Should you consent to be my wife, you will have any number of brothers and sisters to call your own."

"You would use them to persuade me?" she cried.

"Of course. I warned you I would do everything within my power to change your mind."

"Kingslade, it is not so simple."

"No, it is not," he murmured, guiding her firmly up and back and around and around. "You had believed me to be like Mr. Leckford because, in my own fears, I kept myself hidden from you. But no longer, Lydia, and should it require years, I will spend each day happily proving who I am, my worth, my character, my true openness, to you."

Lydia searched his eyes. She saw the depth of his sincerity, and she was moved, immensely so. Still, her fears rose and danced about her head. Images of Harry kissing that young woman burned before her eyes, of Ellis speaking of having been in her room the night of Bentham's murder. "How will I ever really know?" she asked on a whisper.

He did not answer immediately, but led her carefully around and around, up and back to the lovely, marked strains of the music. "I have no answer for you," he said at last. "I resisted you as well, my powerful desire to be with you, to kiss you—that, of course, I did not resist quite as often as I should have. I even chose to misuse you because I was convinced I could never truly trust you. But when you told me about Mr. Leckford's wretched conduct, a voice inside my head dared me to trust again. I saw you through new eyes. I reviewed everything I knew about you and saw that you had never done a single thing to deserve my doubt." Here he smiled ruefully. "I, on the other hand, have hurt you. In that way, I do not deserve you. However, I am willing to spend the rest of my days making up for my stupidity."

Lydia blinked. She had never thought to hear Kingslade refer to himself in such terms. She began to laugh and even missed her steps. "Oh, I am sorry, but I would never have believed my Lord Kingslade would admit to imbecility."

"I take exception to that! I referred to stupidity, not a true lack of intelligence."

"Splitting hairs, Kingslade," she responded.

She watched him draw in a deep breath and then gather her more firmly about the waist. "I do so love how you taunt me. I only wish we were alone, I would taunt you in return."

"Wicked man," she whispered.

Around and around, up and back. "Marry me," he said quietly. "Marry me, Lydia. We shall have adventures, you and I."

"Adventures, you say?" she queried. How tempted she was. How comfortable she was in his arms, dancing with him, brangling, teasing.

"There is something more."

"More?"

He nodded and grew quite serious.

"Oh, dear."

"I have it within my power," he began on a very quiet, subdued tone, "to offer you a post of espionage in the British government."

"What?" she cried.

"Well, you have great talent. I observed as much myself."

"But are there female spies?"

He nodded.

She gasped, and a very strange stream of excitement began coursing through her. She looked about the rooms, at the dancers whirling by her, and felt as though she were not moving at all, as though she were living in a dream. "A spy?"

He nodded again, quite solemnly.

"Oh, Kingslade, you do know how to court a lady."

"Which is the only troublesome aspect of the offer."

"What is that?"

"You will only be allowed to do so as my wife."

She gasped anew. "What a devil you are!" she cried.

"I told you I would do everything in my power to make you my wife."

"Do you know how sorely you tempt me, and in knowing, do you not comprehend that you will never truly be certain just why I agreed to accept of your hand in marriage?"

"I could not care less *why* you marry me, only that you do, for I promise you the next time I am alone with you and take you in my arms, kissing you will be but the first thing I do, and the rest I will not resist."

Her neck grew very warm and the music seemed to have grown reckless. "How can you speak so in an assembly room? You shock me completely."

"I promised myself I would never be reserved with you again. You deserve to know my thoughts, and I tell you now, these are the least of my thoughts where you are concerned."

Lydia had always been drawn to Kingslade, but in this moment, with his eyes burning fire, and his voice melting the frost on her heart, with his cunning offer of spydom and his bed, she found her will absolutely disintegrating about her feet. She glanced at the array of his siblings watching them with amused expressions from the top of the room, and his promise of a family. They were smiling, all of them, as if they already knew what she would do.

She thought of Harry and realized he was a ridiculous man. She recalled the moment she had received the note from Rufus which had exposed Kingslade's misdeed. He had not even attempted to deny what he had done. In that he had been forthright. When she had confronted Harry, he had denied having kissed anyone.

She realized in a startling burst of understanding that Kingslade was nothing at all like Harry Leckford, that he was worth more than a hundred such men. Though he enjoyed the rank of an earldom, a fine estate, a great income, he still had not hesitated in risking his life for his country. But above all things, what returned to her in this moment was how, when he had been carrying her from Almack's a week past, and he had told her to trust him, she had responded without hesitation, "I do."

All her doubts dissipated in this one grand, eloquent moment. Her fears vanished, and in their place was a feeling she could only describe as joy. "Well," she began, the music drawing to a close. "I suppose if I am to be a spy, we ought to be married. After all, it would attract far too much notice for an unmarried lady to go snooping about unattended."

The music ended. The slow fading of the couples to the edges of the room commenced, except that Kingslade did not move. He did not take her hand so as to lead her away. "Will you marry me?" he asked.

She nodded. "Of course I will. I love you beyond imagining. I have from the first as well."

He then did the unthinkable and took her boldly in his arms and kissed her. Somewhere, at the tip of her awareness, she heard the gasps and then the applause of the assembled guests, but for the most part, she found herself drifting higher and higher into the heavens, her heart swelling to a place of tremendous exhilaration.

Only as he finally took his lips from hers, did she return to earth and find that she was still in his arms but surrounded by his family, her aunt, the Almack patronesses—although, some scowling in disapproval—and several score of well-wishers and friends.

A month later, in early June, Lydia bid her husband enter her bedchamber. "Do you think the ambassador will be charmed by this gown?"

He growled. "I would not have it quite so decollate."

"You did not complain last night when I showed it to you."

He smiled in that way of his that promised they would be even later to the ball if she did not immediately change the subject. "So tell me, my darling, what is it you wish to know of him?"

"How many troops Napoleon is amassing."

"Is that all?"

He laughed. "You make a beautiful countess, my Lady Kingslade."

Since by then he had slipped his arms about her waist, she said, "We will be late again," she warned.

"Yes, but that will work better for us, I think, since the ambassador enjoys a great deal of brandy later in the evening."

"Ah," she murmured, as she removed her pearls. "My hair will need to be redone."

"So it will."

With that, Lydia kissed her husband and had all the pleasure of being kissed passionately in return. Brussels was an exciting city at present, with war looming on the horizon and the combined armies gathering in a field near the village of Waterloo.

"I love you, my darling Lydia," he whispered against her cheek.

"And I you."

DO YOU HAVE THE
HOHL COLLECTION?

Discover The Magic of Romance With
Jo Goodman